CW01433215

THE
MANUAL
FOR GOOD
WIVES

Lola Jaye

THE
MANUAL
FOR GOOD
WIVES

MACMILLAN

First published 2025 by Macmillan
an imprint of Pan Macmillan
The Smithson, 6 Briset Street, London EC1M 5NR
EU representative: Macmillan Publishers Ireland Ltd, 1st Floor,
The Liffey Trust Centre, 117–126 Sheriff Street Upper,
Dublin 1, D01 YC43
Associated companies throughout the world
www.panmacmillan.com

ISBN 978-1-5290-6462-9

Copyright © Lola Jaye 2025

The right of Lola Jaye to be identified as the
author of this work has been asserted by her in accordance
with the Copyright, Designs and Patents Act 1988.

All rights reserved. No part of this publication may be reproduced,
stored in a retrieval system, or transmitted, in any form, or by any means
(electronic, mechanical, photocopying, recording or otherwise)
without the prior written permission of the publisher.

Pan Macmillan does not have any control over, or any responsibility for,
any author or third-party websites referred to in or on this book.

1 3 5 7 9 8 6 4 2

A CIP catalogue record for this book is available from the British Library.

Typeset by Palimpsest Book Production Limited, Falkirk, Stirlingshire
Printed and bound by CPI Group (UK) Ltd, Croydon, CR0 4YY

MIX
Paper | Supporting
responsible forestry
FSC
www.fsc.org
FSC® C116313

This book is sold subject to the condition that it shall not, by way of
trade or otherwise, be lent, hired out, or otherwise circulated without
the publisher's prior consent in any form of binding or cover other than
that in which it is published and without a similar condition including
this condition being imposed on the subsequent purchaser.

Visit **www.panmacmillan.com** to read more about all our books
and to buy them. You will also find features, author interviews and
news of any author events, and you can sign up for e-newsletters
so that you're always first to hear about our new releases.

Dedication to come

Prologue

Is this what it felt like, moments from death?

My body rooted to the floor, unable to move, startled by crowds of men. Their hands balled into angry fists, spittle flying from their lips as they shouted my name, along with chants such as 'Liar!' and worse: 'String her up!'

There were reporters too. One of whom had set up one of those new camera contraptions at me, ready to catch me in its gaze.

'Got anything to say for yourself?' said the man in scuffed shoes and an ill-fitting jacket. 'You should be ashamed!'

'It appears you have already made up your mind,' I said calmly. My voice edged with the last of its strength, almost resigned to the fate that awaited me.

'Don't say anything,' said a gruff voice beside me, a hand gripping my elbow.

'Don't you care about what you've done? You're a disgrace!' repeated the man with the shoes. A step closer and he'd almost be touching my face with that bulbous nose, attacking me with his frightful use of the Queen's English.

I widened my eyes expectantly, tilted my head upwards. I would be defiant until the very end.

'Harlot!' said a voice from the left.

'She deserves locking up!' said another from the right.

'Hussy!'

Each voice from the throats of men who I suspected had done much worse than I in their lives. Yet I was the one offered up for judgement. I was the one whose course in life stood on the verge of being altered.

The steps up to the building were vast before me. I had travelled so far in life only to end up here.

'Don't you have any remorse for the pain you caused?' asked another voice. This one sounded a tad kinder, minus the edge of hate.

I looked towards him, smiling ironically. 'Pain?'

What did they know of pain?

What did any of them know of *my* pain?

A strong hand gripped my wrist tightly, forcing me to follow. Normally, I followed no one, because I wasn't a woman to be tamed any more. This time, however, following was possibly for the best, considering the self-righteous mob now clamouring for my blood.

'Lying witch!' said a thunderous voice, just as I took my first steps into that courtroom.

PART ONE

Chapter One

When a young lady is ready to be introduced to polite society,
her sole purpose is to find a husband.

Mrs Adeline Copplefield,
'The Manual for Good Wives' (1888)

Temi
Western Africa, 1860

My earliest memory of him is the sound of his laughter.

A sort of cackle that descends into a throaty, cough-like guffaw. His hand in mine, our toes connecting with the hot sand as we stood at the top of the hill overlooking a hazy yet beautiful horizon.

'What do you think is down there?' It was always the same question as we stood on that hill, never daring to walk any further. My mother would say, 'That *which does not concern you*,' which was always enough to put an end to any further curiosity. Yet with *him*, with Olu, an explanation was always peppered with fantasy and words I could only soak up and devour. His knowledge on matters was impressive, if also concerning, because it came from the pages of an actual book. This boy was never without a book! Whilst I had been forbidden to speak of such things if they were written in English, which my father, the king, said 'should never be allowed to replace our own language'.

Now I had gained a hunger to learn more of these written words simply because this boy I had known my entire life, who now walked around clutching a book, no longer matched me in knowledge. He had surpassed me.

'What is down there is another life. One that is begging to be lived,' he said.

I looked at him with awe. 'Why do you like to read words in another tongue?' I hoped he would not tire of my questions. I had so many, and he was the only person in my life who would ever consider answering them, instead of chastising me for wanting to know of matters that didn't concern a girl such as I. It did not matter that I had been born into nobility, such questions were simply not befitting – yet I did not care!

'A book will tell you there is more . . . beyond what we know.'

'Is it not the white man telling you all of this?'

It was no secret that more and more white men had been seen in the wider village, bringing with them books and odd items of clothing, including something called a bowler hat which I had seen some of the children laughing at.

'Tell me what it is like to read a book,' I said, eyeing the object in his other hand. He seemed to carry one everywhere. 'Tell me.'

He turned to me and his smile widened. 'It is like stepping into a world that is unlike our own, Temi.'

I placed my hand on the book, slowly stroking its cover.

'Take it,' he said.

I scrunched my eyebrows in confusion. 'I cannot.' Not least because I was unable to read a word of it.

'I shall teach you to read,' he said as if reading what I spoke in my head. He opened it and ran his fingers over the words. 'Charles Dickens,' he said.

I mouthed the words and quickly fell into a laughter that was in part embarrassment. Lately, there had been a part of me which wanted to impress this boy I had known since our births fourteen rainy seasons ago. Although he lived in a neighbouring village, we saw one another daily thanks to our mothers being such close friends.

I could never remember a time in this life without this boy named Olu.

As the weeks passed and another season arrived, that book had started to unite us in a new way. Taking us on an unfamiliar journey that felt exciting to walk. Every time I spoke a new word of this language, I saw delight in his eyes, which gave me immense pleasure and a more pressing desire to one day become fluent in this English. Our bond increased along with his deepening voice and the growing curve of my breasts.

Sometimes I felt confused about these changes. The freedom with which we would engage was soon replaced by a silence that felt awkward and full of questions neither of us had the courage to ask.

Our voyages up the hill also lessened, with Olu spending the bulk of the day with the men of the village, whilst I learned from the women the importance of cooking good soup and what it meant to one day be a good wife.

Yet my mind never strayed far away from him. When he wasn't near me, I could feel him next to me. Crave him. And at times he even occupied my dreams.

'Temitope, pay attention now!' shouted Aunty Kike as she bent over the large mortar on the ground.

She had called me by my full name and I sensed trouble. For me.

I pulled my wrapper further upwards, tucking in the ends of the cloth.

'Yes, Aunty Kike.' Saying her name instantly forced a smile onto my lips because *Kike* was pronounced *Kee-kay*. The curve of any lips forced into a smile when her name was spoken, and she was exactly that – a ray of light in my life whom I had adored from the day I had cried my first cry. She'd been the one to care for me with the blessing of my mother. She, the first person I told when I experienced that first flow of blood from my body two rainy seasons ago; she, the only person I needed when feeling forlorn. Aunty Kike was married but had never borne children of her own, so viewed me as her firstborn, whilst I could do nothing but enjoy what she offered me, as unlike with my mother, I did not have to share her with five other siblings sired by the king, my father.

Aunty Kike was simply mine alone.

'Temi, are you listening?' she said with exasperation. 'How are we to prepare you to become a wife if you cannot even listen? Take,' she said, shoving the large and heavy pestle into my hand. One of the maidservants had already placed the steaming yam into the mortar and it was now ready for pounding.

'Oya, cook it now!'

I stared down at the large pestle and tears lodged in my eyes, emotion welling up. I was unsure why.

'What is wrong with you?' she asked.

I shook my head, forgetting this was not how you respond to your elders. Especially one trying to school me on such important matters as cooking for my future husband.

'Eh?' she said, hands on her hips. 'Are you not going to answer me?'

'I am well, ma. Thank you, ma,' I said obediently. I pounded the yam and tried – with great difficulty – not to imagine Olu's big head as the target! Fighting both affection and anger for him, but mostly affection because I simply yearned to be with him. Not used to days not beginning with him as we trekked to the top of the hill at sunrise, talking and reading. Now he had decided I was not worth these precious moments and I'd no idea why.

Aunty Kike pulled the pestle from my tightened grip. 'Whose head are you pounding?' she asked, and I couldn't help the laugh lodged in my throat which forced me to smile.

'What is bothering you, my daughter?' she asked as we sat on the floor.

I was grateful for Aunty Kike. She always knew the temperature of my emotions. We were years apart in age and yet sometimes I would forget and feel her as my peer. Though she was far from this and I could not tell her about my feelings, especially as I myself had yet to understand them.

'Aunty, can I tell you anything that enters my mind?'

Her brows knotted. 'Maybe,' she said. We both knew what that meant. A reminder that some of my thoughts should stay with me. That no matter how different Aunty Kike may be to the other aunties, she was still my senior. That whilst I was her beloved, she still had to make sure my conduct would always be pleasing to the king and befitting that of a future bride.

That night I snuck away to Olu's village. It was not right for a girl to be so far away from home at such a time, but I did not care. I needed to be near this foolish boy once again. To fill the void I had been experiencing since the last time I laid my eyes on him a week ago. Seven whole days without him.

I found him by the bush talking with his elder brothers. I have no idea why I assumed my 'Pssst' would alert him, but it did.

'Temi? What are you doing here?' He ran towards me and I believed my heart would leap through my chest.

I poked my finger into his ribcage. Hard.

'What darkness have I placed upon you?' I spoke in English, sounding like one of his books, I hoped. 'Have I viciously wronged you, Olu?'

The sun may have already said its goodbye, but the moon and parts of the stars decorated his features, so I saw glimpses of him. Those long and thick eyelashes which looked like those of a young girl and that smile which turned into a laugh.

'Don't laugh at me!' I protested.

'You have done nothing to wrong me, Temi.'

'Then why—?'

He moved us away from prying voices, further inside the bush and its limited light. I couldn't see any part of him now, could only hear his breathing and the rustling his feet made on the ground. I could touch him, smell him. His aroma like the tree with the red flowers during the rainy season.

'Temi.'

There was something deliciously unfamiliar about hearing his voice in total darkness. His hands grazing mine. The tips of his fingers moving up and down inside my palms. Feelings I could not describe, travelling throughout my entire body.

I was breathless.

His own breath began to travel the contour of my neck, and my body stiffened as his lips touched the skin on my shoulder. My unexpected shudder, a surprise which felt . . . beautiful.

Then he stopped and we were silent. Only the sound of grasshoppers and maybe the simple beats of our hearts, nothing else.

'Temi?'

'Yes?' I could hardly speak. Had I just felt his lips on my skin?

'I apologize for my absence,' he said.

'Then why . . . ?' I spoke hoarsely, my breathing heavy.

'It is because of you. This,' he said, squeezing my hand.

I knew, we both knew that everything had changed between us . . . and in the most glorious of ways.

'Temi, I . . . I love you.'

I had never heard these words before, and perhaps looking back, these are not even the exact words he spoke to me in the darkness of that bush, during a night that would forever be etched on my mind. What floated between us during those moments felt pure, beautiful and everything I never thought I could feel. A young, tender love between a boy named Olu and a girl named

Temi. A feeling, a state of mind which had been brewing our entire lives and now was finally allowed a voice.

'This is why I have stayed away for so very long,' he said.

He held both my hands now and I felt ready to explode!

'I understand,' I lied. I did not understand why anyone would stay away from a feeling as wonderful as this!

'Temi, you are a princess.'

My mind paid not one ounce of attention as I revelled in what I could only imagine was what the elders had once been privy to before they grew old. His lips had touched my skin! My *bare* skin!

'I am not betrothed to you and you are about to belong to another man,' he said firmly, and this time I awakened from the dream. This time, I realized, he was talking about me.

Chapter Two

*It is unthinkable to marry outside the class you have been born
into. To aspire higher is to be considered an upstart. To marry
beneath you could be your ruin!*

Mrs Adeline Copplefield,
'The Manual for Good Wives' (1893)

Temi
1861

Since that moment standing in darkness, my life had taken on a
brightness I hoped would stay forever.

I could no longer think of Olu as *just a boy*. Now, when I looked
at him, I saw a man and found it difficult to gaze at him without
feeling a flush of heat rush over my cheeks. Fighting this longing
to be close to him, my mood lifting simply at the thought of him.

We began to meet regularly after light turned to black. We'd
talk about the new books Olu had been loaned by the people at
his school. I never asked about these people but I knew they were
from across the sea and were white.

When we began *Romeo and Juliet*, it was clear to me some of
the words used were not the same as what he spoke, or what had
been in the other books he'd been teaching me to read. The words
each sounded beautiful though – and immensely confusing. What
did make sense was the story he reeled off in his own words. Of
two people very much in love and yet threatened to be divided by
others. These thoughts stayed in my head and soon became a

prelude to actions I knew were wrong. Actions allowing me to feel a joy I had never known before. Like holding hands under the moonlight as we talked; pressing our lips together as our eyes closed involuntarily.

The feelings began to feel heavy, yet also light; joyful yet sad.

Sometimes, most times, it felt like no one else lived in this world except the two of us.

Olu and I existing in this ball of our own moonlight.

Just us.

I could never think of my behaviour as defying my parents, because no part of me could see this as wrong. This is what I told myself when we were together. Yet alone, during the night, my mind raced with the reality of my duty as a princess. The destiny of every girl child in my family was to be married and go on to produce a wealth of children. It was no more or less desired of a princess than any other girl in the kingdom, but in my case, the suitor would have to be of good standing and I learned that a chief had already been chosen for me.

Or indeed, *he* had chosen *me*.

My mother was the fifth wife of the king, my father, and there were three more wives after her. We all lived within the walls of a grand palace which stood against a lush forest background generally reserved for my father's outdoor activities.

The palace was surrounded by a high mud-brick wall which towered over the other buildings in the kingdom, remaining the grandest of all. Our everyday needs were generally met by maidservants and an abundance of staff who tended to the palace and its occupants. My mother preferred me not to fraternize too much with my other siblings who were not from her own body. I never understood this silent agreement among the wives but abided by the rules until it came to Taye. She'd been born just two seasons before me and was the exact image of my father, with shining dark skin and a round face (whilst my high cheekbones favoured my mother). We would play in the yard together, laughing as we braided one another's hair. Taye made noises through her nose which made me laugh endlessly and I could honestly say I never thought of the maternal divide between us. When she was found lifeless on the floor one morning, we were all shocked, but my devastation only allowed me to feel numb. Outwardly unmoved. Her mother had screamed that her death was a result of my father's first wife's murderous intent. That Taye's food had been laced with poison. My father shed hard tears for the daughter I always felt had been his favourite simply because of how much she looked like him. Yet all I could do, in the midst of such unbridled grief circling around me, was squeeze my eyes shut and act as if nothing had happened. To behave in the opposite way to everyone else.

Whenever thoughts of Taye entered my head, I would try to simply brush them aside with thoughts of, say, the sweetness of the mango I had eaten that day. Anything but let myself think of the loss of my beloved Taye.

I got used to doing this. To shifting thoughts from my mind when they threatened to engulf me. Just like how I had found it easy to move away from any stray thought of this marriage to the chief and to carry on with my life as normal.

Thankfully, during moments spent with Olu, the question of the future was never spoken. We much preferred the joy of focusing on the sound of our breaths that heightened with each touch; experiencing the intensity of what a simple gaze into each other's eyes would bring. Each tender kiss planting a special memory into my head which would later replay itself over and over again in my thoughts.

'Tem-Tem,' he said, his private name for me, making me tingle with delight. 'When I am away from you it is like a limb is missing from my body.'

I wanted to laugh at this statement whilst simultaneously knowing exactly what he meant. Being without Olu for much of the day and week felt cruel – as if all our time should be spent side by side and basking in a love which seemed to grow stronger each and every day.

One evening, we sat under a multitude of accommodating stars and I dared to place Olu's hand on my chest. 'Can you feel how fast it beats?'

It's then he did something he'd never done before. He moved his palm further down and to the side, cupping the curve of my breast, the whites of his eyes, even in the darkness, questioning. When I nodded my head for him to continue, a surge of desire shot through my body, our lips meeting, but this time more urgently.

Our tongues met for the first time too and we promptly burst into a fit of laughter – part nerves, part happiness.

I felt closer to Olu than ever before and I never wanted to be apart from him again. I moved closer into his arms and that is where I stayed until sunlight.

I shot up from where we lay, rubbing my eyes in confusion.

'Olu, we have slept too long. I must return home!'

He stifled a yawn. 'I will accompany you.'

Clearly, sleep had cleared his head of any common sense.

'No, that is not possible! No one can see you!'

He kissed my forehead and I hurried along the route back to my village, unsure of what would await me.

'Where have you been?' Aunty Kike's features contorted in an anger which simply needed one wrong word from me for it to erupt.

'I went to . . .' The lies refused to appear.

'You are needed at home, something terrible has happened.'

As I rushed in the direction of the palace, I saw the elders had already gathered. I noticed more and more people arriving. Not only my extended family of siblings, cousins, aunties and uncles, but other citizens of the kingdom.

I quickly realized this had nothing to do with me.

The king, my father, spoke first. Then a set of elders. After which, everything began to make sense. Subjects of the kingdom had been colluding with the British regarding the division of the land. Such dealings had been done over many years before, resulting in some of our men and women going missing from our village, taken in chains never to return. My father spoke passionately about this never being allowed to happen again. That citizens of this kingdom would rise up and end such outrage and that the enemy would never win.

I gazed around me at women holding onto one another, some clutching their children tightly. Loud sobbing whilst the men's anger grew. I wasn't sure of my own emotions, perhaps failing to understand the severity of the situation. I had been raised to fear the white man and what he could do to us, yet found it difficult to reconcile with the fact that they also walked freely among us.

The women and children were told to leave the men to continue their discussions.

It was only after some hours that Ade, my eldest sibling and the eldest son of the king, appeared from the courtyard. His words at first did not mean much, but as he continued, soon began to make frightening sense.

'Death to all who attempt to defy the kingdom!' came the throaty roar.

Various menfolk joined him and echoed this sentiment with their own chants, fists in the air, the women shaking their heads in terse agreement.

Ade continued his tirade, now more specific. Each word, every sentence like a dagger to my abdomen.

My mind quickly scrambled for clarity. Unable to erase the

words of my eldest brother: that these 'traitors' had knowingly received gifts from the British such as books and even clothing, and in turn had decided to collude with them. That the majority of these people had come from one specific area.

Olu's village.

Everything had changed.

Women and children were no longer permitted to leave the compound and I'd no idea what was going on outside of it. A sense of mistrust seemed to permeate the atmosphere. I had witnessed a group of young men return with blood caked onto their skin. A result of a fight with a man from Olu's village.

Every night I'd lie awake, hoping my Olu would not get caught up in the fighting, that he was safe. I could not get word to him, communication between us was now impossible.

My mother and Aunty Kike kept asking what was wrong and I could only lie and say it was nothing. I could only hope the strength of my love for Olu was enough to travel through the distance to tell him I was here, waiting for him to return to me.

I could only hope they wouldn't kill him.

Chapter Three

To be a good and dutiful wife requires preparation.
Mrs Adeline Copplefield,
'The Manual for Good Wives' (1890)

Temi
1861

I knelt on the floor of the courtyard in front of four elderly uncles and my father, as they explained their plan for my life.

'You will be married to the chief in sixty days.'

'Sixty days, sir?' I had never been pierced with the horn of a ram before, but I imagined it would have inflicted a similar pain to these words.

'Are your ears clogged with leaves?' said my father, the king, as the others erupted into laughter. My father remained stoic, though, his eyes attempting to read me. For a moment I was scared that, like Olu and Aunty Kike, he possessed such a skill.

The palace was the epicentre of all things judicial and political in regards to the kingdom, much of which I had never been privy to, until now.

'No, sir. I am sorry, sir.'

'Sixty days,' repeated my father, the king, a man who no one ever spoke against. His words penetrated the wall of denial which had served me well up until now.

The maidservants brought kola nuts for the men to chew on and palm wine to drink. My fate was further discussed over delicacies I could never look at in the same way again. The space around me blurring and closing in on me as I remained on my knees, a position to denote respect, now simply resembling a begging pose. And I was doing just that. Begging silently for my life, or at least the life I wanted with Olu, because my mind could never fathom a future not involving him. To be the wife of another. To never hold my Olu again.

This could not happen! said the voice in my head. The laughter of the men loud and piercing as they feasted on each nut and supped on the wine.

The walls began to close in on me, the surrounding trees in the courtyard flapping furiously against an imaginary wind. My breath came in spurts as my name was spoken within a scream . . . my mother's voice, I think. Then my entire body was hitting the floor as I fell into instant darkness.

I awakened to the grainy, textured taste of garri and water being pressed against my lips and someone fanning me with a large leaf. A voice in the background explaining to those gathered that the joy of my impending marriage had been the culprit. That I had simply collapsed with the happiness of it all, because this is what every girl desired. To be wed to a man such as the chief. A privilege, especially as I was not the loveliest of the king's daughters and yet I was the one he had chosen.

The 'good' news of my impending marriage was followed by the doom of another bloody fight which had resulted in one of the king's men being killed.

My mother constantly told us not to fear, even though that death told us otherwise. All of the wives had gathered with the king and had meetings, something not commonplace unless absolutely necessary. My foundations felt shakier than ever without Olu, along with this growing fear for his safety.

Forty days now remained until I would be married to the chief.

He was a man with a booming voice that could cause birds in trees to scatter. His large belly protruded through his agbada like a pregnancy. He was a man I had only ever seen from a distance and whose presence made me feel as if I was shrinking to the size of a black-eyed pea. A man older than my father. A man I knew I could never love as much as Olu, if at all.

Both my mother and Aunty Kike explained more than once that this marriage should not have been a shock to me, that I had known it was inevitable for some time now.

Also that I should smile more.

I couldn't tell them, not even Aunty Kike, the real reason for my misery. That the only man I wanted to marry was Olu and the thought of leaving him felt like the worst of punishments.

I soon realized my usual trick of pretending something wasn't happening had left me. I could rely on it no more.

I was fitted for the matrimonial cloths, made to practise the celebrational dance, and took part in discussions with the elder women on what it took to be a good wife to the chief. To be obedient to my husband was a must, as well as making sure I cooked the meals we shared, even though an abundance of help was available. This in part, explained one of the aunties, was because a man *likes to eat from the hand of his wife*. The other reason, much more sinister.

To prevent poisoning by another wife.

Thirty days now remained.

I began to exist in a dreamlike state, acknowledging my life would never be what I wanted, but instead a nightmare with no end.

With so little time remaining until the marriage, I suddenly became gripped by a fearlessness, by this knowledge of having nothing to lose anymore.

I had a plan.

One last attempt to see my Olu again and to no longer care about the consequences.

Chapter Four

It is wise to take time when selecting a suitable husband. But not too long, so as not to become an old maid.

Mrs Adeline Copplefield,
'The Manual for Good Wives' (1893)

Landri
London, England, present day

'Well?'

She looked down at the man she'd known for half a decade, now propped on one knee in their open-plan kitchen diner and asking her to marry him. A glistening engagement ring nestled inside an open cobalt blue box in his outstretched hand, calling for her attention.

'Landri?'

This may have been her name, but in this surreal and unexpected moment she felt disembodied from that person and ultimately removed from the man asking her this rather important question in front of their friends, all waiting expectantly.

'Landri?' he said again, and all she could think was *why now?* They were both knocking on the door of forty and the last time they'd even broached the subject of marriage was around two years ago, concluding they were happy as they were, thank you very much. So, this act had come as a complete and utter shock, and actually saying yes felt like the most unnatural thing to do.

Their friends' expectant faces weren't budging, though. The

not-so-subtle cough and an actual rattling of fingers on the work-top she'd scrubbed and cleaned that very morning jolted her back to reality.

'Landri?' Ross looked up at her. His voice now with a quiet edge of irritation she recognized all too well. She needed to give an answer. *Now.* It didn't matter that this was the last thing she'd expected at the end of a dinner party which had actually been a success of sorts. The one she'd been stressing about for weeks and had planned meticulously. Constantly thinking about place settings in between work meetings; suddenly remembering she hadn't bought the right type of milk for one of her vegan friends. Springing up out of bed at 5.30 a.m. to chop onions, even though she still had to finish a report for a very important client. This dinner party, work, Ross – she'd been consumed with it all and now, here was something new she had to think about.

An engagement ring.

A potential wedding.

The rest of her life with this man.

She swallowed.

'Landri?' he said impatiently.

'Yes.' Her voice was close to a whisper, so faint even she could hardly hear it.

'Speak up!' said an animated voice from the crowd.

'She said yes!' said Ross happily, as the room finally released the applause they had clearly been holding in. The pop of an obligatory champagne cork and a ring being slipped onto her finger completed this weird and unexpected scenario, and it felt like she was having an out-of-body experience. That this proposal, this spectacle was happening to someone else.

If only it was happening to someone else.

'You're making me the happiest man alive!' Ross declared towards the gathered crowd, without actually looking in her direction. Perhaps if he had, he'd have seen the shock mingled with a look of uncertainty etched clearly on her face.

As her best friend Sadia made her way over, Landri wasn't prepared for the unexpected elevation of her entire body as an excitable Ross, grabbing hold of her, lifted her right off the ground while the room launched into even rowdier applause.

She began to feel an onset of dizziness. 'Put me down, please,' she said slowly.

It was as he lowered her back onto her feet that he moved his cheek next to hers; his voice, a quiet, angry whisper. 'Why are you fucking embarrassing me?'

A collection of heartfelt 'Congratulations!' flooded Landri's space. The handshakes amongst the husbands and partners. The hugs from her closest friends, including Sadia and Claudine, who must have been in on this from the start.

'Sorry . . . I'm not . . .' she whispered back to him.

'Let's get a shot of the happy couple, then!' said Greg, Sadia's husband.

Landri tried her best to curve her mouth into a bigger smile as a succession of mobile phone flashes shone in her eyes.

'Fix your face!' said Sadia.

Landri opened her mouth to speak just as Sadia filled in the blanks with her own interpretation. 'Must be nerves. Don't blame you.'

'Yeah . . . Must be that,' said Landri flatly.

Posing for photos was never a fun pastime and she felt especially rigid as she was told to stand by her 'beloved' and 'give your fiancé a kiss' as flashes engulfed her vision.

They held hands on command, pecked, Ross's grip tightening around her palm.

'One more!' ordered Sadia, pointing her phone in the air.

Then, finally, this excruciating part of the night was over.

'You're getting married!' squealed Claudine, running over and pulling her into an embrace. 'Welcome to the club!'

As her two friends began talking dresses, flower girls, and just how lucky she was to have bagged a man like Ross Sasaki, Landri felt a churning in her stomach. The food she'd eaten swirling about inside of her like a washing machine, her smile locked firmly in place.

Just keep smiling, she told herself, over and over again. *Just keep smiling.*

The night continued with a new energy, Ross clutching her hand for longer than usual periods and planting impromptu kisses onto her cheeks, forehead and even her hand – as if their engagement had energized him. Every single one of their friends, especially hers, ecstatic, as would be her grandma when she got round to calling her to reveal the news.

'To us!' said Ross, when everyone had left and it was just the two of them. They clinked glasses, they kissed again, this time deeply, longer. She pulled her mouth away. Ross said to leave the washing up for now and come to bed so they could discuss the wedding.

'I'm in charge of the cars!' he said happily as he climbed into their bed. His feet were cold, touching the side of hers. 'Oh and Dad will insist on having some Japanese food there whilst Mum and her lot will just be looking at it weirdly like they always do. Can you imagine?'

'Yeah,' she said absently, moving closer to the edge of the bed as she smoothed her satin headscarf onto her newly made pigtail twists.

'The rest of all that girly stuff like flowers and wedding colours can be down to you, Sadia and the girls. I'm sure you'll all enjoy that!'

She nodded her head slowly, the satin headscarf grazing the brown velvet headboard.

He took her hand, the engagement ring with its unapologetic sparkle centre stage.

'What's wrong, baby?' He began to stroke the side of her cheek with such tenderness.

'It's been a long day,' she said with a shrug. The feel of his fingers slightly irritating.

'You're happy, though, right? I mean, I thought you'd like the surprise.'

'It was a bit of a shock.' She turned to the side table and retrieved the tub of cream.

'Yeah, I know. Probably why you took so long to answer. I thought you were going to keep me hanging for a minute there!'

She rubbed a dab of shea butter into her hands. Without it, she'd wake up with tiny white flakes on the knuckles of her light brown skin and she didn't need that on top of this mess. And it was a mess. At least it certainly felt like one.

'I wouldn't have kept you hanging, Ross,' she insisted.

'That's what I thought,' he replied firmly.

She lay down on the bed as Ross continued to talk.

'I just . . . well, I always thought marriage wasn't for us, but you know, why not? We both own this place and we've been together a long time. It just makes sense.'

'I understand that, but we could have at least discussed it first . . .'

Then the silence. She hated this part. The longer than needed pause.

'What do you mean, discussed it? We're on the same page, aren't we?'

That wasn't a question, so to avoid an argument, she said nothing and simply waited for Ross's breathing to slow.

Later, when she'd failed to fall into such an easy sleep, Landri slipped out of the bed, careful not to wake him. In the lounge she stood at the large windows, staring out at the river beyond. The slow rhythm of the water always helped to slow her thoughts and offer a sense of calm. Times like this – of which there had been many lately – reminding her how grateful she was to own a riverside apartment. It had been more expensive than the ones at the back of the building, but she'd insisted and, much to her surprise, Ross had agreed. She hadn't expected him to, considering he was paying sixty per cent of the mortgage repayments. A percentage he'd insisted on when she'd assumed they were going halves. Also odd, considering her pay was now higher than his salary as a recruiter. But as Sadia had said at the time, she was lucky.

Lucky to have a man like Ross.

Lucky.

She unlocked the doors to the balcony, enjoying the crisp air against her skin. She gazed at the ring on her finger. Landri had never been one for jewellery so it felt kind of alien and she felt weighed down a little. No, a lot. This ring on her finger suddenly a huge weight that would simply slow her down and keep her shackled to this man.

Then the guilt. Questioning why she would resist a life with a man who clearly loved her and was offering something she'd never really had – a family. A forever.

Her hand flew to her chest. Her breathing had accelerated.

Could she actually do this? Could she marry him?

The following morning Ross left for work as usual, whistling with contentment.

She'd had a fitful night's sleep and her head ached its disapproval.

Landri pottered into the kitchen, disappointed that last night had not been a dream, judging by the carnage in the kitchen. An overloaded dishwasher, champagne spillages on the dining table. It had happened and was real. The ring on her finger. All of it. Real.

A heat began to rise inside her body, followed by that fast heart rate again.

She ignored whatever was going on inside of her and ripped a black plastic bag off a roll, filling it with the debris from the night before. It was upon realizing she'd accidentally smashed one of the plates that she suddenly felt the need to sit down. Staring at the ring on her finger, she had a feeling of dread, foreboding. Ross would hate that his favourite plate had been broken. The last time she'd smashed a glass, a minor disagreement had turned into an accusation that she, being the higher earner, was prone to chucking their things about with no regard.

Her face fell into her hands.

Sometimes there wasn't even a reason for his anger. He'd just pick a row out of nowhere. Each time making her feel . . .

She walked into the bedroom and stood for a moment, catatonic. Only one thought in her head.

I'm exhausted.

Without thinking, she bent to pull out one of the suitcases from under the bed, recalling a beautiful holiday in Sardinia two years ago. Five days of relaxation and sunshine. Although she had gotten the sunshine, at least half of the trip involved both of them responding to work emails, with Landri stressing about how much work she would return to for daring to take two days off. Then there were the arguments. One specifically on the beach, when Ross had suggested she cover up with a bigger sarong. One that didn't show so much leg. Her rebuff and all that went on afterwards resulted in, yes, a longer sarong that dragged along the sandy beach as she walked.

I'm exhausted.

With her energy on autopilot, she opened up the drawers and then the shared wardrobe, stuffing what she could into the suitcase: dresses, knickers, socks, shoes, not even checking if anything matched. She was simply responding to this rising need to stuff as many clothes into the suitcase as possible, like a thief grabbing her loot.

Less than an hour later, her eyes searched the apartment as she slid her arms through the straps of a small rucksack. The glass cabinet was full of Ross's old county cricket medals, and there stood her one and only prize – a glass, triangular-shaped award with her name on it: *Copywriter of the Year*. It had been a complete and utter shock when she'd even been nominated. She hadn't felt any real joy when she'd gone on to win it, her smile neatly in place as the beaming previous recipient of the award handed it to her. It was when Ross had driven them home that night in silence, without even a congratulations, that she'd first realized something was wrong. Not with him, but with *her*. That she'd been housing more than the usual feelings of not being worthy, even allowing for the imposter syndrome which seemed to plague her almost every day at work. This was more about something deep inside. An emotion she could not access while aware of its potential power and its possibilities.

Now, Landri moved towards the front door, asking herself if she could really do this. If she could really leave him this time. She'd tried before, many times. Pulled back by an invisible force which told her to *be more grateful*. That to be loved in spite of who she was and where she'd come from wasn't an easy thing to achieve.

She placed the note onto the shoe rack. It would be the first thing he saw when slipping out of his shoes. Ross hated people wearing shoes in the lounge. He was very strict about that.

She held onto the front door handle and felt that familiar pull luring her back into the apartment and back into the life she was used to. A picture hung on the wall to her right. Her and Ross smiling at the camera. She remembered that day, the picture taken during a walk in the park on a particularly windy afternoon, during the early days of their relationship when they still did things like that. When he paid her compliments, bought her gifts 'just because' and never ever made her want to cry.

Landri's hand hovered over the door handle now. Breathing intensified. Walls slowly closing in.

She had to get out.

She had to leave, and this time, further than the end of the street. This time, no turning back.

So she did as her body and not her thoughts instructed. She trudged the suitcase and rucksack through the door, shutting it behind her, feeling an instant shot of relief which she believed meant nothing unless she actually made it out . . .

Once in the underground car park, more relief as she stuffed the luggage into the boot of her car and slipped behind the wheel, gripping it tightly. A sharp intake of breath, followed by a long exhale as she slowly backed out of the space and pressed the screen of the built-in GPS.

Where to?

'I have no idea,' she whispered, before quickly driving out of the car park and heading towards nowhere.

Chapter Five

*A young lady must keep a pristine and faultless reputation to
secure a good marriage.*

Mrs Adeline Copplefield,
'The Manual for Good Wives' (1893)

Temi
1861

Sitting on top of a rock, I waited for him to arrive.

I had been slipping away after dark for six nights in a row. Sitting alone in the bush and at the mercy of whatever lived there. Not caring for my safety, my only need to see Olu again. Then, on the seventh night, something miraculous occurred. A rustling sound from the bushes that I hoped was not some wild creature arriving to devour me.

'Temi?'

My stomach constricted into a knot.

'Temi!' Olu now stood in front of me. We wasted no time in launching ourselves into each other's arms.

I spoke in between breaths. 'I have . . . have . . . have been here . . . waiting, hoping.'

I felt a little foolish to be saying such things, yet his response soon began to reassure me.

'We have strict instructions not to head too far away from our village, but I come here often, just in case . . . Just in case you came . . . and you did. You came, my Tem-Tem!'

Time passed; I have no idea how much. The two of us sitting within one another's arms on the ground as unspoken questions lingered in the background.

'When this all ends, we can be together,' I said naively, not even thinking about my marriage ceremony due to take place in just over twenty days.

'Some of the British are attempting to divide us, Temi. To make us enemies with one another.'

'Why would they want to do this?'

'So they can take everything from us. We have many things here they would like.'

'From what I am hearing, men from your village are working with them to overthrow—'

'Temi, do not let this also divide us too. Please.'

I closed my eyes and sank the back of my head into his chest. I would not ask him why he would take books from them. I resented our time being taken up by talking of this anyway. I just wanted everything to be as it was before.

'Temi, we must be careful. You cannot be seen with me. Our people are now enemies.'

I leapt up and faced him, ripples of alarm shooting through my body. 'I cannot stop seeing you, I cannot!'

'We won't. We just have to be careful for now and when everything returns to normal – whenever that will be – we can . . .'

'We can . . . what?'

In that moment I felt even younger than my years, because neither of us was really able to predict what would happen next in our lives. Our fate decided only by others.

'Olu, I have to tell you something— '

Yet before I had even begun to tell him the news of my impending marriage, he silenced me with his lips.

*

Now with just eighteen days to go before the marriage, I knew with every fibre of my being that I had to stop it.

Yet the faces around me, contorted into happiness and spouting words of congratulation wherever I appeared in the compound, disagreed. Even a number of my father's wives acknowledged me with good wishes. Although my mother also revealed some were jealous I had been chosen for such an honour.

Still, happiness was present and I felt responsible for this. The happiness of others.

My father summoned me to the yard where the chief sat with him among others, including my mother.

'What has taken you so long, Temitope?' Like Aunty Kike, my father and mother only spoke my full name when they were close to anger.

'My apologies, sir. I was engaged in my duties, sir.'

'Never mind that, greet the chief, now!'

I sank to my knees and moved awkwardly towards the chief, my soon to be husband, his large frame covered by yards of cloth which thankfully allowed his callused toes to be mostly out of view.

'It is okay. Oya, get up,' said the chief. I had never been addressed by him directly before and it felt as if I were being chastised. 'Don't look so scared,' he said with a gargantuan smile revealing a crooked row of teeth the same colour as the evening sun.

He turned to my father. 'Temi is from a family that is good, just and royal. A proud and wonderful lineage. It is an honour to have her as my wife.'

'Yes, indeed, and many like that Queen Victoria in England should do well to acknowledge this lineage and my position as king here.'

'I agree, Kábíyèsí. So she should also know that with both our families together, we will defeat whatever the British Queen sends our way.'

My father continued. 'It is important to let the British know that even though they are advancing on much of this great country, this is still our land.'

'Correct,' said the chief, nodding vigorously.

My unkind thoughts wished his head would simply nod all the way off!

'Together, we are stronger, and your union with my daughter can only strengthen us!'

More grunts of agreement. I looked at my mother and she was actually smiling, an expression I rarely saw on her face.

'Temi will make you a good wife,' said my father.

'The dowry has already been agreed. I say, with your kind permission, we bring the marriage forward,' said the chief.

My heartbeat skipped. 'Sir?' I said, daring to interrupt the men as they spoke. Thankfully they did not hear me, fully engrossed in this conversation about me, my life and my future.

I had made the assumption it could not get any worse than this; that I still had a chance to convince my father and mother this was not the way forward. My hope, the size of an ant, but present nevertheless.

Yet as soon as the chief spoke his next words, that hope quickly diminished into nothing. 'I would like to take Temi as my wife in seven days.'

Apparently the humiliation of emptying my stomach just a foot away from the chief's ugly feet did nothing to dampen his enthusiasm for making me his wife. The women, including Aunty Kike appearing from nowhere to usher me away, chuckled amongst themselves over my apparent joy. First I had fainted and now this – how overcome I must be!

The pace of excitement within the palace walls accelerated, as my anger simmered in the only place it was allowed to – inside.

It had always been difficult to get my mother alone, let alone gauge her interest in what I was about to say. Indeed, as soon as I had stopped suckling at the breast, I'd been cast aside for the next child, her interest in me waning further once Aunty Kike took over my care.

'My daughter, the question should be, why not you?' said my mother as I engaged in a last-ditch attempt to halt this marriage. 'You are one of the most capable among all your father's daughters, and at this young age, you will guarantee a long line of children.'

'The chief already has eight children,' I mumbled.

'Yes, he has many, many children,' my mother said without chastising my rudeness. 'They are all boys except for one.'

'Is this not preferred?'

'Yes, boys are good to have, especially at first. Though it is the female children who will take care of you in old age. The boys will provide the resource, girls, the love and care.' She began to chuckle, something I seldom saw or heard her do. 'Our family is very blessed when it comes to female babies, as you know.'

My mother and several of my father's other wives had given birth to girls, with only two boys out of eighteen children. There had even been a rumour that the two boys were not from his loins. A rumour I suspected had been started by one of the wives.

I hadn't even thought about how I was to handle the chief's other wives or where I would fit in, because the possibility of this marriage had never seemed real to me.

Until now.

'I heard that when Cousin Bimpe was told to marry, she refused and this was upheld,' I said, trying to hold onto anything. Anything.

'This is not the same,' assured my mother with a hint of exasperation. 'The chief is requesting to marry you during very difficult times. We must have unity against the British. What you are suggesting is unthinkable.'

Why did everyone keep talking of these British? What did they have to do with me and my happiness?

'Cousin Bimpe chose who to marry, ma.'

Her eyebrows raised. 'There is someone else you would like to marry?'

'Erm ... no, ma.' I closed my eyes in shame at lying to my mother and also at denying my love for Olu. Even though speaking of him would put him in danger, this still felt treacherous.

My shoulders slumped and, in a rare show of affection, my mother stroked the side of my neck. I wanted her to hold me in her arms, tell me I did not have to do what was being asked.

'You will marry and you will have a child and you will be happy,' she said.

'Like you?' My final act of defiance.

Her expression went from wide-eyed shock to anger and then to a meekness I hated.

She blinked rapidly, her smile false. 'Yes, like me.'

Once again, evening fell and I was back in the bush, sat on a rock, waiting for my beloved.

When Olu arrived, I fell into his arms, feeling a stab of rejection as he gently pulled away.

'Everybody is talking of you and the chief.'

'I will not marry him. Never!' I said with a passion which up until that point hadn't been allowed a voice.

'Why did you not tell me, Temi?'

I bowed my head in shame. 'I tried ...' His finger tilted my chin upwards. His eyes glistened and I assumed it to be the light from the stars.

'It is the chief, Temi!'

'And?' We both knew that this defiance, this resistance of mine was pointless.

'I want to marry *you*, Olu!' The words which had never had the courage to emerge before had now been spoken.

He took my hand and that familiar fizzle of excitement crept up my body. 'I want that too, but I am the enemy.'

'I only want to be with you.'

'I shall think of something.' He spoke so robustly, I had to believe us being together to be a possibility. I had to trust his words.

It was that very night I decided to confess my terrible predicament to the only one I could trust in my family.

'You are not happy, you say?' said Aunty Kike.

'No, ma.'

'Oh, Temi, I feared this.' Aunty Kike pulled me into her arms in a way my mother never had. This I had not expected. A raised voice at least, maybe even a slap, but not this.

'How did you know, Aunty?'

'I have seen sorrow in your eyes every time he is mentioned and you vomited at his feet!'

'So I don't have to marry the chief?'

Her expression softened even further as she looked straight at me. 'I am afraid, my daughter, you must marry him.'

'Ma?'

'It is all arranged. It is all agreed.'

She embraced me again, mumbling something I didn't care to listen to, as she stroked the back of my head like I were a child. Yet I wasn't a girl any more. I was soon to be a wife, a mother. Whereas I simply wanted to be held and to be comforted.

I could only trust that Olu had a plan.

With five days to go before the marriage ceremony, hope, however small, remained inside of me. Having talked with Olu that very morning as we watched the sunrise together, he spoke confidently of his plan for us to run away together. Shocked at first, it was easy to yield to this plan because we had no choice. Like

Romeo and Juliet, we never wanted to be apart from one another again.

Looking back on that beautiful sunrise, I wish I had truly savoured each second and minute. I wished I had allowed him to hold my hand just a little longer. To have kept my head resting on his shoulder until it ached.

If only, if only, if only . . .

If only I had known that soon nothing would ever be the same again.

It was not uncommon for the chief to summon someone from the village, but a girl of my years, his soon to be wife? This was not usual.

My breathing quickened as my mother and I took the path to his compound, her own silence unnerving. My newly plaited hair was causing my head to itch, newly applied oil fresh from the karité trees dripping down the sides of my face and mingling with nervous sweat.

'Mama, do you know what this can be about?'

'We do not question the chief, we just go,' she said. 'Don't look so worried, Temi. Your father is the king. He would never allow you to come to harm.'

I stood yards away as the chief and my mother spoke hurriedly but quietly. They must have been speaking in jest because she began chuckling in that false way only my mother could muster.

She turned to me, her voice raised. 'The chief will ensure you return home.'

'Mama, where are you going?'

'Don't worry,' she said, moving away from me. 'I will be with you tomorrow after sunset.'

I had planned to see Olu at that time to discuss his big plan for us. I could not be at the chief's compound all that time.

I opened my mouth to call out to her, but was silenced by the sound of the chief's booming, irritating voice. 'There is nothing to fear. You will soon be my wife and this, your home!'

I turned to him, this stranger.

'It is good to familiarize yourself.' The chief had hardly ever spoken directly to me before and I did not know how to position myself. I hadn't even greeted him in the formal way yet. I dropped to my knees quickly.

'That's all right, get up,' he said quietly. I became even more overcome with panic as this all felt strange. I longed for my mother to return. The confusion must have been evident on my face, yet the chief could only chuckle. Until he didn't.

'Temi!' he said, as my eyes followed the path my mother had taken, away from me.

'Temi!' he reiterated. When the chief spoke, you listened, yet all I could hear were the screams inside of my head.

'Yes, sir?'

'Come.' He held out his hand. The last thing I wanted to do was to touch him, yet it was unthinkable to say no. So I took his large hand, his skin clammy to the touch, and allowed him to lead me away. I had never been alone in close proximity to this man before.

'It has come to my attention you are having doubts of our union.'

From the corner of my eye, I could see one of his men standing guard.

My thoughts immediately turned to Olu, wondering if he was safe.

'You are the king's daughter. A beautiful princess. A treasure. I want you to be satisfied the right decision has been made for you.'

No words were forming in my head, just a fear rising in my body. Fear for Olu, a longing for my mother and Aunty Kike.

We walked through to his courtyard and slowly past the animal murals, carved posts, and a collection of onlookers who I could only imagine were his wives and their children. Some of the older wives turned their faces away from me, whilst greeting the chief respectfully.

'Enter,' he said, in front of a doorway away from the main throng. It was a large room, much grander than the courtyard, with statues adorning both ends and, in the middle, a raised floor covered by a woven mat and a soft material.

'This is where you will sleep.'

Even I knew it was not befitting for a man of his stature to be showing me his home like a mere servant would.

'Thank you, sir . . . for your kindness.'

'Sit,' he said. I did so immediately, on the edge of the woven mat where he had pointed. The material on top was the softest I had ever felt against my skin. He was indeed a grand man who owned beautiful possessions.

He sat beside me. 'As you can see, I want only the best.'

I nodded my head.

'You, Temi, my princess, are the best. The most beautiful of all my wives.'

I wanted to remind him I was not yet his wife.

'So very beautiful,' he said, shifting in closer, his hot breath now bathing my neck.

I hadn't noticed his hand on my knee, which quickly moved up my thigh and to the place between my legs. A place Aunty Kike said was sacred. A place not even Olu had ever touched.

My entire body felt like one of the rocks at the top of the hill, my mind unable to think of anything when his finger began to probe my sacred place.

A flash of utter disbelief gripped me as I silently questioned what was happening.

Then an intense fear gripped my entire body, rendering me helpless, even though I wanted to run. Instead I squeezed my eyes shut, not remembering to even breathe, and when he gently pushed me back onto the soft material covering the hard surface below, it was time to activate something within me. Something which said this was not actually happening. That none of this could be real.

I thought of the morning sun as his hands slowly pulled open my wrapper.

I thought of the taste of freshly cooked rice and soup as his 'thing' slowly brushed up against my thigh.

I thought about plaiting Taye's hair, as the chief's voice spoke into my ear. 'Just calm yourself.'

Those words were the last I remember. My view overtaken by that of a white bird with an orange ring around its eyes.

Was it real? To me, it was. Flying gracefully up above, hovering, and staring down onto the compound and into this room.

It was not my body being smothered by this gigantic man; not my legs and wrists gripped by fattened hands – they belonged to someone else, another person, a girl whose name I did not know. Whilst I . . . I was just that beautiful feathery white bird with an orange ring around her eyes, flying towards that deep blue sky.

I was free.

Chapter Six

You are your husband's most delicate, precious possession. You belong wholly to him.

Mrs Adeline Copplefield,
'The Manual for Good Wives' (1891)

Temi
1861

That white bird stayed with me, watching as the minutes, hours and days of my life sped past in what felt like the speed of lightning during a harsh storm.

It watched me being dressed in lavish garments for the introduction and marriage ceremonies. It watched the beads being placed around my neck as I rigidly stood in front of the chief and someone announced I was now a wife.

'We can be stronger than ever before!' announced my father, as the chief and I sat side by side in our ceremonial necklaces. The hair near my temple that Aunty Kike had plaited too tightly was not aching as much as the sensation in my chest. I could not look at the chief, nor my father, a sense of injustice no one told me I had a right to nestling inside of me.

Sometimes the bird was tired and would refuse to fly. When this happened, my heart would beat furiously and my neck moisten even though there was a cool stream of air from the desert a long journey away. Sometimes my breath would catch in my throat and it would feel like my time on earth was about to end.

A constant battle of thoughts and feelings which mostly felt out of my control.

Since the marriage day, the chief had not let me alone on any night. Continuously summoning me to that space on the floor with the hard surface and soft material. A contrast of surfaces existing as one. Reminding me of the first time he had done *that* to me.

Unlike the first time, he no longer needed to remove my garments without asking, as now I did so without question.

I no longer remembered the girl I had been before. The joy and the light bled dry from my body. Any real feeling inside of me gone, locked away in a box I could never open again. Even the way I walked had changed: slow, as if dragging my full weight under sufferance. My voice too was now a low whisper and devoid of any strength.

I belonged to my husband. A man who did what he wanted with my body and whenever he wanted. That was my life now.

Thoughts appeared to me in the darkness as the chief lay beside me, snoring loudly after yet another laborious onslaught on my body. Thoughts ranging from how it would feel to place bits of cloth into his mouth and watch him struggle to breathe his very last breath, to that of my own demise.

Sometimes I'd think of Olu. An image of him somewhere in my mind, yet I was unable to truly connect with it. Too frightened to even dare.

What a relief when the chief finally stopped calling me to lie with him. Instead spending many nights with his second wife, Fola, the one many felt him to be truly in love with.

'Aunty Kike,' I said, unable to conjure up any excitement at seeing a familiar face.

'Temi, we miss you,' she said, putting her basket on the floor.

Questions rested on my lips that were dry from the afternoon sun. Questions which were futile now. Gone, the chatty child of yesteryear.

'Your mother sends her greetings.'

I do not care.

'Look at me.' She gently pulled my shoulder towards her and I hated the treacherous tear which appeared in my eye.

'Oh, Temi, why do you cry? You are a married woman now; you should be happy!'

'Why do I cry?' My voice was low, conflicted on whether to show respect to my elder. How could I, though, when I could no longer even respect myself?

Then something extraordinary happened. Aunty Kike's eyes began to water. The only time I'd ever seen a woman in my kingdom shed tears was at a death and nothing less than that.

'Why do you cry?' I asked, not bothering to hide the disdain in my voice.

She beckoned me to a mat on the floor and we sat. At first saying nothing and then she pulled out of the basket a mango, which she placed into my hand.

I looked towards her and then at the mango, my eyes widening in disbelief.

'Forgive me,' she said.

I looked again at the mango. This was my favourite fruit and Aunty Kike and I had spent many moments devouring its sweet nectar. She would often bring them to me after a bout of illness when my appetite returned.

'It is sweet,' she said. 'You will feel better.'

My brows knotted. I looked towards her. Words lodged in my throat. Disrespectful words I could never speak to an aunty.

I looked back at the mango again, wishing it could cure all ills. Or at the very least, choke me as I ate, so that I could breathe no more.

Chapter Seven

To ensure your own happiness, you must always put your husband's first.

Mrs Adeline Copplefield,
'The Manual for Good Wives' (1891)

Landri
Present day

She'd been driving for hours. Mostly in circles and ending up nowhere. Leaving London, then taking a motorway exit that brought her straight back into the capital. As if she hadn't quite summoned the energy to commit to a destination. Stopping only to eat at a nondescript greasy spoon, hardly touching her food, and that blasted mobile phone pinging incessantly.

The first few messages had been from well-wishers, news of the engagement having reached her wider circle of friends. Also a group chat had been created by Sadia – entitled *Landri's wedding brunch prep!* – to which all their friends had been invited, many of whom she hadn't seen in years.

A number of messages were also from Ross.

Babe, missing you.

Guilt flickered within her. Ross would sometimes send these messages during one of his particularly boring work days, less so when he was busy. Today was clearly a slow one because five had buzzed through even before midday. It was as if he knew something had gone off in her head. As if he knew she'd been driving around for hours, second guessing her decision.

At the lights, she stared at the phone expectantly. The tone of the messages had changed.

Where are you?
I called you twice??

It was now three o'clock. By this time, as was their pattern, she would have checked back in with Ross. He'd always insist she 'respond within a timely manner', as he liked to call it. Many times she'd be in a meeting but as long as she'd pre-warned him of this, he was fine. Otherwise, he'd question why she hadn't responded quickly enough.

Now she wasn't responding at all.

WHERE ARE YOU?

This caused her to almost rear-end the car in front. The loudness of the capital letters. His obvious frustration.

She placed the phone into the glove box, berating herself for looking at messages whilst driving. Ross was due home around six and as soon as he saw the note, he would know. She could turn around now and be home in time for his return. Blame her lack of communication on a dead battery. She could do it; she could turn back and behave as if none of this had happened.

She continued to drive. Aimless. Stopping only to call work. Thankfully, Monday was a work from home day.

It wasn't as if she had any family she really spoke to in England and her grandma was the only relative consistently present in her life. Pity she lived in a quiet, picturesque village all the way in Italy!

As for her friends, they wouldn't actually understand if she showed up on their doorstep less than twenty-four hours after getting engaged.

There was somewhere she could go, though.

A house.

A property she made sure to hardly ever think about because the memories attached to it were still raw all these years later.

A house she'd owned since the age of five, yet hadn't set foot inside for over ten years. Even then, a quick once-over as she'd signed an updated contract with the property management company. Over the years, she'd made sure to have nothing much to do with it where possible. There had mostly been long-term tenants staying an average of five years, but the email she'd received only last week had reminded her of the fact it had been empty for a month. She'd responded with a shrug of the shoulders, at peace with the knowledge it was mortgage-free, and had simply continued with her day – oblivious to the smallest of seeds that email had planted in her mind.

Now she was headed towards a destination. Just on the outskirts of London. Far enough away, yet not too far.

The car no longer driving at speed, she took in the unfamiliar area which had a country feel to it, even though she could be at a Tube station within fifteen minutes by car. The houses were mostly quite large, some with gravel driveways, others with brightly coloured flowering bushes decorating the front. Even the sky looked bluer here, with a sense of freshness permeating the surroundings. She couldn't understand why she hadn't thought of it before. Especially as, for once, the timings had aligned: the property was empty for the first time in years.

'Will you be staying long?' asked the bemused Mr Shilling, one half of the team who owned Shilling and Jones property managers. Landri gazed out of the shop window and onto the quaint little high street with a barber, artisan bakery and a fancy gift shop called Chimes & Things.

'Miss Sommers?'

'I'm not sure,' said Landri. He clearly wasn't happy with the vagueness of the answer but was at least appeased when she assured him their services would still be needed and the house was still very much on the market as a short- or long-term property letting.

Landri told herself she'd only need to stay for a few nights. Maybe a week tops. Or a week or two. She wasn't much sure of anything in that moment, only that she never thought things would end up like this when she'd met Ross five years ago.

It had all begun on an online dating site, although no one except Sadia knew this. According to everyone else, they'd first locked eyes across the room of a fancy Thai restaurant where Landri had taken herself on a 'date' after yet another succession of failed first dates. The Thai restaurant part was true. That night she'd felt emotionally battered, reminding herself she was an idiot to think any good man would want her. Even her own parents hadn't thought much of her, so why should a stranger on an app? She'd violently dunked her rice-paper roll into the dipping sauce, repeating the mantra 'no more dating'. She was done. It was over and she could only feel exhausted at the prospect of any more. Then, a ping. From the dating app she'd forgotten to uninstall on her phone. It was a message from 'too good to be true' Ross. She thought *what the heck*, and responded, and in person he'd surprised her by being even better than his profile suggested. Apart from the beautiful aesthetics (dark hair, clear skin and tall, athletic frame), he came from an intact family of mum, dad and two sisters, having grown up in an idyllic little house in the countryside. His parents still adored one another and in time he said they'd love her too. This was more of a pull than anything else. The chance to be part of a real family.

During their first few dates, Ross continually explained that, for him, the only thing missing was someone to share his life with. Landri meanwhile had always operated as a one-woman show. Yet Ross, being the attentive, generous and loving boyfriend he came to be, forced her to believe she could exist with another person and with one who loved her fiercely, and more importantly, might just stick around.

Ross was a man everyone loved. His charm matched his looks and he had the power to make you feel like the only other person in the room. Oozing not only confidence but an air of vulnerability that made you want to also protect and nurture him.

It had been easy to fall for him. Make him the centre of her world whilst losing something much, much more precious.

Now, as she sat in her car outside a house called Tumbleberry, her one wish was to be as far away from him as possible.

Chapter Eight

A wife's sole concerns should be for her husband and for her children.

Mrs Adeline Copplefield,
'The Manual for Good Wives' (1891)

Temi
1862

The day the baby came, we experienced a downpour and a swathe of sunlight appearing at the very same time.

My desire, of course, was to close my eyes and remove myself from what was happening to my body. To blot out each stab of pain, the pulling ache down below. Only, this time, I could not avoid reality and even the white bird had deserted me. I would have to acknowledge what was happening.

'She is here!' my mother kept saying, along with satisfied murmurings of the women who had gathered, including Aunty Kike. At first I thought she was referring to me, but her gaze rested on a tiny bundle wrapped in her arms.

Some of the women began to dance, as if filled with the greatest of joy.

'Don't worry,' said one. 'Your next will be a boy!'

It was with immediacy that my mother corrected her. Saying the chief already had an abundance of sons and a daughter was what he desired most. I couldn't help but hope that now he had what he wanted, he'd no longer need to lie with me.

Lola Jaye

I lay back on the mat. This body I inhabited seldom felt like a part of me, just a tool the chief had used for his own pleasure. Now, with what had just happened, it felt even less a part of me. As if something much more had been taken.

Regardless of how I felt, nothing could stop the festivities which continued in earnest around me. I was a thousand miles away from it all, though. From everything. Not wanting to connect with anyone's gaze, whilst at the same time looking for any sign of Olu, my eyes fixed on one of the trees outside my quarters.

My Olu. I had not seen him in so very long. Not since before that night, when the chief . . .

Why would Olu want to see me anyway? I was no longer the same person he used to meet in the bush. Why would he even want to be near me again? I had betrayed him. Unwillingly perhaps, but my body now belonged to the chief to do with what he pleased. Why would Olu want anything to do with me again?

A loud wailing turned my gaze away from the tree.

'Look,' said Aunty Kike. Something moved in her hands, wrapped in cloth.

I looked up and she moved the bundle towards me.

I turned away from her and back to the tree.

'Take,' said my mother, placing the baby into my arms one day. Soon, the forty days would be over and I would be expected to return to the chief's quarters.

'Are you not going to feed this child?' she said.

As I had done the first time my mother had placed her in my arms, I pulled her closely to my chest, my gaze straight ahead.

'Why do you not even look at her?' asked my mother.

'I am doing what you ask of me. I cannot do any more.'

'What did I do to have a child like you?'

I blinked back a tear.

'Temitope? What have they done to you? I don't want them to take you like they did Taye.'

I flinched at the sound of her name. *Taye*. The one who was lost. Gone. Could I not be lost too? Why had the wives spared me?

'They have poisoned you like they did her, but Taye's demise was quick. I don't know what this can be!' My mother fell at my feet, the loudness of her voice not enough to shake me out of this haze which nowadays seemed to pursue me everywhere, as I moved, tried to sleep. This heaviness sitting in every part of me. Refusing to leave me.

I held tightly onto the baby as she nursed, staring straight ahead.

Nothing appeared to change. Every time the baby was placed in my arms, I failed to make the faces I had seen on other women when they held their babies. They would always smile, their voices turned up to almost shrill and then rocking would ensue. Gentle movement for a newborn, a slight bounce for an older child.

'Do you hate her? Tell me you do not hate her?' asked my mother not for the first time.

I looked at the baby briefly, but not for too long. Then I turned to my mother. There were no words, but if there had been, I would have told my mother that I didn't hate the baby but I fiercely, and without apology, truly hated myself.

'You must know how blessed you are?' said Aunty Kike one evening. Even she had lost patience with me and I couldn't help the extra layer of guilt at the tone of her voice. She'd been married for a very long time now and had failed to give her husband a child. He had since married another wife who had conceived three children, whilst Aunty Kike remained a source of gossip and unkindness amongst the other women, including her siblings, my father's sisters.

I wanted for her sake to be better than this. To show her how

I could be with the baby. That I could nurture her, hold her close to me without fighting the need to hand her to someone else. I desperately wanted to show my aunt how I could be *good*, when in reality, I wasn't sure I could.

'This is how you hold her,' said Aunty Kike, holding the baby so effortlessly and in a way I never could. Rubbing her hands up and down her back and placing her lips softly on the top of the child's head.

'Here,' she said, moving her towards me. 'Take.'

I took the child from her again and placed her on my lap.

'No, Temi. Hold her like this.' Aunty Kike pressed her palms to her chest.

'I have just fed her!' I cried.

I felt impotent.

'Hold her. Like a mother holds a child!'

I slowly placed the child to my breast, her legs wriggling slightly with a small cry, a heartbeat. She smelled of a freshness I hadn't noticed before, her tiny eyes looking up at me expectantly. She needed attention, feeding and care . . . all the things I knew I could never provide for her.

'Temi?'

As soon as she took her again from my trembling arms, I saw myself in the distance, flying away. To oblivion. Yes, that.

The bird was back.

I crept between sleep and a painful consciousness, just as I did every night.

The tap on my shoulder startled me. I saw Aunty Kike's face. She had clearly been crying, yet I couldn't summon the energy to care for the reason for her tears.

'I am full of remorse for what I did,' she said.

I sat up and reached for the baby. Then I remembered she was with my mother.

'What did you do, Aunty?' I rubbed at my eyes.

'I was the one to tell them of Olu. This is why they changed the date of the marriage.'

My heart leapt at the sound of his name. Yet my energy remained weak. 'Aunty, it is in the past.' My words were forgiving but my mind recalled the chief summoning me to his quarters. Doing what he did perhaps because he knew my secret. I closed my eyes. 'Aunty, please, I am very tired.'

'Today, I spoke with him.'

I dared to believe what I had just heard. 'With . . . with Olu?'

'Yes, with Olu.'

I sat up straight. 'Did . . . did he ask of me?'

She nodded her head.

'What did he say?'

'Temi, you are a married woman. After your father, your husband is the most respected and most powerful man in the kingdom.' She took my hand and squeezed. Her voice now low. 'If you were to stay with me tonight and then go to the bush before sunlight, I will never tell them I knew.'

I finally woke up to what she was saying.

'Do you understand me?' she said, leaning close. Her lips brushed against my ear as she spoke. 'Olu will be there, waiting for you.'

Rushing but in a dreamlike state, I wandered the familiar route that would lead me through the bush and to the rocks. My mind refused to believe I was actually there; perhaps this was a dream, a participation in something which did not exist. But when I finally saw him, my mind cleared of the debris which had dominated my thoughts. His perfect back towards me, I simply caught my breath in my throat and closed my eyes, fearing if I moved closer, he'd disappear like a firefly.

When he turned to face me, his smile was wide. 'Temi?'

I rushed towards him as his arms opened, then stopped to drink in those beautifully long eyelashes, strong nostrils and skin which glistened despite the lack of light.

When he cupped my face, my tears refused to stay put, his own eyes shining too.

I had so much to tell him yet no words were spoken. As if speaking would break something.

Our cheeks were touching now and our bodies so close, we could have blended into one person.

'My Tem-Tem,' he said, and I never wanted to be anywhere else again.

Chapter Nine

Any man will be seeking purity and innocence in a potential bride.

Adeline Copplefield,
'The Manual for Good Wives' (1893)

Temi
1862

My life no longer felt like this endless, hopeless journey into what I could not see.

It now contained a rush of hope and meaning because Olu was once again a part of it.

It felt as if no time had passed between us, even though I had got married and given birth during our time apart. As for Olu, he now attended a school run by the British which had clearly brought a change in him. I saw a fire in his eyes as he spoke incessantly about lands far away and his increased love of books and the written word.

He also explained that, all that time ago, he'd hatched a plan for us to flee to a neighbouring village. A plan full of flaws, he said, and perhaps it was just time that we had needed. I could never agree with that, because given the chance to erase all which had happened to me from that night onwards, I would.

'You are a wife now, Temi.'

I hated being called a wife and even more so when it came from his lips.

'How are you keeping?'

No one had ever asked me this, but had just assumed I was 'keeping well' or didn't care for the answer anyway. I wanted to break down in his arms and tell him everything – what the chief had done to me and how it had felt afterwards. Yet how could I, without telling a story showing me in a way I never wanted Olu to see me?

I had to focus on the future now. Something I suddenly had the ability to do, as after this unexpected reunion, I felt myself coming back to life again.

'She likes the water,' I said, as Aunty Kike wrapped the baby in cloth after bathing her. An act which appeared to make the baby smile incessantly. I hadn't noticed this before. Or perhaps she had been doing it for some time now and I simply hadn't been awake enough to appreciate such a gesture.

Sometimes I longed to gaze at her the way Aunty Kike and even my mother did. With a love that could not be articulated. Yet on the rare occasions I allowed myself to look at the baby, my body would simply stiffen.

I took her, still damp, from Aunty Kike's arms.

'I knew it!' said Aunty Kike.

'Ma?'

'The wives were saying you hated your own child. I was always defending you, telling them this wasn't true.'

'I could never hate her,' I said tenderly, bouncing her gently on my knee. She was indeed a beautiful baby. Favouring my side of the family with her darker complexion and widened nose like my father's. Yet I still could not look at her at length without recalling the pain; a part of my life I would rather did not exist.

In fact, I loved her enough to know that she deserved much better than that.

She deserved better than *me*.

*

It was another seven days until I was able to see my Olu again.

'I will come back for you after dark,' said Aunty Kike.

'Aunty, why are you helping us? I believed you did not approve . . .'

'I do not, but I look at you now and already, since Olu's return . . . you have changed.'

I understood this.

'You are still not the same as you once were . . . no longer the young girl I watched grow. The light . . .'

'Light?'

'Your eyes used to be shining . . . like that moon. Now your eyes have no light, Temi. Only when you are with him.'

My feet followed beside her and my heart sang inside my chest. This was happiness. The expectation of something good. Hope. Not the dread I was used to whenever I thought of the chief, not the fear when yet another aunty chastised me for being an indifferent mother.

Yet just minutes into seeing him again, my world was about to be shattered once more.

'Temi, I am leaving,' he said.

I unfurled myself from his embrace and just stared.

'Temi, my love, I am leaving our beloved country!'

I needed to stay present, to hear his words, however much they felt like daggers sliding into my heart. They may as well be daggers because without him, I would have nothing left. The chief had already been asking my father when I would be returning to his quarters, having been gone much longer than the required forty days. The thought of ever lying beside him again filled me with a revulsion so powerful, it threatened to topple me where I stood.

'You are . . . leaving me?'

'I cannot stay here. There is a vast world far away from here, Temi. Remember the books we read together? Besides, I do not see the troubles within our villages changing. I feel they are getting worse. Also, if anyone were to find out about us meeting . . . I know we do not discuss this, but you are married, Temi. To the chief. And we are still at war.'

'They are at war, not us!' I said passionately.

'There is a ship leaving for England and it is my intention to be on it.'

'A ship? Like the ones who took our people in chains?' I had heard these stories my entire life, though was never privy to when the men discussed it in meetings. The women spoke of it in hushed voices, the grief forever etched on their faces. The mothers, wives, siblings. Forever retelling the story of our kin who were placed in shackles on ships, never to return.

'It is not like that, Temi.'

'Then what is it like?'

'Mr Carmichael is a good man and will give me work as a ship's boy.'

I may not have been privy to men talk, but had deciphered that the British were supposed to be the enemy, even if they no longer came with chains. If so, why would Olu be joining them on a big ship? None of this mattered in that moment as the emotion in my chest felt seconds away from erupting. I was losing him all over again and for a very long time . . . possibly forever.

'Wh-when will you return?'

'I do not know.'

We stood facing one another, our hands entwined. This could not be the last time. My life could not go back to simply being confined to the chief. No.

'You can't leave!'

'Temi, please be calm.'

My palms pressed to my face where I willed the tears to stop. I was tired of crying. 'You are never to come back, are you?'

His facial expression told me what I feared the most.

'Please do not do this. Please, Olu! Please don't leave me with him!'

'Temi, I am going nowhere without you!'

Silence.

'So you will not go?'

'Oh, I'm going. Only, you are coming with me.'

Chapter Ten

To be truly respectable in the eyes of society, a woman must marry and marry well.

Mrs Adeline Copplefield,
'The Manual for Good Wives' (1888)

Landri
Present day

Landri exhaled.

Just standing in front of that house, having made a decision, allowed the tension in her scalp and forehead to ease and her shoulders to move downwards.

This was a good idea, she realized, pulling the suitcase out of the boot.

'Hello there!' An older woman waved at her from across the street and began slowly walking towards her.

'Hello,' replied Landri brusquely, hoping she'd take the hint. She did not have the energy or inclination for chit-chat.

'Moving in?' said the woman anyway.

'Sort of,' she said, quickly regretting the ambiguity that would now require more of an explanation.

'Hope you're better than the last lot!' said the woman, her bouffant-styled grey and black hair blowing in the slight breeze. 'A family of four. The couple were nice enough but the kids were so rowdy. Playing football in the road and kicking the ball onto my front lawn a couple of times, just narrowly missing my window.'

'It's my house actually.'

'Oh,' said the woman, and Landri hoped that would be the end of it.

'Need any help with your stuff?'

'No, that's all right. I'm good.' She could feel the woman's eyes on her as she grappled with the rucksack and case, then struggled up the steps to the arched front door.

'I'm just across the road if you need anything!'

Landri zoned her out, as she took in the front door of the house. She'd forgotten how impressive it looked, especially with its recent light-grey paint job. Luckily, the name of the house, Tumbleberry, was still visible on the arch.

On this particular street, the houses were a mixture of pastel colours – she'd even spotted a pink one on the drive up. The trees were neatly trimmed, the pavements smooth, and she'd only seen one car drive past. She suspected it didn't look that much different than it had a hundred or so years ago, and it felt like she'd possibly stepped into a time warp.

Landri had always resented the spare key on the I Love Miami key ring she carried everywhere, a constant reminder of the weight of responsibility in owning a property she'd never wanted. Now, as she turned that key in the lock, Landri felt only gratitude for it and for the woman who had bequeathed it all those years ago.

She was immediately hit by the smell of lavender air freshener. A long corridor led to a bright kitchen and, on the right, a flight of wooden stairs. She was grateful the cleaners had obviously been in to prepare for the next tenant.

Neutral tones decorated every inch of the house. Off-whites and beige – perfect colours for renting apparently, but precisely what Landri needed. A total antithesis to the riverside apartment full of Afrofuturist artwork and colourful tiles she'd left behind.

The original fireplace in the living room activated a memory of one of the times she'd spent Christmas here. Back then, her child's imagination had focused on how a very round Father Christmas could ever have fit down the chimney and out of that fireplace. It was something she'd gone over for the entire holiday, perhaps failing to notice anything different about her mother. Not knowing what was to come and that it would be the last Christmas they would ever spend inside this house together.

The kitchen had been completely remodelled and whilst this made sense, it didn't seem to go with the rest of the house, which appeared to still be locked in a centuries-old world. She was relieved to see it contained all the appliances she'd need, though, including a top-notch air fryer like everyone seemed to have these days. The main bedroom was sparse, with no personal touches. The property was just a neat shell of a house which had once been a home.

There wasn't much point in going into the other rooms, as she just needed a bed and a bathroom anyway. Until she figured out her next move.

Landri lay down on the bed, her phone buzzing beside her. A call. She stared at the name.

Ross.

It stopped and began to buzz again.

It was now seven o'clock and he'd be at home. He was meticulous with time keeping. Got the same train every day, and if he was running late would let her know with a message. He never deviated from anything, their lives ordered in a way which at times felt suffocating.

7.10 p.m. He'd be calling Sadia now, to find out if they were together. Sadia would then ring her.

As predicted, Sadia's text message pinged its arrival.

Sadia: U OK?

Ross: Where are you??

Landri's throat turned dry. She picked up the phone and threw it against the wall in a fit of unexpected rage.

Of course she wasn't okay! Hadn't been for a long time. She'd been drowning, suffocating in a life of her own making. A life she had slipped into without warning. A life she no longer enjoyed, only tolerated.

She fell face down on the bed, hands balled into fists, the pillow muffling tiny, tiny sobs.

She wasn't actually sure what the tears were for, only of how much they needed to be shed.

Chapter Eleven

If you do not possess the feminine qualities desired by society,
you will not only be dismissed as an unsuitable woman, but
also as a potential wife.

Mrs Adeline Copplefield,
'The Manual for Good Wives' (1890)

Temi
1862

I held the baby close to me and for once my mind did not drift.

I willed my thoughts to stay on her, to drink in every inch of her, when usually I would close my eyes and welcome the retreat. This time, I looked down at her in my arms. Really looked. Conceding she was indeed beautiful. She was indeed worthy of a good mother.

I looked up at Aunty Kike. 'They will no longer condemn you, call you names. You will be her mother,' I said.

Aunty Kike blinked rapidly, my words finally getting through.

'You will be to her what you have always been to me.'

'Are you certain of this, Temi?'

'She needs a mother. A good mother. I am not that.'

The silence which followed was only punctuated by the sound of a persistent mosquito buzzing between us. A moderator. A judge.

'Temi . . .' she said quietly.

'Aunty, please . . .' We both knew I was not capable of

mothering this beautiful child. 'You are a better mother than I. You take care of her most of the time anyway.'

'That is what I am supposed to do.'

'Yes, but you do more than you should and you do it without complaint. You cannot be apart from her without longing. I see it in your eyes, every day. Whereas I don't feel this way.'

'Temi . . .'

'Aunty . . . Please, take her. Whilst I am in England, please look after her for me. She will know her father, the chief.' I swallowed, knowing full well he wouldn't have much to do with her and part of me was glad of this. 'She will know you and you can keep her safe from everyone.'

'When will you return?'

'I can't ever return, if I do this. The chief, his people, the family will all punish me.'

'So I will send her to you on a ship?' Her forehead crinkled.

'Yes, Aunty. Or maybe you will come with her.'

'I don't want to ever go there, to England. I fear the white man.'

Frustration began to build inside of me. I needed her to agree to take the baby and tell no one of my plans.

'How do you know I won't tell them?' she said.

'It is something you have done in the past. I cannot be sure.' Indeed, I was hovering over the line of disrespect, but I would speak like my life depended on it. 'If you choose to do so again, Aunty, know that you would be condemning me to a life with a man who takes what he wants from me, even if I do not permit it . . .'

'Temi . . .'

'Each night he hurts my body. Every night. Even when I was with child.'

She turned away.

'Now, when I have been eating with him, he has started to beg me to lie with him and I have refused. How long until he stops begging and just takes what he wants again? How long?'

The tears drenching my face surprised me because I had only meant to produce them to ensure my aunty would bend my way. Yet the pain was there, real, raw and threatening to overtake me if I allowed it.

If I stayed.

The corner of her mouth twitched. 'Is he not your husband? Is it not your duty?'

Her questions enraged me so I ventured into the tactic I knew would result in what I needed in order to save my life.

'Even before he was my husband, Aunty . . . he took me in his bed. After you told them I had doubts about wanting to marry.' My words continued, with unplanned anger. 'I hate him! I truly hate him and I would rather die than lie with him again!'

'Temi, stop with this, please! I will do what you have asked. Whatever you want, I shall do it.' Her own tears came thick and fast, mingling with my own as our foreheads touched, our bodies shaking with emotion. She was sorry for what she had done, I could see it in her eyes. Her apologies meaningless, if she prevented me from leaving.

'There is sweet fruit I have packed for you,' said Aunty Kike, placing a sack into my hand. I already had a change of clothes in the other. Olu said we must travel lightly.

The chief had mentioned me joining him tonight. His tones less of understanding and more of a command. This day could not have come soon enough.

'It is time.' Aunty Kike's tone sounded as bitter as a kola nut, whilst I felt a sadness at this possibly being the last time I'd lay eyes on her for a very long time. Perhaps even forever.

'Say your farewell to the baby.'

'Will she not be unhappy if you awaken her?'

'You have to bid her farewell!' The venom in her voice alerted me to the shame I had felt from the moment the baby was born. The shame attached to the knowledge that I am not a good mother.

When Aunty Kike placed her in my arms, I felt an emotion for the baby but in a new way. Like a sibling or a cousin. She belonged to Aunty Kike now. Everything I had done for her had been a poor imitation of what Aunty could and would do. She needed her more than me, which was why it felt so easy to hand her back to Aunty Kike, her mother. Her *real* mother.

'Temi, I will return for you long after the sun has left. Be ready,' she said.

I stood there, watching her walk away with the baby in her arms. Silently, I mouthed two words I had been unable to articulate. Words laced with a hope that, one day, the baby would understand.

'I'm sorry.'

That evening I sat with my mother as she complained about one of my father's wives. My mother had only been a little older than I when she'd borne her first child and now looked more advanced than her years. Tired. She would say over and over again how hard it was to be the wife of a king. Now when she said it, I'd fight the need to add: 'It is equally difficult to be the wife of a chief. It is lonely, it is painful on both my body and my mind, and it is everything I would never wish upon another woman.' Instead, that last night with my mother, I whispered a silent goodbye to her as she continued her chatter.

As for my father, he was tending to business in another village. Although I had not been able to sing a silent farewell, it felt as if I had done so a long time ago. Our distance perhaps heightened the moment he insisted I marry the chief.

I could not blame him for his actions, though. My father was the king, just as his father before him and his father before him. I was from a long line of princesses with a duty to uphold, a birthright.

Yet I wanted none of it. I was willing to walk away from it all for the chance of a happy life with Olu.

The sun had not yet appeared, locked in that time between darkness and light. However, there was enough light to see Aunty Kike's tears after she embraced me.

'Go and find your happiness,' she said. I had not expected this. The women in our family were not expected to be happy. They were expected to ensure their husbands were happy, to sire children, boys to continue their husband's line and girls they could raise to do it all over again for another man.

I moved away from her, as if already stepping into another country. I had no desire to return to the one in which I had lived for my entire short life.

Now, barefoot as I ran to meet him, I felt as if I were rising from the dead and running into a new life.

Through the bushes, past the ube trees, my toes connected with the sharp-edged stones and the softness of fallen fruit. The newly risen sun guided me as my heart pulsated under the thin layers of cloth covering my body. When I made it to the top of the hill overlooking a large body of sea and its angry waves, I allowed myself to exhale. Seized by a gust of freedom I'd never felt before in my life.

Then that voice, deep and alert, spoke my name. 'Temi.'

My eyelids opened in gratitude, my mouth smiling automatically as both of us held out our hands. My name on his lips sounding like a song and bringing with it a sense of warmth and security I had all but forgotten.

'Let us go,' he said with an injection of assertiveness I needed to take that final step away from absolutely everything. Away from my home, Aunty Kike . . . and my child.

'Are you sure you want to do this?' he said.

I nodded vehemently.

'What of the child?'

'She is with my Aunty who will care for her. One day I shall return for her. Or Aunty Kike will arrange her journey. Olu, please, let us just go and think of the plans at a later time. Please!' The panic rose in my voice and his face remained stern.

'Temi, I must be sure because if we do this, there is no way to turn back.'

'Yes!' I screamed with absolute abandon. I had been in bondage for as long as I could remember and it was time for the freedom which had until now been elusive. 'I am sure! I am sure! I am sure!'

He squeezed my hand and, in that moment, I knew without any doubt that whatever faced us on the other side of that water, it had to be better than what I was leaving behind.

PART TWO

Chapter Twelve

A woman must remain ladylike at all times, with a soft tone of voice and genteel manner.

Mrs Adeline Copplefield,
'The Manual for Good Wives' (1888)

Temi
1862

'Boy!' spoke the gruff voice from behind me.

I stared out at the horizon, the large expanse and endless flow of water still managing to surprise me with its mindless beauty. I was still unable to decipher how this large vessel named *The Foundlander* had the ability to keep us above the surface. This wasn't the only time I'd seen such a beast, but it was my first time actually being on one. Living on one. People in the kingdom would often describe them as *bad*, as they brought enemies to our shores when we had not asked for them. Yet the moment Olu and I had boarded one, it felt more like something good that could take us on a journey far away from anything I had ever known. A chance for Olu and me to live out a story book of our very own. A story not yet written.

'Boy!' said the voice again. I turned around.

'You hard of hearing?' said the white man with a tufty beard drooping at the bottom of his face. His skin had pockmarks around his cheeks, wiry hair framing an oblong face.

'I . . . Yes, sir,' I said in a deepened voice, perfected with Olu just days before leaving.

'You have no place up here. You should be down below with the others.'

I nodded, careful not to meet his gaze so as not to reveal what I had already been able to conceal for days now. I dressed as a boy because women were not permitted on *The Foundlander*.

In the galley of the ship, Olu sorted the freshly caught fish I knew would never reach my lips as they were reserved for others. Also on board were live chickens which we used for eggs. I longed for one to be killed so I could tear into its succulent meat and fill my belly. It was during such moments of hunger I missed the taste and aroma of home.

There was indeed a hierarchy of who had what, though, with a handful of men like Mr Carmichael, the owner of the ship, indulging in the fish and the rest of us left to eat salted beef and hard ship's biscuits, which I hated. I could not begrudge the rules, just be grateful to be on this ship and moving away from *that* life.

Mr Carmichael appeared to be a good man. He and Olu had met when he began gifting materials to the school Olu attended. Apparently stunned by Olu's 'tenacity' – a word Olu explained to me – he promised him work in England if he so wished and to accompany him on the voyage back.

'How do you know he does not wish to place you in chains?' I had said, to which Olu laughed and then with all seriousness said: 'Mr Carmichael is not that type of white man.'

So far, I had seen nothing to contradict Olu's assessment of this man.

I made my way below and caught sight of Olu talking to one of the other ship hands. He looked up and I smiled slightly. A silent intimacy between us.

When we'd first considered this plan just days earlier, it had sounded ludicrous. Yet after stepping into the clothing of a white man, which included hard-wearing shoes and a cotton shirt which covered every element of my shape, I felt confident of what lay ahead. Then, just as I had assumed my disguise complete, Olu had produced a thin knife.

'This blade will rid you of your hair. I will use it with the soap Mr Carmichael has given to me.'

I had placed my hand to my head, slowly pulling away my headscarf. My mother had always commented on how beautiful and thick my hair was. *A window into your beauty*, she would say. What if my hair had attracted the attentions of the chief?

'I am very sorry to have to do this to you,' said Olu. 'But it will grow back.'

I ran my fingers through my hair and a smile had formed.

'Take the hair off. All of it!' For the first time in so long, I had felt a surge of power in my body. Believing the shedding of my hair a way of being reborn. To start again.

As he had smoothed away the strands of my hair, a story was also disappearing. I was Omo Oba, a daughter of a king. First name Adekunbe by my father and Temitope by my mother. I was sixteen years old. A wife. A mother. One of six siblings from my mother, one of eighteen for my father. I hailed from a proud royal lineage with expectations and traditions I was bound to.

Would the erasure of my hair take all of this away?

I hoped so.

As the days wore on, Olu insisted on taking over most of my heavy duties on the ship, even though I assured him I was capable of the work.

'You are a princess,' he whispered.

'No, here I am not. I am just me. Besides, we can't let anyone know that I am a woman, let alone a princess.'

He would not listen and the extra work often resulted in a weariness in his eyes and constant yawning. I did what I could, of course, and would slip him some of my food, pretending I wasn't hungry. In truth I found the food tasteless anyway.

Mr Carmichael would read during down time, with Olu following suit, whilst the others all preferred to drink alcohol and sing at the tops of their voices. It was clear to me and the others that Olu was Mr Carmichael's favourite, and this soon benefited us both as we were sometimes allowed to eat some of the leftover fish. It didn't taste that much better than the salted beef, but I pretended to like it. Something much harder than pretending to be a boy!

When it was time to sleep beside the mass of snoring bodies, Olu would sometimes reach for my hand which I would gently pull away. It's not that I didn't want to touch him. I did. I also did not.

When my monthly visit arrived, it was Olu who gathered up extra cloth for me to place inside my trousers. It was Olu who disposed of the soiled cloth by mixing it with the fish guts and throwing them overboard so as not to cause suspicion. When the flow was light, he was able to wash them easily, explain the stains as being remnants of an injury. There was no time for coyness with him, I had to reveal every part of myself and, in doing so, did not have time for the shame I knew lurked within me. The shame that would find me as we slept on board that ship. When Olu would fall asleep beside me. When thoughts entered my head. Of her. Of the baby I had left behind. It would only happen at night when sleep would not come – generally most nights. Her face appearing in my thoughts as a single tear fell towards the floor. While I told myself I had left her with someone who could love her more than I, my heart ached in a way I had not expected.

As time continued on *The Foundlander*, Mr Carmichael began to single out Olu more and more for easier tasks and I'd sometimes catch the two of them whispering or engaging in guffaws. Olu was different when in Mr Carmichael's company. More *English-like*, I imagined. It would appear I wasn't the only one pretending to be someone else just to get by.

On my knees, scrubbing the cabin floor, I quickly noticed a pair of hard-toed boots and looked up to see Simon, one of the other ship's boys, stood in front of me. As far as I knew, he was from Olu's village and they had known one another before boarding the ship.

'I know your secret,' he said in my native tongue.

I'd been trying so hard to learn English and this was all we spoke, yet hearing my mother tongue spoken with perfection sounded comforting for a moment . . . until I realized what he had said.

He bent down, squatting beside me.

'It's quite a sight. A real princess on her knees, cleaning the floor like a common servant!'

I gasped.

'Do not worry, I will not tell anyone,' he said in English, speaking in a raspy voice I instantly hated.

I carried on moving the brush up and down the floor until he had gone, then stopped to sit back, my heart racing.

Olu insisted Simon was harmless. His reassurances did nothing to curb the stabs of fear that appeared whenever Simon glanced my way.

Thankfully, later that very day Mr Carmichael announced our arrival in England was imminent. The loud cheer which followed from the mouths of all the men echoed what I felt inside. An excitement over a new life I had thought about every single day on this ship.

I only had to keep this 'disguise' up for a small amount of time and then it could begin.

Just a little while longer.

Chapter Thirteen

It is said, self-denial or self-control does not come easily to a man.

Mrs Adeline Copplefield,
'The Manual for Good Wives' (1889)

Temi
1862

'What will you give me to stay quiet?'

The quickness with which he moved shocked me, as did the putrid smell of his breath as the tip of his nose touched mine.

It was already dark; we were alone save for the loud singing and the clanging of bottles coming from below deck.

'I said, what will you give me, Temitope?' I resented him saying my full name almost as much as being alone with him. Especially as Olu was nowhere to be seen.

Simon reached for my arm and I immediately stiffened. In the darkness, I could only see the chief's hands tearing at my clothing and his ugly murmurings of satisfaction, as his sweat dripped onto my face.

'No,' I said quietly.

'What?' he said with laughter in his voice.

'NO!' I roared towards Simon, just as my knee rose to connect with that part of him between his legs that I hated.

The howl of pain from Simon's mouth was drowned out by the singing on the ship. Yet I was certain it could never match the sound inside of me as I watched him double over. Tempted to pound my fists into his back and inflict as much pain on him as I felt had been done to me. Instead, I rushed to find Olu, who sat with the white men as they drank.

We stared at one another – in silent communication – and he stood up abruptly, placing his cup to the side. Without saying one word, we moved away from the throng.

'You are shaking,' he said, hands steadying my shoulders. I had not even noticed. 'Talk to me, Temi.'

'I cannot,' I said. 'You would not be able to receive such news.'

'Of course I can. I do not consume what is in those cups. Alcohol will never touch my lips. I am of sound mind.'

I could see Simon in the distance. Limping by, his expression one of hatred.

'Temi, please!'

I spoke a lie, insisted the rocking motion of the ship had rendered me ill.

'If only I could hold you,' he said.

I nodded my head in agreement. Wishing we could touch, relieved we could not.

Luckily, I didn't have the burden of keeping Simon at bay for long because *The Foundlander* finally arrived in Great Britain a day later.

The last of us had disembarked and Simon stood beside me.

'You should thank me,' he said in that raspy voice. 'If I had revealed your identity, they would have thrown you overboard and not before doing much worse to you. The white sailors believe a woman on board is bad luck.'

Olu was in the distance, shaking the hand of Mr Carmichael.

I turned to Simon. 'I owe you nothing,' I replied in English, my stature defiant, my voice firm like an unripe plantain. I had forgotten what it felt like to speak above a whisper in my own voice. It felt good.

'Is that so?' Simon sucked his teeth the way my mother would when angry with me, whilst I calmly walked away, instantly forgetting his face as I took in the sights before me. Of this Great Britain. Currently full of a grey mist that seemed to cover everything, including the other moored ships, as menfolk exited or boarded. Men, Black and white, carrying goods from ships to land. The smell in the air putrid, although never as bad as the odours below deck. That mixture of alcohol, sweat and excrement something I was not about to forget in a hurry.

Olu's widening smile and obvious excitement as he spoke with Mr Carmichael was something I could not match.

We had left the beauty of our land for . . . this?

'Temi,' he said.

My teeth began to chatter. The cold air a shock as I'd assumed such temperatures were only confined to parts of the journey. It never occurred to me England would also be this cold.

Olu's hand then discreetly touched my back and I felt a reassurance in that touch. A belief we had made it. That we'd be successful in everything and anything we tried to do. I'd left everything behind, risked being uncovered on the ship, and now – many, many days away from the land where I drew my first breath – I simply had no choice but to be hopeful for everything which came next.

Chapter Fourteen

As a wife, do not dwell too long on heightened emotion. A husband needs serenity in the home.

Mrs Adeline Copplefield,
'The Manual for Good Wives' (1889)

Landri
Present day

Her eyelids flickered open and at first she couldn't quite believe the time displayed on the white circular alarm clock on the wooden bedside table.

She'd been asleep for almost twelve hours.

A gorgeous ray of sunlight crept through the white net curtains and she pulled them apart to peer out at the view of her car on an empty street. The pastel houses and gravel driveways seemed almost like a giant dolls' house utopia. It was sweet, quaint, and so not her! She was all about apartment living, working in the city and surviving on lattes. She'd landed a job as a junior copywriter at E&S, one of the UK's largest advertising agencies, straight out of university. She'd made it to senior advertising director on sheer hard work and now ran a team of eight and had come up with some of the best slogans in the business. She'd always loved writing, being creative, and at times – especially in the beginning – couldn't believe she was actually being paid a lot of money to do so. Her team consisted mostly of men, with Landri being lauded as the first 'woman of colour' (how she hated that term) to reach such a senior level.

Yet no one had told her that after fifteen years of doing this job, any creativity would have been sucked out of her. That the higher up she climbed, the less joy she would feel walking into a plush office with her name on the door. That she'd be exhausted from working twelve-hour days as well as fighting a constant feeling of not being good enough.

Both in the office *and* at home.

Landri was grateful she'd packed her new gym kit, bought in a moment of madness. When it had arrived a month ago, Ross had gone from congratulating her on finally joining a gym to asserting how trashy the gym clothes made her look. 'It's a bit tight and might give the gym rats the wrong idea,' he'd said.

She'd never taken it out of the drawer again.

Now she viewed it with a fresh lens. The leggings would look fab with the leopard-print hoody. At least that would cover most of the top. Ross had always commented that her bum and thighs were what needed the most work, and maybe he was right.

Peering into the fridge, she was faced with a pint of long-life orange juice and a pot of raspberry preserve clearly left behind by the last tenant, and this pushed her into action. She checked her delivery apps for any local services, which proved pointless, reminding her of this weird time zone she'd stepped into. Perhaps this was a good thing. Maybe she could pretend her real life outside of it did not exist.

Closing the front door behind her, she felt both silly and smug in her get-up, more used to wearing uncomfortable high heels for over twenty years, along with the business suits and tailored skirts.

'Looking for something?' said the neighbour she'd met the day before.

'Sort of,' she replied with a hint of embarrassment. 'Is there a local shop nearby or should I just drive to the high street?'

'The ones on the high street are the only set of shops around here.'

'I was hoping for a corner shop or something.'

The woman shook her head slowly. 'Not if you want something quick, my love. Anyway, looks like you're ready for a walk in your lovely tracksuit.'

Landri smiled awkwardly, regretting her choice of outfit.

'The high street isn't that far away. Less than a mile. My daughter picks me up once every two weeks and takes me for a big shop further away. If you need something quickly, there's one of those fancy farm artisan thingies. You can get all you need there.'

'Right.'

'Judging by that car you can probably afford those prices anyway!'

Landri glanced at the gleaming red Alfa Romeo Giulia Sport. A gift to herself after the promotion two years ago.

'My name's Gwendolyn, by the way.' The name sounded old-fashioned, like everything else in her new surroundings. 'You can call me Gwen.'

They exchanged pleasantries and Gwen gave her a quick run-down of the area she referred to as 'a little bit of the countryside just outside London'. Landri suspected the woman would be a source of important information if she decided to stay longer.

If.

Landri assured Gwen she'd take her advice and walk along the cricket fields too. She wasn't going to add that cricket reminded her of Ross.

'So, I take it you are one of the family?' said Gwen.

'Excuse me?'

'You said you own the house . . . so you're part of that family.'

'No, the family who were here were long-term renters.'

'I know that! I meant the original owners of the home. *That* family.'

She nodded awkwardly as she wondered why this woman was making her family sound like part of the Mafia. Also, she'd never truly felt part of any family, which made the conversation even odder.

Gwen continued. 'It's a very famous house around here, you see. My mum – God bless her soul – told me so many stories about the place. How the original owner buried three husbands and went to prison for killing one. Or was it two husbands and one went missing? Can't remember, but it was a very big scandal.'

'Really? I mean, I did hear something. I think it's just hearsay, though.' Landri was caught in the space of wanting to be respectful to the woman who had first owned the house and also . . . a little curious.

'Fascinating story,' said Gwen as Landri glanced at her watch, which had just alerted her to a text message.

'Boring you, am I? I thought you'd be interested.'

'No, not at all . . .'

'Only joking. I like to do that sometimes.'

Landri smiled.

'It's good to finally meet someone connected to the place. All we get in there are a succession of people. Some stay a good few years, while more recently some have come through those app things and just stayed a few days. Not sure what that's all about, but I'm pretty certain the original owner wanted more for it than that.'

Landri shrugged her shoulders. She knew nothing much about the original owner of the house, only that she was her great-great-great-grandmother, who had run away to England with her lover. She'd heard rumours about the husband she may have 'killed', but there being more than one husband was news to her!

Gwen continued. 'A woman who looks like us, living in this type of street in Victorian times was virtually unheard of. She wasn't an average person, you know . . . She came from good stock, which means you do too.'

Landri had never thought of it that way. Always shrugging off that part of her history and often feeling too far removed to be touched by it.

'I can imagine,' she said absently, the growling in her tummy louder than ever.

'Why do you think I made a beeline for you yesterday? Even today it's an anomaly around here. Oh, and the things she must have got up to! What a woman!'

'She sounds really interesting. I'm sure I'll find out lots about her,' she said hurriedly.

'What a strange thing to say. She's part of your family.'

'My family aren't what you'd call close and there aren't many of us,' said Landri by way of explanation, which still sounded inadequate. Yet it was the truth. She'd never had much to do with her mother's or even her father's side of the family – who were white, and not that open-minded about him choosing her Black mother all those years ago. Or maybe she'd just assumed that. Besides, he couldn't confirm or deny considering he was some-where in the world living out his older years as a bassist for an equally ageing band, whilst her mother . . .

Gwen continued. 'I've lived in this street all my life. My mum used to know the lady – your great-great-great-grandmother – who lived there. Used to call her "the old lady across the street". Don't recall her name, though . . . ?'

Landri shrugged her shoulders, partly in embarrassment at not having the answers. She'd been told names in the past and quickly forgotten them.

Gwen's voice dropped. 'The lady was very good to my mum. I wish I could remember some of the things she told me . . . but like most things, the conversations start to leave your memory.'

The air was suddenly solemn and Landri felt a wave of full-blown guilt at not actually knowing anything about the woman who first owned this house hundreds of years ago, or whenever.

'My grandma, she knows a lot more about the original owner. I'll ask her,' she said.

'You mean, she knows more about your great-great-great-grandmother,' corrected Gwen, who tutted her disproval. 'How could you not know her name?'

'Do you know the name of your great-great-great-grandmother?'

'Why no, but I probably would if she'd left me a house!'

Deep breath, thought Landri. This was not a battle she wanted or needed to fight. There was simply no space for extra guilt in that head of hers. It was full.

Gwen thankfully walked away at last, something about patties overcooking in the oven.

The 'artisan thingy' turned out to be a small shop full of delicious-smelling pastries, organic fruit and veg and pots of organic pesto and the like. Ridiculously overpriced, it was at least all Landri needed to feed herself for a few days. She walked past the storefront for Shilling and Jones and made a mental note to one day take a tour of Chimes & Things.

After a hearty lunch of pancetta omelette and a pot of rooibos tea, Landri headed out of the door for the second time, but this time in the opposite direction from the shops and towards that cricket field.

Gwen was right, the scenery was breathtaking, a large green expanse giving way to a view that prompted her to try to work out the direction of the apartment. The office. Her job. Her life. She ignored that feeling of dread forming in her tummy at just the mere thought of work . . . and Ross, instead breathing in a gust of fresh air.

She thought about the woman Gwen spoke so fondly of – a person neither of them had ever met. All she did know was this woman, her great-great-great-grandmother, had given strict instructions that the house stay in the family, in trust, and be used for the 'betterment of the women'. Also, that it could only be inherited by the firstborn daughter of each generation.

Landri smiled at how radical that statement must have sounded then – and even now. She liked this woman already! So what if she'd possibly left three dead husbands in her wake? One in what sounded like very suspicious circumstances.

Whatever this woman's reasons for anything, in that moment, Landri was truly, truly grateful to her.

Chapter Fifteen

A good wife should constantly praise the man of the house whilst sympathizing with his complaints.

Mrs Adeline Copplefield,
'The Manual for Good Wives' (1890)

Temi
1863

My life settled into a routine which felt comforting in its predictability.

Our one-room home started off bleak and devoid of sunlight, but with regular cleaning and scrubbing, I was able to transport it into some sort of haven which represented safety for me and a place for Olu to return to from work. Sometimes he arrived when I had already begun to sleep. Other times, I pretended to be asleep so he would not require affection I was not ready to give.

I soon got used to the many layers of attire needed to simply stay warm in the house. The bonnet strings on my head were always a nuisance as they untied themselves quite regularly. I was grateful, however, for the long skirts and knitted shawl the land-lady, Mrs Bryers, had loaned me.

With Olu bringing home leftover food and cleaning supplies provided by Mrs Bryers, I had no real reason to venture past the front door. Besides, I enjoyed sitting down to read one of the books Mr Carmichael had given to Olu. Attempting to write down new words in this English that was fast becoming easy on my tongue. I began to crave the company of others, though, even if no words were spoken. Just their presence.

At the end of the street were a couple of shops selling meat we could not afford. It felt like an adventure to venture there even if just to stare longingly through the window. I began to do this around twice a week.

Thanks to the constant reading, writing, and daily chats with Mrs Bryers and a handful of curious traders, my English began to improve greatly. What came from that was also knowing which *type* of English I desired to learn.

At times, though, I still fought a loneliness I could not describe. A longing to hear Aunty Kike's laugh; the sound of a baby gurgling. My baby.

'Are you longing for the child, my Tem-Tem?' said Olu. He knew me so well.

I did not answer.

'Mr Carmichael has promised me more responsibility at work which means extra income and then we may send for her. You will not have to be without her for much longer, I will make sure of it.'

I smiled thinly. This boarding house where we made our home did not seem conducive to raising a small child used to outside space. Yet this wasn't the reason for my reluctance. How could I tell Olu the truth? That I had given the baby, *my baby*, to Aunty Kike and that I had resigned myself to her calling her mother for ever more and having no memory of me. Her knowledge of me would come solely from the mouths of others, which unfortunately could include many of my father's wives and even that of the chief. If they allowed themselves to talk of me at all, that is.

'I promise you, Temi, this will not be our life for ever. We shall stay here in the boarding house for just a small while longer. I will work very hard so that we will have a life you would never have dreamed of. Then we will send for her.'

'Yes, Olu . . .'

'There is something else. I can read this by your expression.'

'Like a book?' I said.

'Yes, like a book.'

I stared towards the bed I'd occupied alone since we had arrived just over a month ago. Olu slept on a small woven mat on the floor, insisting this is what he was used to back home anyway. But after a long day's toil, I wanted him to experience the comfort of a bed. I had never slept on one before arriving in England and could honestly say, I would not want to sleep on a floor ever again. Yet he had done so, for me.

'There is simply no rush, my love,' he said, looking towards the bed. 'We are not even married.'

'What of when we are . . . ?'

'Temi, I am simply honoured and ecstatic to be with you. Our love will be forever. We have no need to rush anything.'

That night, as was usual, I failed to close my eyes long enough to embrace sleep. I hated Olu having to be on the floor instead of inside the bed. I longed to join him on the floor, hold his hand, just like we did back home before everything had changed. Yet now, even after all that time on the ship and now just over a month on dry land, I still couldn't be sure he wouldn't change and turn on me if we shared a bed.

I hated that I couldn't trust him.

I hated myself even more.

The days and nights in England grew colder. Something I did not think could be possible. So it became a necessity, and at my insistence we began the habit of huddling together on the bed, a blanket covering us.

I sometimes felt him harden in his sleep and I would quickly leave him sleeping to lie on the mat, my bones chattering with cold.

*

'Tem-Tem, I have news!' said Olu one evening. Mrs Bryers once again had allowed me to help her prepare a dish of bread and dripping, which Olu and I both found delicious. Yet I hungered for the fresh meat and fruit I saw on my twice weekly jaunts.

'Temi, I have been promoted!' said Olu, a look of excitement on his face.

'What does this mean?' Although my English improved daily, some words still eluded me.

'I will be in charge of the men at the docks and I will be rewarded accordingly. Which means ...' In that moment, he scooped me up in his arms in a way I could only conclude he'd seen his workmates doing. 'We will be able to afford new and more comfortable lodgings.'

Thankfully my elevation into the air was short-lived, with Olu coming to his senses and placing me back on the floor.

'We can finally marry. If ... if you so want me, that is ...' he said, searching my face.

'Olu ... I ...'

'I know what you are thinking, Tem-Tem.'

I loved that he still called me this. A name he was unable to use on the ship and which lovingly poured from his lips almost daily now. Yet the sweetness of his words did nothing to hide what was inevitable.

I was already married. A man may be permitted to have multiple wives, but a woman ...

He grabbed both my hands with such enthusiasm. 'I endeavoured to make some enquiries and we are able to marry in Britain, you and I ... Your marriage to the chief is not recognized by British courts. I wanted to make sure or else I would have married you as soon as *The Foundlander* moored!'

'Does this mean ...?'

'It will be a legal marriage here, yes! You would not be committing any crime.'

Lola Jaye

What of the crimes I had already committed? Running away from my village, shaming my family . . . Leaving my child?

Getting married now would be based on a web of deceit and the unhappiness of others, and yet . . . looking into the eyes of the man I still very much loved, it was easy to incorporate my usual trick of placing all my fearful thoughts into a box far away from my heart.

'Also, my love, we will need a new name to signal our new lives in this country.'

No matter how Olu tried to present this, it was indeed prudent to change our names, for many, many reasons. One of which was my father being a very important man across the seas. If we had been able to cross the waters unscathed, what of the king's men? Or other members of the tribe?

'Do you have a preference for our new name?' he said.

It still surprised me just how much Olu included me in decisions. As the female child of a king, I and any other woman or girl in the royal family would have no say in anything official. Only male children of the king were allowed such a privilege.

'Mr Carmichael has suggested a number of names . . .'

'Olu, can we choose our own name?' I suggested boldly.

'Of course we can . . . he was just suggesting . . .'

I had heard enough back in my kingdom to want to instantly resist an English person naming us. Added to the fact that in our culture names are important and have meaning, this decision should fall with Olu and myself only.

This would be a name that in no way could be linked to my past, but would reflect what I wanted for our future: *for Olu and I to be masters of our own destiny.*

'Masters. Olu and Temi Masters,' I said grandly.

Olu's lips curved into a smile. 'I like this. I really like it.'

'And yes, Olu, I will marry you!' I said, smiling.

He scooped me up in his arms again, an act I could never get used to, and he squealed with delight. A strange noise in which I joined him. The two of us squealing together!

Just seven weeks after arriving on *The Foundlander* ship, Olu and I were married as Mr and Mrs Masters. I wore a very British white gown edged in lace that Mrs Bryers had kindly loaned me via her daughter-in-law. An outfit so at odds with the many bridal outfits I had worn for the chief. Apparently this was the type of gown Queen Victoria had worn at her own wedding twenty years before and was still a popular style among brides. My eagerness to emulate this had more to do with its utter erasure of what had come before, because I wanted no trace of home or *that man*.

The afternoon of the small wedding ceremony, the sun shone upon us (something of a rarity in this country) whilst a cloud also appeared in the shape of Simon, who now went by the name of Simon Wetherell and who Olu insisted on being one of the witnesses. I knew they worked together still but their closeness had come as a shock to me.

'He is from back home and at times this is comforting,' Olu had said once I expressed concern. Such concern focused on him knowing of my past life as the wife of the chief.

'Don't worry about all of that. I trust him,' he'd said.

My attempts to ignore Simon's presence on this most important of days came with difficulty at first. But as soon as Olu and I were legally announced as man and wife, I managed to remove him from my thoughts, focusing my attention on the fact that I was now the legal wife of Mr Olu Masters.

That night we returned to our lodgings. The feelings of elation slowly evaporating once we entered the room.

'I am the happiest man alive,' Olu kept repeating. The more he said it, the more my nerves increased.

I slipped out of my dress and lay back on what was now to be my marital bed, not realizing my eyes were closed until Olu spoke to me. 'Temi, open your eyes.'

I was surprised to see him still fully clothed in his trousers, single-breasted jacket and waistcoat.

'Are you not going to disrobe?' I asked.

He sat beside me on the bed, shaking his head slowly. 'I want to be with you, Temi, but not like this. It is like you fear me.'

'We are married. It is my duty.'

'No.'

I sat up, my semi-nakedness making me feel a little foolish.

'No, Temi, not like this.'

'Do you not desire me?' I pulled the blanket over me.

'I desire you greatly, but nothing will occur unless the feeling is mutual.'

My brows knotted with confusion. 'Tonight is our wedding night, Olu. It is expected.'

'It is, but only if you so permit it.'

That I had a choice had not once occurred to me. Not once.

'I am content to hold you for as long as you feel comfortable. Like we sometimes do when we are cold. Or if you do not want this, that will be just fine too.'

'How can this be enough for a husband?'

'Temi, if I only get to hold you for the rest of our lives, I will take it.'

I had been building myself up for something that was physical, an act that could possibly bring me to tears. I'd never imagined what would produce the tears was this absolute outpouring of love I felt emanating from my husband. I hadn't envisaged any of this. I had underestimated him.

'I do not know what went on with the chief and you may never tell me and that is your right too, but I love you, Tem-Tem, and I will protect you with my life.'

That night, our wedding night, he repeated this vow over and over again as we simply lay side by side. Repeating words of love until I fell asleep comfortably and contently in my husband's arms.

Chapter Sixteen

As a married woman, your status is raised.

Mrs Adeline Copplefield,

'The Manual for Good Wives' (1889)

Landri
Present day

In the space of forty-eight hours, Landri felt less weighed down, but boredom had kicked in.

So used to being active and on the go, this stillness felt weird.

She'd heard it said that being busy does not mean being productive, but in her case she begged to differ. In her normal life, by now she would already have bought and cooked food for the entire week and visited Ross's parents fourteen miles away, a monthly scheduled trip. On Mondays, she'd work from home, which actually meant back-to-back online meetings and very little creative work. Sometimes finishing at around 10 p.m. if she wasn't careful. Steve, her so-called partner in various projects, never seemed to be around much during the initial heavy lifting, but when it came to recognition, he'd appear quick enough, at times taking ownership of some of the work she'd led on. Ross once called her weak for allowing this to happen and sometimes she'd agreed with him.

As for friends, she never saw them as much as she'd like, but Sadia and sometimes Claudine would make an effort. Everyone was busy and that included her. On the rare occasion she was off, she'd post in the group chat about making a dinner date, with most coming back with a no.

With Sadia, it was different. The girl she'd known since the age of twelve after getting locked in the girls' toilet at school together. Sadia who had just re-sent her an invite to that irritating group chat!

> Save the date guys for our first session of wedding planning!

Five of their closest friends she hadn't seen in over a year had already clicked yes, whilst Landri fantasized what it would be like to respond with a no. Instead, she sent an email to HR and her boss saying she wouldn't be in for the rest of the week due to illness.

When the phone began to buzz incessantly, Ross's name flashed on the screen along with a picture of them wrapped in each other's arms. Happier times.

Ross, once her anchor, now feeling like an albatross around her neck.

'Hello Ross.'

'Where have you been? Why won't you talk to me?' His words were rushed.

'As I said on the text message, I'm fine.'

'I didn't know what to think. You leave me some letter and just disappear. Where are you? Let me come and get you.'

The ensuing silence felt deafening to her ears. Words unspoken and yet with so much needing to be said.

Her voice was a whisper now. 'No.' She hated the way she sounded. As if silently pleading for permission to live exactly how she wanted to in her own life.

'I want you home,' he said.

Her tummy scrunched.

How had they got here? She'd agreed to move in with him because she loved him. Both able to raise a decent mortgage as first-time buyers and a sizeable deposit thanks, she realized, to the money she earned on the house she had inherited. Eventually settling on a luxury off-plan riverside apartment which felt like a dream. Landri was never one to believe in fairy-tale endings, yet meeting Ross had the potential to be hers. Believing that, like Sadia and Claudine, she too had met her prince charming.

Ross was the man to give her the love she never thought she'd needed. Opening her up to a family who adored her. His mother Kath constantly knitting her scarves and his dad Riku referring to her as *their daughter*. Spending Christmases with them, having spent so many alone. Hosting dinner parties with their friends twice a year and fitting into the couples clique she'd often observed from the outside.

Everyone constantly said what an amazing couple they were.

Landri and Ross, the true definition of a power couple. Ross the perfect man. And on paper he was.

What she'd loved about those early days were the endless kisses and hand-holding, the affection which allowed her to feel constantly wanted. Now he hardly kissed her, unless it was a sure-fire lead into sex.

'I wish you could . . . you could just hold me sometimes?' she'd said once.

The look he'd shot back had sliced right through her. A look which told her she wasn't worthy of a hug, a kiss or any sort of affection. A look which reminded her he was right. Yet days or even a week later, he'd be back with the affection, all over her. Making her feel warm and wanted again. Those were the moments she'd begun to crave from him and, when they came, she would forget how he sometimes made her feel.

Then there was the jealousy. At first, she'd been flattered he cared so much about where she was going and what time she'd be back. Desperate to be around her all the time. He loved her and was simply showing her how much.

Yet Sadia and Claudine's husbands didn't behave that way, and it soon began to make her feel uncomfortable and at times stifled.

She told herself that in the grand scheme of life these were small things. That a man who wanted to be with her for the rest of her life wasn't something to just dismiss.

Also, he wasn't just any man.

He had a great job, was gorgeous to look at, and was often funny, articulate and caring. The last trait, she soon began to realize, had to be on his terms, though.

'When?' he reiterated. 'When are you coming home?' His voice had grown louder. 'Landri!'

'I've got to go.' She didn't want to hang up on him, but she would. She could.

As soon as the call was over, with Landri apologizing as she indeed ended the call, she did something she would have considered inconceivable just forty-eight hours ago. She switched off the mobile phone, pulled off her smartwatch and placed them both into the drawer of the bedside table.

Then she exhaled.

Chapter Seventeen

The act of intercourse is for a husband's pleasure and for a wife, her duty.

Mrs Adeline Copplefield,
'The Manual for Good Wives' (1888)

Temi
1863

I was now a wife and yet could not even lie with my husband.

I apologized almost daily, even though Olu never made me feel any of the guilt I felt inside.

Two weeks after the marriage ceremony, we moved into a slightly bigger dwelling. There, I could prepare our food much more comfortably, and this also meant I no longer had to only stare longingly at the fresh food, but could purchase it. Olu's raise in income had afforded this, but we were still on a ration as we needed to save diligently for our own home. A proper house like the one Mr Carmichael and his wife Mary Ellen occupied. Then, and only then, could we send for the baby, Olu kept saying.

The market was congested, noisy and full of odours. With traders shouting to sell their wares, wet fish gathered on top of one another as women handled them, shouting to be heard. It was clear I looked nothing like anyone else in the vicinity, my eyes turning this way and that, just to see if anyone actually did look like me.

''Scuse me, love,' said a voice belonging to an unkempt woman. She appeared just a few years older than me, but it was hard to tell. 'You look a bit lost. You all right?' Her dress was clean enough, but her hair was a little untidy and she had a number of teeth missing at the front.

I started to walk in the opposite direction, then turned back again, my options limited. 'I wish to purchase food. Meat. Or fish.'

'Stay with me, I'll 'elp yer!' she said.

That she did, and by evening, Olu came home to a cooked meal of fish and potatoes. Tasteless fare yet something I was proud of nevertheless. The woman named Olive had helped secure everything I needed along with a promise to meet her at the same market in seven days' time at 9 a.m.

Olive's tour of the markets sometimes took us further away to much larger ones. The smells even more repugnant, the voices of the traders more animated. She once bought from a vendor two cooked sheep's' trotters which we ate in what she referred to as 'the woods'. I was not partial to this rather unusual-tasting meat but I obliged out of gratefulness, more concerned we were sitting on a patch of damp grass that would discolour my garments. I had to admit, despite it all, spending time with Olive was an enjoyable experience, even if her incorrect use of the English language sometimes irritated me. Reminding me more of how the men spoke on *The Foundlander* and less like the learned women in the books I read!

Inside the woods, we'd pick flowers to brighten up our dwellings, something we both enjoyed.

'No, don't touch that!' she said, smacking my hand away. Olive always appeared full of energy.

'Whyever not?'

Her voice was a whisper. 'No, we don't touch that, Temi, love. It's what they call the Lords-and-ladies berry and it's very dangerous!'

I stared, confused at the stem of brightly coloured berries which looked good enough to consume.

'Word has it, old Maud Parker poisoned her husband with those. Just wanted to scare him after finding out about his bit on the side. Ended up making him really poorly. She's lucky no one called the coppers on her . . .'

'What happened to him?'

'Had all these blisters. Bit of swelling too. Poor bastard was dead in no time.'

'Do you mean to tell me, if I had touched those berries, I would have died?'

'No, you silly mare. You'd have to take a mouthful at least, I would have thought. Best keep away from it.'

'Of course . . .' I thought about the herbs and plants back in the old country. Taye's demise. It had never occurred to me such poisons could also be found in this Great Britain.

'Come on, let's see what we can find over 'ere,' said Olive.

My days of exploration were not only confined to forests and markets. The day I came across a free public lending library was probably one of the happiest days of my life since marrying Olu.

When I asked Olive about it, she simply said 'It's not for the likes of us!', whilst I begged to differ. Olu and I were lovers of the written word and to be around such an array of books and not have to go hungry to pay for them was an unexpected treat.

After I had drummed up enough courage to enter the library, I discovered I could borrow books to my heart's content. I of course began to spend all of my free time inside that building. Fairy tales fast became my favourite book of choice, because even when horror is experienced, everything always ends in the most wonderful of ways. I hoped my own life would mirror this because I was more than ready for a happy ending with Olu.

The discovery of fairy tales allowed images to form in my

mind, of a big house where we would raise children, living a long and prosperous life together. Oh, and we'd also own a large library of our very own. That would be a given.

For any of this to be possible, there would need to be a compromise.

'What if I too worked?' I asked.

'There is no need, Temi. Besides, I have vowed to take care of you.'

'I will simply die of boredom!' I wasn't sure what book I had read this phrase in but it suddenly sounded disrespectful out loud.

Instead, Olu simply laughed. 'Fine, my dear, but the only gainful employment I see of women of our hue is that of a maid and you will never be that to anyone!'

The strength in his voice assured me this meant as much to him as it did to me.

'How about I assist you in your work? Did you not say you were thinking of pursuing your own business away from Mr Carmichael?'

'Yes . . .'

'Then I will learn bookkeeping or whatever it takes to assist you in achieving this faster. I can pick up some books at the beautiful library and what I cannot find, we shall buy. We came to this country together and we will rise together, my love.'

'You are a princess . . . Have I not taken you away from enough?'

I placed my finger onto his lips, to shut out the words. 'We shall do this, together.'

Such confident words from a girl who just months ago had hardly known any English, yet each word spoken I meant and could visualize. My future, here with this wonderful man, where I would contribute to securing our very own fairy tale.

That night, in our rickety bed, I whispered into my husband's ear that I was ready.

'Are you sure?' he said.

I shifted my body close to him and, placing my lips on his, I did not wince. I wanted to be with him. The voice in my head said I did, as did the feeling in my heart.

'We don't have to. Please don't think you have to.'

'I want to. I want this.'

His fingertips were at the hem of my nightgown. 'May I?'

I giggled slightly, part nervousness. 'Yes.'

'Are you sure?'

'I am sure.'

That night, after sixty-two days of marriage, our wedding night was patient, gentle and everything I needed it to be.

1868

Five years after arriving in England, Olu was indeed on his way to becoming a wealthy man. When I said this, though, he'd quickly correct me. 'No, *you* are a part of this as much as me. I would not have achieved half of it without you.'

He'd been promoted multiple times before starting a separate seafaring business with Mr Carmichael, and as bookkeeper of the business, I knew what was made and what went out. Our fortunes were substantial and growing month by month. This meant finally moving into our fifth dwelling in five years. A house we would finally own and that I believed would remain our home forever and a far cry from anywhere we'd lived before.

The house boasted a long staircase with large rounded windows in each carpeted room, a huge fireplace and an archway outside which led to the front door.

'A house with a name!' I squealed in delight. The word *Tumbleberry* etched into the arched brickwork thrilled me so much, yet I couldn't even say why.

Thanks to the trappings of *our* success, we were able to furnish the house with the best of items, including furniture made from quality dark woods like mahogany, giving each of the rooms an elegant, regal feel. As did the impressive crystal chandeliers hanging from the ceiling that shone a light upon the Minton tiled floor. This, all of it, showing the world we had means.

The favourite room in the house for us both was the library. Two large wooden bookcases adorned the walls and were lined with a selection of our favourite books and some we had yet to read. *Romeo and Juliet*, of course, had been the first purchase, and a number of editions at that.

Olu had insisted on a collection of carvings he'd purchased from a seafarer who had recently travelled to Africa. The irony was not lost on either of us. The oblong mask had little in common with our tribes back home, but as Olu insisted, 'It is something.'

Whilst Olu appeared desperate to hold onto pieces from our past, I was keener to do the opposite . . .

Olu and I had only grown closer over the years. After our wedding night, lying with my husband had not been such an easy task for me, but gradually he'd reminded me that love was more than just a word. That it represented itself in how one is treated. And how this man treated me was so opposite to the chief, I could no longer compare both marriages. For the first time in my life, I felt truly loved. Oh, how I felt loved!

Love was an emotion which sang from him whenever he looked at me, how he held me and reassured me that he would never leave me. A reminder his love would never be dependent on my lying with him. So in time, I actually began to enjoy his caresses, his tender and feather-light kisses on my body, no longer associating such acts with pain, but with care, security and, dare I say it, pleasure.

Now, when we lay together, it was the sweetest of experiences, sometimes peppered lightly by a memory that occurred many years ago, but such emotions no longer held me captive.

'My darling, I have something to discuss with you,' I said, patting the front of my silk day dress trimmed with beads. I moved to one of the large bay windows and looked out onto the smart, tree-lined road. The sun, even in the winter, seemed to shine more in this street than anywhere else we had lived. This house, this street, radiated happiness, with every part of me certain this was where I would raise our children and live out our fairy tale.

Olu placed his hands on the back of my shoulders as I gazed through the window.

I turned to him noticing once again those beautiful long eyelashes. 'What is it, Tem-Tem?'

I placed his hand on my growing stomach and his eyes widened.

I nodded.

This was one of the things I loved about my husband and I – we could communicate without words.

'Temi, say it isn't so?' His smile was wide. I loved to see him so happy.

'Yes,' I confirmed.

When he pulled me into his arms, it was shocking to feel his wet tears against my cheek. Men were not supposed to cry and yet Olu was constantly showing me my idea of what a man should be could not be confined to my father and the chief, continuing every day to confuse me in so many delicious ways.

As he kissed every part of my face, I never believed I could feel as happy as in that very moment.

I was wrong, of course.

When our little baby arrived, I realized it was possible to feel a happiness which eclipsed anything I had ever felt before in my life.

Because, the minute I held her, I became flooded with a feeling I had feared would never materialize. Throughout the pregnancy I'd been afraid. So every afraid that what had gripped me the first time I was with child would return.

Instead, on a sweaty bed still daubed with my bodily fluids, I could think of no other place I wanted to be. It was with her. This beautiful little dark brown baby girl with a shock of curly hair and a mouth not unlike her father's, snug in my arms. Her warmth and fresh scent radiating from every inch of her. A love, a complete-ness I never knew existed. I loved Olu, but in a different way and not like this. I wanted, no, I *needed* to protect her and would do anything to keep her safe. She was mine and I had never loved anyone on this earth more.

At that thought, a prickling invaded my skin. I had held a baby, *my* baby in my arms once before and yet it had never felt like this. Indeed, I had never allowed myself to feel anything close to this. A part of me wondered if I had deprived myself. Yes, I certainly had, because this felt precious. Yet I had allowed other thoughts to invade it all.

Not this time.

When this tiny infant suckled on my breast it was as if she erased all the pain the chief had inflicted upon my body. All the pain in my heart.

I felt new.

Amelia Kikelomo Masters changed my life for the better. The word *me* etched into her name as she was the reason I had found myself again.

Her middle name, after my beloved aunty, meant 'a child des-tined to be pampered' – something I intended to make sure I did on a daily basis. Also, Olu and I both wanted her to have some-thing from the country we'd left behind; just as her British-*sounding* first name reflected where she needed to go.

Chapter Eighteen

The domestic sphere is of great importance to a wife: the centre of her entire existence.

Mrs Adeline Copplefield,
'The Manual for Good Wives' (1892)

Temi
1869

It wasn't hard to see that people found my husband's meteoric rise surprising. An African man with the audacity to attain wealth in a country he had only arrived in a few short years ago.

I made it a point never to contradict anyone who commented on what a hard-working man he must be to have secured such a thriving business. I was not in the habit of trying to explain to them we worked together as a couple and my contribution was just as valuable and needed. Many times, Olu would include me in such conversations with other men, yet be dismissed with: 'Well, she has other duties to contend with now, like motherhood, which I am sure she does excellently!'

Again, I made it a point never to contradict. It wasn't hard work alone that had brought us to our current position of owning a nice home (plus my collection of gowns made of silk, adorned with ribbon, hanging luxuriously in our large mahogany wardrobe), it was also the connections. Many of these people held onto their own prejudices, which did not concern me in the slightest, my silence a small price to pay for the dividends. It was Mr

Carmichael who had continued to introduce Olu to the right people, mainly his rich and powerful associates. People who, perhaps without his introductions, would have turned their noses up at this 'little negro boy' as I had more than once heard him referred to. Others remained curious and at times respectful, especially when they heard the rumours that I was the daughter of a king. This seemed to bring instant respect in such circles, or perhaps an unrealistic fantasy of what it meant. When asked about my tribal name and lineage, I would most often revert to lying – careful not to be identified and connected to a dynasty I had fled. A family I had disgraced.

'This house is simply gorgeous!' said Ellen in an accent I had yet to become accustomed to. Mary Ellen Carmichael was Mr Carmichael's much younger wife who I had taken an instant dislike to when we first met. Indeed, as the wife of Olu's business partner, I had learned to grit my teeth whilst behaving courteously. Her clothes were always impeccable and she appeared to smell of luxury, a trait I found to be both vulgar and alluring.

The constant sarcasm to her tone I could also do without. 'It's always a misconception, isn't it?' she said.

'Dare I ask of this misconception?' I said.

She slid her perfect fingers over the shiny wooden cabinet. Her silk gown draped on the floor. Her fine hair was worn with a centre parting and tied into low chignons at the nape of the neck, curly ringlets around her ears.

'Is it that a woman of my colour can live this way?' This clearly had been resting on her lips and it was up to me to release the words.

She turned to me. 'Not at all. Where I'm from there are plenty people who look like you in beautiful homes. Plenty free people.'

I wasn't sure what she meant by 'free people', but her tone sounded condescending. Or perhaps I was being sensitive. It's not as if she didn't speak to her own husband in the same way!

'I mean, it's a misconception that any place can feel like home.'

'I don't understand.'

'If not for Mr Carmichael I would have sailed back to my beloved United States of America some time ago.'

'I believe love has kept you bound to England.'

She turned to me, lips protruding. 'Now, now, Temi dear, love is the least of reasons.'

'I do not understand such a woman!' I said as I joined Olu at the dining table that evening. Amelia was asleep in her perambulator.

'I have always worried about you not having a companion. It is important you have a confidante like Ellen.'

'I am content with you and Amelia, my darling.'

'Ellen is very fond of you and I will be away quite a lot. Especially if the shipping business continues in the current direction.'

'I can survive without you for a week!' I lied. Every time he was away, I would spend the nights awake in our bed, willing him to return, but grateful for the company of our daughter. I just needed to be near him. To touch him; even if it was just the cuff of his finely tailored jacket or my palm on the small of his back. I needed to know he was there.

'The nights away may become more frequent, Tem-Tem. I may have to travel to other continents.'

I stared down at my plate.

'I made you a promise on our wedding day – that you would want for nothing, my love.'

'I have all I want. You, Amelia, a fine living . . .'

'I also know you desire the trappings people like Mrs Carmichael have and that is understandable. Why do we not deserve such things?'

I nodded.

'Also, I have been thinking about the child,' he said.

'Amelia is fine.'

'I am speaking of the child we unfortunately had to leave behind. Of course, no longer a baby!'

My body tensed. 'It is I who left her with my aunty.'

'Yet over the years I have also felt that burden. The guilt of leaving a part of you so far away from us. I know, over the years, it has not felt like the right time for you . . . but I think this has changed now?'

The question hung in the air, testing me, goading me.

'Temi?' He took my hand. 'We are very comfortable now and, well, we should think about sending for her. She is a part of you, which means she is also a part of me. Let us send for her.'

It always sounded strange when Olu referred to the baby in this way. As if I had not birthed a child for another man seven years ago. As if that man had not almost killed me with his treatment.

Whilst I appreciated Olu's words, I also didn't wish to hear them.

'I believe I should spend as much time with Amelia alone first . . . Then we shall send for her . . .'

'I understand your point, but Amelia should be raised with her sibling, don't you think? It would be such a sight to have them both here under one roof, playing together. I'm sure the governess can cope with two children!'

'Yes . . . of course . . .'

'We will be one big happy family.'

'They will never let her go, the chief and his people.'

'She is travelling to see her mother. Whyever not? Tem-Tem, we can but try?'

I knew Olu would be a wonderful father to her just as he was to Amelia. He loved her fiercely and thought nothing of joining her on the floor and singing to her as she laughed in appreciation. Back home, I had never seen men engage with their children as he did. Their contribution was limited to ensuring their safety and full bellies, whilst Olu would read stories to Amelia in a wonderfully silly voice and hold her close at night when she refused to sleep. I felt unease at first because this wasn't the done thing for a man. But Amelia's responses to her father made me realize there was no way it could be wrong.

When Amelia was four years old, Olu insisted we speak to her about her *sibling across the water*. Her response was one of incredible nonchalance.

During the following years, Olu continued to do exceptionally well at the shipping company. He often spoke about the number of Black men they employed and he made sure they were paid the same as the others. He took great comfort in being with those who spoke similar mother tongues, whilst I shied away from it all. Instead, taking silent comfort in spotting other Black people at any given moment. I could be shopping for garments in the high street and one would walk by, my heart swelling with warmth and pride. Fighting the need to walk up to them and ask questions about what had led them here. But the risk in doing so felt too high.

I was now a British lady. One who employed a governess for her child and a personal maid. That job had gone to Olive, the woman I had met in the market when I had newly arrived in England. She may have been a bit slower than I would have liked, but it felt like the honourable thing to do. Her family were constantly struggling and she had assisted me when I had once been in the same position.

Some of my most precious moments were sitting on the lawn, my dress spread out around me as Amelia sat on my lap. I would tell her all about the flowers, marvel at the colours of each and even allow her to pick some for the house. She wasn't as interested in gardening as I, but those moments together, away from the house and everyone else, just us, were my favourite of the day.

The Manual for Good Wives

1874

As Amelia grew into a precocious and intelligent little girl, I hired her a tutor, and it was during this time that I'd sometimes find myself at a loss. As well as catching up on my beloved reading, I would occasionally slip my thoughts onto paper and just stare at the words.

Love.
Amelia.
Olu.
Wealth.
Comfort.
Home.

For the first time in so long, I finally had a life that felt like *home*, and hardly ever gave much thought to the one I'd left behind. When Amelia would surprise me with something so beautifully childish, like a drawing or a line of a song, my mind would move to the baby I'd left behind. She would have no memory of me and deserved to not be plucked from all she had ever known. Besides, I had no idea what I would find if I tried to disturb that particular hornets' nest. The chief, although not the king, was a powerful man and retribution surely awaited me if I ever tried to reconnect to my country.

Thankfully, Olu hardly ever brought up the subject of sending for her after my initial reluctance and when he did, I'd murmur a 'maybe', confident he was often too consumed in his work to continue with the conversation. At times I thought about whether we would have another child. A son. Olu assured me the sex of the baby was immaterial, but I wasn't sure I believed this. Mr Carmichael had sons, some of whom worked at the shipping company. As much as I had learned and assisted with Olu's business, as much as Amelia would learn, attend the finest college and become well read, it would still be a man who would be allowed to put such an education to its full use.

'Mummy, mummy!' sang Amelia as she ran into the drawing room, a piece of paper in her hand. 'Look, I have finished my arithmetic!'

'Splendid, my darling,' I said, placing her beside me. As I gazed at the collection of crooked numbers, she suddenly wrapped her arms around my neck, kissing it in spurts. I pulled her close to me, inhaling the scent of her, filled with a happiness I never wanted to end.

Chapter Nineteen

Before the marriage, it is wise to seek the counsel of your mother in regards to your marital obligations.

Mrs Adeline Copplefield,
'The Manual for Good Wives' (1891)

Landri
Present day

Landri hated the effect Ross had on her.

That one phone call threatened to take her back to a place of feeling she had somehow let him down and was not the person he deserved.

She'd run out on him a day after their engagement party – what type of person did that?

It was another twelve hours before she switched her mobile back on and it immediately began to buzz. Her stomach churned as she saw the voicemail icon.

When she returned the call, Steve, her colleague at E&S, spoke in a slow tone she did not recognize. 'I hear you're unwell . . . I just wanted to make sure you were all right?'

'Because it's not like me to take time off?'

'Something like that.' Indeed, she was used to taking meetings whilst in bed with flu – not that she hardly ever got ill. Not physically anyway.

'You don't sound ill . . .?'

She made up an excuse about getting over the latest bug

that was doing the rounds. 'Now, if you don't mind, I am off sick . . .'

'Yeah, I know . . . I just wanted to ask if you were going to be well enough to make the meeting tomorrow with Gorings.'

Landri recalled the days and nights spent formulating a proposal for that particular company. The worry and the stress involved.

Steve continued, 'I mean it's a big one and they really like ou . . .'

'You can handle it, Steve.' She said this before she could take any of the words back. What was she doing? This was her baby, not Steve's.

'Are you sure?'

'The ground work's all done, all you need is to execute it.'

'Without you?'

'Yes, without me,' she said firmly. Was she tempted to give up on this running away stuff, step into her trouser suit and roll into the office first thing tomorrow morning? Yes. But she physically did not have the strength to do so. The thought of it brought fresh nausea to her throat.

'Can I call on you if I need anything?' he said pathetically. This was the same man who just last year had taken the credit for their last major project, even though it had been a result of all her hard work. She'd had to sit in that boardroom full of men and watch the high-fives among them, her role reduced. Then, an unexpressed anger had cut her to the core as she remained powerless to speak. She'd let it go because Landri had learnt over the years to choose her battles and she'd envisaged much larger ones ahead.

'Steve, you're a big boy, I'm sure you can handle it.' They both laughed but hers was false. She simply wanted him off the phone so she could get back to . . . well, she didn't know what. Breathing. Yes, breathing out loud.

As soon as the call ended, she placed the phone back into the drawer with a curt reminder to herself that the world did not stop just because she wasn't actively checking emails and text messages. Nothing would come to a halt in her absence. Steve would handle the client and everything would be okay. *Right?*

If not, she wasn't even sure she cared anymore.

Something had already shifted inside of her and Landri Sommers couldn't articulate what. All she was certain of was the fact she lived in a house named Tumbleberry and the only person she'd spoken to at any length was a pensioner called Gwen from across the road. This was her now for the foreseeable future and, to be honest, it felt like all she could or wanted to cope with.

Chapter Twenty

*How can there be harmony in a home when a woman con-
cerns herself with finances and expenses?*

Mrs Adeline Copplefield,
'The Manual for Good Wives' (1888)

Temi
1874

Most if not all of the wives I had ever encountered, through Ellen,
were blind to the finances of their own household. They pottered
around making sure their hair remained neat, clothes pressed, yet
asked no questions when it came to much else. I generally loathed
being in their company and always left them with a feeling of
pride in what I had achieved within my own marriage. What *we*,
as a couple, had achieved.

Ellen was different, though. Making sure she was up to speed
on every one of her husband's dealings and advising me to do the
same. I didn't have the heart to tell her this advice was a waste
because my husband consulted me on everything. We held no
secrets from one another and, above all, we were happy.

Ellen and I had now been friends for some time, yet she continued to be an anomaly to me, as well as a contradiction.

'I know I intrigue you,' she often said, sipping her drink
demurely. Her actions were so ladylike, yet what sometimes came
out of her mouth sounded boorish. 'You intrigue me too. The
African princess.'

She often mentioned being born into a wealthy Bostonian family and how much she missed her home in the United States of America. Perhaps this is what drew us together. The feeling of displacement even though we were in a country we had chosen. Or a country which had chosen us.

One day, we had been sipping tea and talking about her new drapes that would be arriving from Italy, when Amelia ran in, the governess trying – and failing – to keep up behind her.

'Oh, Amelia, you are such a delight!' said Ellen.

'I'm six!' said Amelia proudly. Her hair in two bunches wrapped in ribbons, my little girl was indeed a delight. A beautiful child who now resembled my mother in her features.

'It's all right, you can leave her with us,' I said to the governess, Edna.

Amelia stood next to Ellen, resting herself against Ellen's jacquard woven silk dress trimmed with lace.

'I cannot wait for Amy to return from school,' said Ellen of her daughter. The two girls had become firm friends over the years, albeit they hardly saw one another as Amy was away at school most of the year.

'Lucky for you, the governess is homely,' said Ellen in a whisper. 'You hear stories, you know, about the husbands having relations with the governesses and the maids – all of them!' I didn't understand the laugh that followed. 'Can't be an issue with that maid of yours. She is so . . .'

'Olive is a dear woman. Please do not speak ill of her,' I said politely.

When Amelia left to find her doll, I attempted to satisfy my curiosity.

'Has Mr Carmichael—?'

'Oh no, he would not dare. A man like him is fortunate a woman like me would even give him the time of day.'

'Is it because of the age difference?'

'Oh, he just looks much older than he is. All that travelling to remote areas. There's only ten years between us. He married his first wife very young.'

My mind briefly drifted to the chief. There must have been as much as a forty-year difference in our ages.

'What I mean is, I'm from a very good family in Boston and I could have had my pick when it was my season.'

'Dare I say it, but Mr Carmichael is a good man. He's always been very kind.'

'You describe my husband very well. Daddy was beside himself, though. Wanted someone of a higher class.'

'Then why did you marry him? Were you forced?' I asked tentatively.

'Why, of course not! What he lacks in breeding he more than makes up for in wealth. It would be stupid to marry a man unable to keep me in a particular style, don't you think?'

'That I wouldn't know,' I said truthfully, which appeared to bring on a barrage of laughter.

'Oh, Temi, you are a delight. What have I done without you all those years?'

I was relieved when she left as I always felt a layer of exhaustion after her visits, whilst at the same time looking forward to the next one.

1880

When Amelia was twelve, she went away to boarding school. I hadn't wanted her to go, but she and her dad had been in cahoots and I relented, not able to voice the reality of wanting her around me forever. That I couldn't bear to be parted from my little girl.

It was Ellen who assured me this would be wonderful for Amelia and Amy would take good care of her. She also assured me this was the only way for Amelia to become the refined young lady she was destined to be. Something I had always wanted for her.

'My little princess,' I said, grief nesting in my heart as I stroked her hair. She would always be my little princess. A title I had denied her. A lineage she knew nothing about.

The morning she left with her father, I took to my bed. Of course I could have accompanied them, but the last thing I wanted was to show such emotion in public and in front of a school principal or my child. I stayed at home and sobbed into my pillow with Olive insisting I eat some of her chicken soup.

'Oh, Olive, what will I do without her?'

As she looked into my eyes, I felt a wave of guilt. Olive had confided having lost three children during childbirth and that her only surviving child, Ellie, was her pride and joy. What right did I have to mourn a child that still lived? Indeed, I had left a child across the sea and had never mourned her absence in this way.

'I apologize, Olive,' I said. She said nothing and simply forced a smile.

When Olu returned, not even he could console me. Something had awakened inside of me. I told him to leave me be and infuriatingly he did just that. Left me to think about my mother, father, siblings, and Aunty Kike. Recalling that look of anger in their expressions as one by one I had disappointed them. Something lodged in my throat when I pictured her. The baby. How she had looked then and not how she must do now, at the age of eighteen. My thoughts turned to anger, hatred even. All the emotions I had stored up, had managed to keep inside now escaping. Like a living gun, it felt like a trigger had been pulled and my emotions were now being released against my will.

The child. I had left my child.

I moved to the dressing-table mirror. An image of my widened eyes stared back at me, the reflection of a person I hated.

I pulled at my neatly constructed hair, tugging at the coily strands until they fell stiffly to the side. My hands, fists as they now grabbed at the strands, pulling my head from side to side; the sound of my voice loud and uncaring:

'How could you?'

The house was big enough for Olu not to hear me, with the rest of the staff busy in the kitchen or garden. My voice releasing a loud shriek as I fell onto my bed and covered my face with one of the silk pillows. The sound muffled, yet the loudest, angriest sound I had ever produced.

Chapter Twenty-One

Entrusting your heart to your husband is a sacred act. You can at least expect his devotion to keeping it whole.

Mrs Adeline Copplefield,
'The Manual for Good Wives' (1893)

Temi
1880

The letters Amelia sent told me she was having a wonderful time at her school. Olu, sensing my discomfort with our little girl being away from home, began to work shorter hours, choosing to spend more time with me than usual. At times, he would join me in the garden and help to pick lavender, one of my favourites, or we would read together liked we used to. We told one another of our week so far, as well as the brighter memories of the past – like the way we would meet before sunrise. That first kiss by the tree.

'I knew even then you were the only one for me, Tem-Tem.'

'Do you ever wonder what it would have been like for you to experience the affections of another? I have been married before . . .'

'Temi, that was not a marriage. It was a prison. Besides, you are all I have ever wanted,' he said, pulling me in for a kiss. The aroma of lavender and fresh flowers surrounded us, the sun warm on our backs.

*

On yet another gloriously sunny morning, Olive insisted I come to the door.

'I am resting!' I said.

'But ma'am, she won't take no for an answer.'

'And it's not Mrs Carmichael?'

'No, ma'am . . . this lady, she looks . . .' Olive gazed at the floor.

'What?'

She ran a finger across the top of her hand.

'She's Black?' I said.

Olive nodded and a shot of alarm sped through my body.

'Says she has important news from across the seas.'

I swallowed.

'Said her name is Iybee or something. Sorry, ma'am, I can't remember.'

The room began to spin.

'Show . . . show her in. I will be downstairs shortly.'

I had known this day would come.

'Good day,' she said simply. Her skin was the colour of midnight, her cheekbones high, like mine, hair neatly held in a bun. Her clothes had clearly seen better days, but were not from home. So many questions littered my mind, yet only one would leave my lips.

'Is it you?' I said in a language I had not used for years.

'Yes, Mother, it is I. Your daughter, Iyabo,' came my daughter's reply in a broken English I understood clearly.

Chapter Twenty-Two

Marriage is said to be the pinnacle of a woman's hopes and dreams.

Mrs Adeline Copplefield,
'The Manual for Good Wives' (1893)

Landri
Present day

The wall-mounted phone in the kitchen had been a weird surprise, but it allowed Landri the option to call people, without having to be fully 'on'. That's if she could remember anyone's number. She could not.

She unlocked the back door which led into a large, well-kept garden. Having never cared about having a garden, she had to admit the pink, yellow and orange roses adorning the flower beds were gorgeous. Then there were the sweet-smelling lavender bushes planted in different spots, along with a number of flowers she did not recognize: purple, yellow, bell-shaped, circular ones. While the gardeners the agency hired had clearly taken care of the garden over the years, it was also clear that much thought had gone into its original design and she did wonder if this great-great-great-grandmother, whose name she did not know or had once known and forgotten, had lovingly tended to it.

She pulled out one of the white wrought-iron garden chairs in front of a matching circular table and sat down.

She actually owned this house. The enormity of that fact only hit her now. The early rental money had gone into a trust for her until the age of twenty-one, when she was able to draw it out, invest it, and use the bulk as part deposit for the riverside apartment she now owned with Ross. She had benefited greatly from this house and had never given a thought to its original owner. The person who made it all happen. She had managed to place any such thoughts into an unmarked box and simply chuck away the key; a box containing all the other family history she didn't particularly want to face.

Sadia loved asking her the question of what she'd do if she won the lottery and didn't have to work. Sadia's response was always to shop until all the best shoes in the world were in the walk-in closet she had in the mansion she could now afford. Whilst Landri's answer always raised an eyebrow: 'I'd read.'

'Boring!' Sadia would say.

'I'd re-read Maya Angelou's entire works and then maybe some contemporary romance, oh and a bit of YA.'

'What's YA?'

'Young adult,' Landri had said, rolling her eyes. 'I would just read every single day.'

So, walking into what she'd thought was another bedroom but was, instead, a library, she felt like she'd woken up on Christmas morning.

The space was a bright room with two large antique-looking wooden bookcases adorning the walls, each lined with oodles of books. Some were very old but she doubted there were any rare first editions of anything. *Although you never know*, she thought.

She pulled out a succession of books, some of which Landri knew she wouldn't be reading, others added to the 'maybe' list. Whoever had lived here clearly loved *Romeo and Juliet* as there were three separate editions. There were other classics from

Charles Dickens but also Jackie Collins, Virginia Andrews, Toni Morrison and her beloved Maya Angelou! She pulled out *I Know Why the Caged Bird Sings*, sad at the film of dust decorating the cover. The date inside the book read 1969.

This could have belonged to Mum.

She carefully placed the book back onto the shelf, blinking furiously, a well of emotion sitting in her throat. Indeed, her mother could have touched this book, opened it and read part or all of it. This very book. She picked it up again and held it to her chest. The emotion still refusing to surface.

The glorious reading nook under the window had previously missed her gaze. An oblong cushioned seat which she could see had hardly been used. She sat on it, the book in her hand and, feeling a surge of contentment, opened it up. She may not have won the lottery but she was going to take advantage of this time to simply read in this gorgeous room.

Landri's love affair with reading had begun at the age of six. She hadn't been speaking much, sometimes not at all, and found reading a way to block out the noise which seemed to follow her everywhere. The noise mainly from her grandma, but occasionally existing in her own head.

Reading had allowed her to enter a fantasy and simply escape.

Landri had no idea how many hours had passed.

I Know Why the Caged Bird Sings was a book she had first read as a teenager and now, with the eyes of an adult, she was able to find new meaning in it. After closing it at the last page, she felt a tiny strengthening of her resolve. That maybe she could go it alone after all – leave the man who'd been her partner for five years. Do what she'd thought about more than once over the years yet never actioned, shamed into going back to what made her unhappy simply because of her own fears.

*

After a very quick dinner, she returned to the library. The emotional pull tying her to that room felt even stronger. Perhaps a little more than her love of books, it was the knowledge that some of her ancestors may have touched these books.

Mum had touched some of these books.

Landri noticed something poking out of the top of one of the bookcases, its hiding place disturbed by her manic grabbing of the books earlier.

It was a book-shaped object wrapped in old, yellowed newspapers.

'What's this then?' she said.

Unwrapping the dusty package like a bizarre game of pass the parcel, what was revealed inside looked like a leather notebook. Old, yet in good condition. The softness of the leather suggested it must have been an expensive buy in its day.

Landri stared at the notebook for at least thirty seconds.

By unwrapping it she was now duty bound to see what was inside, but something pulled her back. Perhaps not wanting to intrude on whatever secrets lay within.

That night, the hailstones began outside and Landri found it difficult to sleep. She sat up, switching on the side lamp and, once again, gazed down at the notebook she had retrieved from its paper prison. It now sat on the bedside table and she looked at it, sleeplessness giving her a new vision.

Picking it up very carefully, she padded downstairs and sat facing the fireplace, heart suddenly racing with excitement.

It was bound together with some sort of material she could not identify. Muslin or satin ribbon perhaps. Once a beautiful object, she could tell, the effects of age only diminishing its beauty minutely.

Landri exhaled as she slowly opened the first page.

Chapter Twenty-Three

A marriage is seldom without loss.

Mrs Adeline Copplefield,
'The Manual for Good Wives' (1891)

Temi
1880

During the first days after Iyabo's arrival, I felt like a bystander.

Watching as Olu, delighted with her appearance, constantly apologized to her for not sending for her earlier. What with his contacts in the seafaring trade, it had been easy for him to communicate with members of his family as well as Iyabo, who was now a young woman. He'd kept this as a 'lovely surprise', which it had been – I simply needed time to adjust.

'We can't wait for you to meet Amelia!' he said.

'I did not know I have sister,' she said, beaming. Her accent was strong, yet I was curious as to how she had learned English. Also, how was Aunty Kike? Was it easy to just leave? So many questions.

Days passed and I started to feel even more like an outsider in my own life. When Olu was away for two days on business, it finally felt right to speak with Iyabo, my daughter.

'I am happy you are here,' I stated. I was concerned I hadn't said it with enough passion before, keen not to disappoint her.

'I wanted to meet you, Ma. For so very long. I could not do it until my father was gone.'

I stopped.

'The chief is . . . dead?'

'Yes, Ma.'

I did not allow this news to touch any part of me.

'What about . . . my mother and my father, the king . . . are they well?' I had thought of them over the years but admittedly not often. The fear they had come to harm was mixed in with the unforgivable shame I had heaped upon them both.

'They are well. Everybody is well,' she confirmed.

'What of Aunty Kike?'

Without answering, she ran into my surprised embrace and I patted her back tenderly.

'Let us not talk of that right now,' she said firmly.

Of course I would do anything she asked. I owed her that and so much more.

What Iyabo did reveal that day was the fact she'd yet to be betrothed, what with the death of her father taking up most of her and the family's concerns. She'd learned English courtesy of a British trader whom she befriended. I wanted to know more about this man, but Iyabo refused to elaborate further, simply adding he was 'a nice man' who gave her items others envied. Like a pair of white silk gloves, which would have been pointless under such a searing sun. Yet here in England they were much more suitable, remaining one of her most prized possessions.

'Did the family not question your association with this white man? What you were . . . to him?'

Her eyes narrowed. 'Many things have changed since you leave me.'

That stung harsher than a bee sting. I had left her. That was my sin.

I ceased with the questions, placing my hand on her back gently for the third time that day, expressing how overcome with happiness I was to see her.

Olu promised to find her work at the shipping company whenever she wanted but Iyabo seemed happy to run errands and assist Olive around the house. Something I kept telling her she did not have to do.

'I like to help you, Ma. I enjoy helping Aunty Kike.'

My heart leapt at the sound of her name. Finally! Out of all the people I had left behind, she was the one I longed to hear about, and yet having been here a week Iyabo had hardly mentioned her name.

'How is my aunty?'

'She is well . . . though . . .'

'What is it?'

'She has baby now.'

'Aunty Kike has a child?'

'She has three. The first one arriving when I was small.'

It was always understood in the family that Aunty Kike could not conceive. This was the reason I had allowed her to take Iyabo in the first place. Or perhaps I simply believed what I wanted to in order to achieve my wishes.

'After she have the child, she different.'

I tilted my head. 'In what way?'

'She is not good to me. She don't care for me. I ran to live with my father's family but they always say bad things about you. They hate you. So I go back and she . . .'

I swallowed as Iyabo looked towards me.

'And what?' I said, my mind a scramble. Because the woman she described was not the gentle aunty who had brought me up as her own. None of this made any sense. Was this a lie? If so, why? 'Iyabo . . .' I began, doubtfully.

She cut me off and shook her head. 'Do not be sad, Ma. I am here now,' she said, resting her head on my shoulder. 'I am here now.'

Life had now taken on a new rhythm.

Iyabo was a presence around the house I had not planned for, yet now welcomed. Especially as she appeared to forgive all I had put her through, even though I had failed to do so for myself. This was a penance I would live with. One I deserved.

With it being less likely I would give birth to another child, it seemed to please Olu that our family was now 'complete'.

Then, one day at breakfast, Olu shattered this rhythm with some very unwelcome news.

'I will be away my love, for upwards of six months.'

Olive placed the bread rolls on the table and then discreetly left the room.

Iyabo was helping in the kitchen, even though I had told her not to.

'That's such a long time.' I gulped down the remainder of my tea, suddenly preoccupied with how long he had known about this.

'My love, this voyage will mean securing goods that will ensure our wealth is doubled, perhaps even tripled. Also, ensuring the future of our girls and even their children and children's children! Isn't this what we planned for ourselves?'

I thought of the beautiful house and the clothes, the staff, our daughter's school. None of it really meant anything without Olu by my side.

'It is only six months,' he said as Iyabo entered the room carrying a plate of fruit. She sat down at the table.

'Amelia will be back for the holidays soon; you can sort out the garden and Iyabo will keep you company through it all. I will be back in no time at all.'

'Indeed,' I said, with a quick glance at Iyabo. She never spoke much, but liked to smile – a smile that made me feel uneasy for reasons I couldn't quite place my finger on.

I turned back to my husband. 'I will miss you.'

'I will miss you double.' He moved his hand across the table and took mine. As usual, an act that calmed the pressure I felt building inside of me.

'I suppose we can write to one another,' I said.

'Well . . . I'll be stopping off at various ports. You know what the ships are like. Correspondence will be difficult but not impossible.'

I allowed myself to get sucked into the reasoning surrounding the trip when all I wanted was my husband. Is this not one of the most infuriating aspects of love? Always wanting the other person to be happy? I could see what this meant to him. It was reflected in his eyes when he spoke about always having to prove himself among his peers; striving to be three times better to get even a quarter of the respect. This way, people would finally be forced to respect him.

The day before Olu left, I lay in his arms in our bed. We'd been to Amelia's school with Iyabo to visit with her and Olu had decided not to tell her he was going away for such a long time. He'd just wanted to see her before he left. The visit had also given me a chance to finally see the school – and it was grand. With the carefully tended lawns and shiny iron gates, it was a reminder of the trappings Olu worked so hard for, whilst also reminding me that Iyabo had never experienced such things.

Now, Olu and I had less than twenty-four hours together.

'Close your eyes!' he said, leaning to the edge of the bed.

'Olu, what is it?'

'Did I not say to close your eyes?' He smiled.

I did as told and quickly felt an object pressed against my hands.

'Now, open them.'

I thought about just how much I would miss that voice.

Six whole months.

I opened my eyes, running my fingers against the warm leather covering the book-shaped object.

'A notebook. For you to write down all the letters you wish to send me and, when I return home, I promise to read every single one of them.'

Something lodged inside my throat as I carefully opened the leather-bound notebook, and brought it to my nose. The smell of fresh pages and leather all combining to bring me the sweetest of aromas. 'This is beautiful.'

'Read the first page.'

To my wife Mrs Temi Masters. My one and only love. Now and forever.

My heart swelled. 'Oh, Olu.'

He brought his body against mine and that's where we stayed, the notebook pressed between our beating chests.

Olu had been at sea for almost a week now and for the most part I felt able to get on with my life. Partly because he'd been away for up to a month before. So, the way I viewed this, I would at least be able to get through four weeks. Then darling Amelia would arrive and then . . . well, I couldn't think that far ahead because it then started to feel too painful.

I opened up the notebook from time to time, but nothing would appear in my head. There was always something which needed doing, like instructing the gardener and Olive on their duties. Then the task of assimilating Iyabo in our way of life here. Whether this be teaching her the correct pronunciation of words or how to conduct herself as a young lady.

I was thankful for Ellen's visits, which became more frequent, and I started to look forward to them.

'Oh, you'll get used to it! The long absence of a husband!' she said. A large emerald necklace shone from her neck beneath the cream silk and velvet coat trimmed with Arctic fox fur she wore. She often wore the finest things but this could hold an audience on its own.

'Your outfit is divine!'

'Straight from Paris!'

'Your necklace, exquisite,' I said.

She brushed her fingers across her neck. 'Oh this lil' thang.' I wasn't sure what the chuckle meant. There was so much I didn't understand about this woman.

'Mr Carmichael likes to give me gifts when he goes on one of his voyages. This one being six months means a bigger gift. That's all.' She shrugged. 'What did your husband get you?'

I thought about the leather-bound notebook sat against that beautiful necklace. 'A few things. My husband is always generous, so he doesn't need to . . .'

'My, my, have you seen the rain out there? My hair has just been newly done too.'

For once I was glad Ellen did her usual act of changing the subject to herself. I also wouldn't be pointing out that as she got in and out of her carriage, her hair would be protected by an umbrella held by her coachman. Indeed, it was my hair that would suffer the most from British rain, shrinking to the size of my fists and rendered unmanageable for the rest of the day! What did Ellen Carmichael know about wet hair? I checked the anger brewing inside of me. I wasn't one for envy. My marriage to Olu was what she should envy, considering she always complained about her husband. Yet that sparkling necklace was something I would like perhaps to own one day and, according to Olu, this voyage was the very thing that would make something like that possible. Catapulting us up to a higher status. One where I would sit comfortably side by side with the likes of Ellen Carmichael. I and my family, secure for years to come.

I had left my country carrying the biggest burden of shame I could think of, and perhaps attaining such a level of success would somehow make it worthwhile.

Chapter Twenty-Four

If three seasons after being presented as a debutante, a young woman remains unmarried, she may have to consider the consolation of spinsterhood.

Mrs Adeline Copplefield,
'The Manual for Good Wives' (1891)

Temi
1880

When Amelia came home for a visit, I noticed she was not the same.

Not just physically, as was normal for a girl going on thirteen, but she also no longer sought comfort in my arms, instead sitting at a distance whilst updating me on all her shenanigans at this school. The friends she'd made, her difficulty with some of the subjects and the teacher she favoured the most. Of course, I was interested but much preferred her to tell me while wrapped in my arms. I missed the smell of her, that wonderful laugh illuminating any room she entered. Now it would appear she also held some malice because of my part in not telling her how long Olu was going to be away.

'You lied to me, Mother!'

'What happened to *Mummy*? Now I am Mother?'

'I cannot believe you didn't tell me!'

'Your father thought it best we didn't say anything. We just wanted you to enjoy the day.'

'Nothing is the same anymore. I even have a sister!'

'You have always known of her.'

'That is hardly the point, Mother!' She looked at me with her eyes almost closed. I'd noticed her do this earlier but had not chastised her then.

'Amelia, you are being very disrespectful.'

She huffed with exasperation as she stood up.

'Where are you going?'

'To my room, if that's still there!'

'Sit down, we haven't finished speaking.'

She sat down and I spoke. 'I will tell Olive to prepare your favourite, the charlotte russe. She's finally managed to perfect it.'

'That's not my favourite anymore.'

'Oh, so what is?'

Her silence and refusal to look in my direction was the only answer she cared to give. Back in the old country, she would have been beaten for such behaviour and, even here, I could have spanked her myself, but would never inflict such pain on my child. An image of Iyabo entered my head then. Of what she must have endured after running away. Because even if aunty Kike had not hurt her, an elder would have. *'I ran to live with my father's family but they always say bad things about you. They hate you. So I go back and . . .'*

'You can go to your room, Amelia, and don't forget to wash for dinner.'

She mumbled something under her breath as she hurried away, rushing past Iyabo at the door.

'Is everything all right, Ma?'

'Yes, of course,' I lied. Not wanting to think about Iyabo's time without me or what aunty Kike could or could not have been complicit in. I simply wished Olu was here to shoulder some of this. To hold me in the darkness and remind me that all this confusion in my mind would be resolved. Olu clearly the forever hopeful one in our union.

*

When Amelia had been home a week, I believed she began to thaw towards me, even though she hardly spoke with Iyabo. She even helped with the weeding in the garden as we chatted about her father.

'This isn't very ladylike, is it?' she said.

'This is true, but I like it . . . It relaxes me.'

'I won't tell if you don't.'

I liked that some semblance of my daughter was back, albeit for how long, I just couldn't be sure.

'When Daddy gets home, we'll have the biggest party!'

'Yes, why not? We'll invite Ellen and Amy.'

'No, not her,' said Amelia.

'Have you and Amy fallen out?'

'No, I just see a lot of her at school. I don't need to see her here also.'

As understandable as the statement sounded, it wasn't long until our mother–daughter idyll was broken by the sound of Iyabo announcing Mary Ellen Carmichael's arrival.

'Iyabo, Olive is more than capable of announcing guests,' I said quickly, as I wiped down my dress.

'I am wanting to be helpful to you, Ma. If you prefer not . . .'

'I just don't want you to think you need to work here. You are my daughter.'

It seemed like such the wrong moment to announce this, with Amelia sitting there in the garden, but it needed to be said. Iyabo was my daughter too and I wanted her to have the best, just like Amelia.

'Thank you, Ma,' said Iyabo.

'There you are!' said Ellen as Amy trailed behind her. I felt a flush of embarrassment, quite sure the Carmichaels employed an excellent gardener for such chores.

'I think my girl was missing Amelia,' she said. Amy was a thin child with long yellow hair which always looked unkempt.

'Hello, my dear,' I said to Amy, then clocked Amelia's uninterested expression.

'Now, you two young ladies run along. Mrs Masters and I have matters to discuss.'

Amelia dragged her feet to the door, with Amy following behind. As soon as they left, I noticed a troubled look on Ellen's face.

'I am afraid I have news to share about Mr Carmichael and your dear husband.' She shot a suspicious look at Iyabo.

'I would like her to stay. What is it? What has happened?' I said.

'*The Foundlander* is missing.'

'What?' I screamed at her. My insides gripped with fear. 'What do you mean, missing?'

Iyabo stood beside me and held onto my stiffened hand.

'Calm down, Temi, please. Maybe we should go inside.'

'No. Tell me now!'

'This has happened before. When you're a seafarer's wife it's par for the course. Last time was a few years ago, when they went off course, and they were located a few weeks later. Luckily for Mr Carmichael, he got word back to me. Your husband wasn't a part of that trip so you wouldn't have known.'

Nothing she said made any sort of sense. Why wasn't she panicking? Why so calm?

'Ellen, where is my husband?'

'At this point no one knows.'

Chapter Twenty-Five

A wife would be wise enough not to be more knowledgeable than her husband. Especially in company.

Mrs Adeline Copplefield,
'The Manual for Good Wives' (1888)

Landri
Present day

That first page of the notebook transported Landri to a time when people wrote. *Really wrote* and took care in *how* they wrote. The strong curves of each word written carefully in ink an actual delight to look at, even if it was difficult to make out some of the words.

Squinting, she took in the words printed on the very first page. An inscription. 'To my . . .' she tried to mouth the words but they were too hard to make out.

To my w—e M— —e—i M—s. My o—e — o—y—. N—w — for—ver.

Some of the letters that would have given her something were now beyond recognition. Yet this made it all the more intriguing.

Who had this notebook belonged to?

She pulled open the second page, this time very slowly, as if handling tissue paper. The words flying off the page perfectly, each letter clear in its construction. She braced herself, ready to take everything in, just as she heard a phone ring.

At first Landri believed she was imagining the sound. Then she remembered the land line. The phone stopped ringing only to start again as she entered the kitchen.

'Landri, is that you? I'm so glad I was right and you're at the house.'

'Gran . . . how—?'

'Remember, you told me you needed the landline to get this Wi-Fi installed and I told you to give me the number?' Her grandma's part Italian, part British accent echoed down the line.

'Sure,' she said dejectedly.

'So what I want to know is, what is going on? I've had Ross on the phone to me asking where you are. Is everything all right?'

'It's nothing.'

'Nothing?'

'I just—'

'You don't tell me anything, so how am I supposed to defend you when he calls me?'

'I don't need defending, Grandma. We're taking a break. You don't need to get involved. I'll . . . I'll sort it out.'

'I'm not surprised you don't tell me anything, we hardly speak anyway.'

And there it was. Landri detested the pangs of guilt which emerged at having not visited her grandma in so long. That strange dichotomy of being scared that one day her grandma wouldn't be around anymore, whilst resisting the thought of spending time in her company. The excuse she was too far away in Italy had been wearing thin for a while now.

The long sigh on the other end was something Landri was used to. 'As long as you're all right. I couldn't bear anything to happen to you. . . .'

Landri resisted any response to that statement, so she switched lanes.

'Gran, what do you know about your relative who owned this house?'

'You mean my great-grandmother?'

'Do you remember her?'

'Not a lot – I'm not that ancient!'

Landri couldn't help but smile. If she took away all the negativity, her grandma was still one of the funniest people she knew. 'I mean, I have heard a lot about her. She's famous in this family. An African princess.'

'So that's actually true? We do actually hail from royalty?'

'Of course!' I always told you that when you were little.'

Landri wanted to dispute that. To say they hardly spoke when she was little. That her grandma hardly looked at her those first few years.

Grandma continued. 'She killed three husbands apparently.'

'What? Come on!'

'Oh, I don't know. It was a very long time ago and there was a trial and everything.'

'Surely a Black female serial killer from the Victorian era would have made headlines, Gran.'

'You are probably right. Maybe it was just the one husband. She was a bit of a character, though.'

Or a bit of a badass, thought Landri as she listened. Her grandma spoke of her with a hushed embarrassment, whilst all Landri could feel was pride at having such a radical ancestor who dared to own property and leave it to only the women in the family.

'What was her name?' asked Landri.

'I swear I have told you this many times before. Why is my memory better than yours?'

Landri rolled her eyes.

'Your great-great-great-grandmother was called Temi.'

Chapter Twenty-Six

With lineages inspected and financial accounts studied, the next stage is engagement and then marriage. But what of love?

Mrs Adeline Copplefield,
'The Manual for Good Wives' (1893)

Temi
1880

If Ellen could not see a problem with the ship's disappearance, I wouldn't either.

So, I filled the next two days with simply trying not to think about it and spending time with Iyabo and also Amelia who would soon be returning to school.

'Would you like to tell me about the problem with you and Amy?' I said.

She shrugged her shoulders, which nowadays I realized meant yes.

'Did you have an argument? You know it isn't ladylike to argue.'

Her look was something I would also throw if someone had said this to me.

'You can tell me anything, Amelia.'

'I was waiting for Daddy to get home, so I could tell him.'

I had always been proud of the unusual relationship Amelia had with her father, yet sometimes felt envious. 'Will I do?'

She exhaled. 'The girls at school are mean!'

'Amy?'

She shook her head. 'No, she has never said anything horrible to me.'

I squeezed her hand, willing her to go on.

'When the other girls are mean to me, she says nothing, though. She stands by and says nothing, Mummy.'

I closed my eyes, aching for my child and feeling every emotion she felt. 'Did anyone come to your aid? The headmaster?'

'I didn't tell him.'

'Whyever not?'

She shifted in closer to me. 'Mummy, I don't like it there. Please don't make me go back.'

There was so much information hitting me all at once. Someone had been mean to my daughter and she did not want to return to the school we had done so much to secure for her.

'Please, Mummy,' she said, her hot tears dampening my arm.

'I will wait for your father to return and we will discuss it.'

'So I'll still have to go back before he returns?'

I suddenly felt overwhelmed with having to make decisions for my daughter alone, without her father. 'Yes, my darling.'

That night I opened the notebook. Since Olu had left on the voyage, I'd only managed a few lines here and there. The very first pages contained letters I hoped to read to him upon his return, as he had suggested.

My dearest Olu,

I never knew it possible my love could grow for you, yet in your absence, this is a certainty.

Dare I count the days to your return, whilst not knowing when that will be? I can only hope it is soon . . .

As the days wore on, I no longer constructed letters, more my thoughts, responses to what had happened on any given day.

Amelia is missing you desperately.
My life feels only half of one without you here. Come home soon, my dear love.

I awakened to a chill, the notebook on the bedside table. I moved over to the window, pulling open the drapes and peered out into the morning sunlight. The street was almost empty save for the paperboy running from house to house, the sound of birdsong disturbing the eerie quiet.

I was still awake when Olive showed a young man into the hallway. His face was ashen as he avoided my gaze.

'Madam,' he said. That is all I recall, because the moment the next set of words left his lips, I could no longer claim consciousness. My body hit the ground without warning just as I heard gasps and a scream.

With no idea how much time had passed, I was sitting in bed propped up by pillows. My first thought was who had carried me up those stairs and into the sheets, and had they seen my corset? Heads would roll for this.

I called out for Olive. When she appeared her face was tear-stained.

'Whyever are you crying, Olive?'

Her eyes widened and she did not speak.

'What is happening? Where is Amelia?' I had a need to be near my daughter, to hold her in my arms. To protect her from a danger I felt in every part of me.

'She is in her room, ma'am.'

I placed my hand to my head. Nothing was making sense.

'The doctor is downstairs talking with Iyabo. He has been waiting for you.'

Before I could ask why the doctor was waiting downstairs, he appeared in the doorway as Iyabo rushed inside.

'Ma!' She knelt beside the bed and placed her forehead on my lap. Why was she behaving like this?

'I am so terribly sorry about the news,' said the doctor.

My eyebrows crinkled. 'What news?'

'Your beloved husband.'

I looked down at Iyabo who said nothing, her head still on my lap. All I could think of was how bizarrely everyone was behaving. Iyabo, Olive, the doctor who I hadn't even seen since Amelia was a baby!

'Oh, ma'am. Mr Masters . . .' said Olive, tears streaming down her face. Iyabo's head on my lap, the sound of her own weeping now clear.

'What of him?' I said.

Then silence, like a loud echo in that room. The room in which my husband had held me in his arms. The room where we made plans for the future. A room now polluted with a horde of people who had no business being in here.

'The young man gave you some news not half an hour ago. Do you remember?' The doctor talked to me as if I were a child.

'What news?'

The doctor nodded towards Iyabo, who I realized had now raised her head.

'Olive, please go and fetch the young man from the downstairs,' said the doctor.

Moments later the boy stood at the foot of my bed. Another intrusion into my most private of rooms. 'I have in my hands a telegram, madam. News of the fate of *The Foundlander* ship and its passengers.'

The ship which brought Olu and I to this vast land. The one—

He continued. 'It is with utmost regret that I must tell you the ship and its passengers are missing, presumed sunken off the shore of—'

I closed my eyes. Squeezed them so tightly, as if to open them would mean the words of this boy, this stranger could penetrate into my being. I could not allow that. I could not allow anyone to tell me my Olu was never coming back.

Chapter Twenty-Seven

Naivety in a potential wife is attractive to a man.
Mrs Adeline Copplefield,
'The Manual for Good Wives' (1890)

Landri
Present day

The inscription in the notebook could contain the word Temi. Or not.

But it was on the second and third pages that Landri had the confirmation she needed. The beginning of a series of what looked to be love letters addressed to an Olu and signed by Temi. These were love letters between her great-great-great-grandparents!

My dearest Olu,
  I never knew it possible my love could grow for you, yet in your ab—e, this is a certainty.
  Da—e I count the days to your —rn, whilst not knowing when that will be? I can only hope it is s—n.

As Landri opened each page, she noticed less damage, the words becoming clearer.

My dearest Olu,
  I have spent most of the day consoling Amelia who appears

lost without you. Iyabo is a wonderful help to me, her affections having grown.
This is more than I deserve.

Landri had assumed this would be a book of love letters, but she was wrong. After the first three letters, the tone and style seemed to change. Each page contained either a set of words or rogue sentences. Some pages had been torn out. What had they contained?

Now only eight pages in, Landri already felt like she'd dabbled too far. This was an ancient book sat here for possibly centuries and here she was devouring it like a gossip mag. She had to take her time with this precious item and savour each and every word. Landri was actually reading the words of her great-great-great-grandmother, a princess, a woman she had never once set eyes on in the flesh or in photos. A woman who had unknowingly, all those years ago, bequeathed her this very house.

This was mind-blowing. So much so, she needed to share this momentous news with someone.

Carefully placing the notebook onto the side table, an inadequate resting place for something so old and so valuable, she moved to the window and caught a glimpse of Gwen through the net curtains, carrying two bags of shopping.

Landri rushed outside. 'Here, let me help you!'

'There's really no need,' Gwen said as they both looked up at the set of steps leading to her front door. 'Seemed like a good idea at the time, those stairs,' she said with a shrug.

Gwen stepped aside as Landri picked up one of the bags.

'My daughters wanted me to sell this place and get somewhere smaller near them, but I grew up here with my mother. It has sentimental value. I'll leave here in a box, I tell them.'

'I bet that doesn't go down well,' said Landri taking in the decor of Gwen's home for the very first time. Warm brown and terracotta walls and the sweet aroma of turmeric- and garlic-infused home cooking.

'Make yourself at home.'

They sat at the square wooden dining table in the kitchen. Beside them, the fridge was adorned with pictures of small children and a small furry dog.

'They your grandchildren?' asked Landri as a way of buying time, because she wasn't actually sure how or where to begin. She had found a notebook dating back to possibly – if her maths and the newspaper it was wrapped in were right – the late 1800s. Written by an ancestor who Gwen believed was responsible for killing three husbands.

'Yes, Nella is all grown up now, sixteen going on thirty, and Charmaine is eleven. Tea?'

'Please.'

'I don't have the fancy stuff, just regular builders' tea.'

'That will work,' Landri said. Unlike the kitchen across the road, Gwen's had been well lived in. Mementoes collected across time, including a set of china horses by the kettle. Children's paintings on the cupboards. A school swimming certificate and a young woman dressed in cap and robe holding a degree scroll hanging on the living room wall. Gwen had and was still experiencing the type of family life that Ross, Sadia and a lot of her friends were used to. At a young age, Landri couldn't recall ever experiencing that. Becoming self-sufficient at the age of five, really, in spite of her grandma and grandfather being present. Doing it for real at the age of seventeen when she finally moved out and it was just her.

'The dog you see there is my little Rascal. That was his name. My boy named her. My girls wanted to call her Daisy! Oh, the commotion that caused, even though they were all grown up at the time. He was a wonderful companion. Me and my husband Herman got him together after saying for years he didn't want a dog. He must have known he hadn't long on this earth because he died six months later. That dog helped me through the worst of it.'

'Oh, I'm sorry, Gwen.'

'Don't be. My Herman was the best husband I could have asked for and we had a wonderful life together, even though he died relatively young.'

Landri was horrified when Gwen began to weep. She hadn't come here to reduce Gwen to tears.

'Don't worry, these are happy tears. I miss him every single day, but the years we shared together more than make up for the loss.'

She thought about the love Temi and Olu shared. A deep love, if the letters were anything to go by.

'I found a notebook,' said Landri suddenly.

Gwen raised her eyebrows, and Landri continued. 'It contains a few love letters written by my great-great-great-grandmother.'

'The lady who used to live there?'

'Her name was Temi Masters.'

Gwen's hand flew to her mouth. 'That's it! That was her name, yes! Temi. How did I forget that?' Gwen's smile widened. 'Now tell me about this notebook!'

'It's really old.'

'Naturally.' Gwen smiled.

'Contains a few sentences, words . . . but also these love letters written to my great-great-great-grandfather, Olu Masters.'

'Oh my! A love story. A real-life love story. Wait, my mother never mentioned there being a man living at the house. Only the nice lady.'

'Well, that's it, you see . . . the love letters stop and there are all these words and what I've read so far is quite dark.'

'Do you think she poisoned him, like they said?'

'Like who said?' Landri felt affronted that Gwen could bring up such gossip in this moment. Here she was talking about a great love story between two Black people in the Victoria era and Gwen was attempting to muddy that.

'Sorry, carry on,' said Gwen, not oblivious to the faux pas.

'It's so beautiful, the words . . . the love . . .'

'Do you think it's a forgery?' said Gwen.

'No . . . why would someone do that?' Landri was getting sick of Gwen's negativity and wished she hadn't mentioned the notebook. 'It was wrapped in really old newspaper. That proves it's old too. Right?'

'It does sound fascinating, Landri. I wish I could say more about her, but if my old mum was here she could tell you. I think she used to tell her stories about Africa. Yes, maybe that. Obviously my mother was from the Caribbean and the old lady from Africa, but that of course didn't matter. They were one people.'

'I've only read a few pages . . . Still seems a bit intrusive, to be honest.'

'Depends how you look at it. Just think, you're reading a slice of history. Not just a part of *your* history, but *all* our histories.'

Chapter Twenty-Eight

Unlike the ritual and preparation of becoming a wife or a mother, widowhood occurs without warning and without mercy.
Mrs Adeline Copplefield,
'The Manual for Good Wives' (1888)

Temi
1881

A few days, a week or maybe even a month had passed.

My daily routine consisting of lying in bed as Olive and Iyabo took it in turns to feed, clothe and even bathe me. Iyabo insisted on me walking down the stairs and into the garden one day and, for the very first time, the garden failed to fill me with the joy it once had.

It was simply another place I could not find my Olu.

When I would hear Amelia's loud sobbing, I blotted out the sounds by resting my face down on the pillow with a hand across each ear. A pent-up rage inside of me simply wanted a space to explode.

A letter arriving from Simon Wetherell angered me further. Unread, I tore it into tiny shreds, watching as the pieces slowly flickered to the ground.

Grief exhausted me. Like an enormous weight, a piece of luggage strapped to my back, sapping every ounce of energy I possessed. It was lonely. Yes, Olive and Iyabo had been very good to me, but they could not possibly feel an ounce of what I felt. I had known this beautiful man since we were little more than children. With his long eyelashes and calm nature. I'd never loved any other man in my life. He had been my absolute everything and I failed to glimpse a future that did not include him.

It was only the thought of Amelia and Iyabo which kept me from jumping into the sea and never looking back.

People kept telling me to speak, to say something. Say what? Whenever I asked where my husband was, I was always met with a blank stare. So it was best to say nothing.

Yet being selective about who I spoke to was not going to be helpful long-term, I knew that. But I needed it. I needed the silence.

Iyabo was a wonderful help during those early days. Making sure the house ran as usual, sitting by my side, watching as I sipped the broth she'd brought in from the kitchen.

I'm not sure what was worse, the grief or the guilt. Making my husband feel such pressure as to provide the standard of living I craved and envied. Forcing him to embark on such a dangerous trip. Guilt every time Iyabo performed an act of nurture as it simply reminded me of when I had all but abandoned her.

I couldn't be sure, but there were times as I lay silently in bed, eyes wide open and raised towards the ceiling, that Iyabo would detail what had happened to her in my absence. Of being beaten and sometimes going hungry. This could have been my imagination, though; I was not always sure of what was real and what was not.

I touched a strand of her braided hair one day. 'I'm sorry,' I whispered. Hearing my own voice sounded odd. A chill ran through my body. Iyabo pulled away, returning with a blanket which she draped over me. It smelled of Olu.

'You should rest,' she said in that accent which reminded me of home. One Olu and I had tried so hard to lose, just so that we could fit into the thin lines of life in England. Part of me wished she would shed it too, so that I wouldn't have to think of what I had left behind.

'I'm sorry,' I said.

She smiled.

One day something happened.

'You do not eat unless I feed you. You do not drink. What if I stop, Ma? Will you die too? Will you leave me again?'

It was Iyabo.

My eyes blinked rapidly as her words began to penetrate. She was right. If I didn't allow myself to feel even a smidgen of who I once was, I would die. And I couldn't do that to my daughters.

I nodded in agreement. Not really knowing if I could, only that it was time for me to shed this coat of grief and get on with life – whatever *life* was.

It was another week until I finally began to face this new world. My utterances turning into full sentences, the need for simple broth turning into an appetite for roast chicken. Ellen Carmichael had sent word to me and I had responded with something similar – expressing condolences. Yet this did not send me into the stupor it could have done.

Amelia stayed in her room most days, refusing to interact with anyone unless it was at dinner – which I insisted the three of us took as a family. Olu's empty chair was a stark reminder of his absence. One evening, she refused to join us as we sat before Olive's freshly roasted chicken with vegetables.

'May I go and fetch her?' asked Iyabo.

'No, you wait here.' I patted the front of my dress down as I stood. In Amelia's room, I found my youngest child lying on her front and, for one terrifying moment, I thought she was dead.

'Darling?' I said, moving quickly to her. When she turned around, her eyes were reddened, her hair dishevelled.

'What do you want?' she said.

Once, such a response would have hurt me deeply, yet now and what with the pain already endured, this was bearable.

'I am here to bring you down to dinner,' I said calmly.

'I'm not hungry.'

'You must eat, Amelia.'

'How can you have an appetite? I understand why Iyabo can eat, she doesn't care, but you . . . you were supposed to love him!'

'I do love him.' I swallowed. 'I will always love him.'

She turned away from me and onto her side. I placed my hand onto her shoulder; she shrugged it away. I was wrong, that one action shattered my heart into tiny pieces and it felt as if I was also losing my daughter and I could not have that. I could not lose yet another person in my life.

'Amelia . . .'

'How could you?'

I know she blamed me for Olu leaving us and she was right: I had always wanted the finer things in life, with him just wanting to please me.

'How could you make me sit at that table night after night, chewing food whilst looking at that empty chair? My daddy's chair! Knowing he's never going to sit in it again. It's cruel. You're a monster and so is she!'

'Who?'

'Iyabo or whatever her name is. She's glad he's gone. She doesn't even care, does she?'

Amelia pushed her face into her pillow and I was glad to only hear the muffled sounds of her pain, her distress. What had I done? I had simply wanted some normality in a house that had been plunged into turmoil. To allow my daughters to know I was carrying on . . . for their sakes. I patted her shoulder, which still heaved with emotion.

'I will tell Olive to leave your food covered for later.'

Yet still she sobbed and I simply wanted to grab hold of her and soothe away her tears like I did when she was little. Yet I couldn't. Afraid I would crumble too and this would benefit no one. I had to remain stoic. I must not crumble.

That evening, Iyabo heartily ate every morsel on her plate, whilst I took twice as long to chew and consume a few potatoes. Amelia had been right about one thing: Iyabo did not feel the pain we did, having only known Olu for months.

'Ma, are you feeling a little better?' she said with a sweetness in her voice.

'Yes, my dear.' My smile was false, but I had begun to suspect hers was too.

Chapter Twenty-Nine

If a woman be deemed too emotional and incapable of making
rational decisions in marriage, what then of widowhood?
Mrs Adeline Copplefield,
'The Manual for Good Wives' (1893)

Temi
1882

The first bill came via a nice young man who said he regrettably
would have to seize items of property if I did not pay. It would
seem that when any nice young man came to my door, it was usually with bad news.

Soon, the delivery of fresh produce ceased and at one point I
had to decide whether to purchase food or coal for the fire. To use
the tasteless metaphor of a ship – the cause of all this in the first
place – my fortunes were sinking fast.

If not for Amelia and Iyabo, I probably would have curled into
a ball and waited to be moved into an asylum, but my daughters
continued to push me, albeit in different ways.

With Amelia, although she hardly spoke to me anymore, I
wanted to make sure I could provide for her in the way her father
always had. I needed to make sure she was fed, clothed and was
safe. Iyabo pushed me in ways I only now realize were so very
helpful. Her tone harsh whenever I did something attuned to
giving up – like lying in bed a moment after 5 a.m.

*

Lola Jaye

'Aunty Kike beat me.'

'Aunty Kike gave me no food.'

'She mark my back.'

I used to wonder if those words were part of a delirium I had welcomed during the initial loss of Olu.

Now, months later, those terrible words had reappeared in my thoughts. Clearer this time.

'Iyabo, may we speak?'

She was sat on the chair with her embroidery.

'Ma, what is it?'

'You said . . . you said Aunty Kike behaved cruelly towards you.'

She placed the embroidery to one side and I waited.

Iyabo closed her eyes slowly and then opened them. 'Yes, but it is in the past, Ma. I am here with you now.'

My denial may previously have been fierce, but now, the need to finally know the truth felt stronger. 'Please, please tell me what happened to you, Iyabo.'

She hesitated.

'Please,' I urged.

'Aunty Kike was a cruel woman. When she birth her own child, she no longer care for me. She make me work for her, like a common house girl. Washing, cooking – serving her, her husband and the child. She beat me with a branch from the tree. She mark my back.'

I closed my own eyes and exhaled with utter sadness. 'She said she would love you as her own . . . I didn't know . . .'

'If you had known, would you have allow her to take me?'

The sentence shocked me into silence. A silence which Iyabo received the wrong way.

She stood up abruptly. 'I have to see what food there is so we can eat tonight,' she said.

'Iyabo, we are talking.'

She sat back down. 'Yes, Ma,' she said respectfully.

'If I had known of course I wouldn't have—'

'You love Amelia more than me.'

'No!' I protested.

'It is true. Now, look at us. She doesn't even talk to you and it is I who tend to you.'

I remained silent, her words sinking in.

'Is this not the truth?' Her narrow eyes searched mine.

'Yes.'

'I am here. No one else.'

Her politeness was clearly masking something more sinister. Something I had suspected since the very first day she'd walked through the front door.

Deep down, Iyabo hated me.

Chapter Thirty

*The respectable widow is solely dressed in black for a time of
two years. Fabrics permitted are those without shine or lustre
and devoid of any fancifulness or fripperies. Not unlike her
life.*

Mrs Adeline Copplefield,
'The Manual for Good Wives' (1891)

Landri
Present day

Sitting on her bed reading the thoughts of a Victorian woman
wasn't how she'd seen this 'break' pan out.

Yet Landri couldn't wait to shower, eat breakfast and then to curl
up in the nook in her library and read a new page of the notebook.
She only allowed herself one page a day, and then to go back to
previous pages. This notebook deserved to be savoured, each word
tasted and not devoured. It was difficult to be so restrained, but it
was necessary. The written words of Temi Masters, her great-great-
great-grandmother, were too precious to rush.

Landri hadn't felt this excited about anything in a long while.
Realizing she had just been plodding along, her moods never quite
rising above the lines in which she allowed herself to exist. The
last year or so feeling more 'meh' than anything else. Being in this
house – reading this notebook – was reviving her in ways she had
not expected and she suspected there was much more to come.

She figured it was time to switch her phone back on,

considering it had been off for a while. And as it flashed into life, a barrage of pings flooded the room, with each one, her body tensing further, a nauseating swirl in her tummy.

Three messages from Sadia and five from Ross.

Another voicemail from work.

'Landri, you have to come back to work!' said Steve. After their last call, she wasn't quite sure what was so urgent. Regardless, the feeling of guilt was immediate. As if she was in some way letting everyone at the company down.

'What's happened?' she asked Steve once he picked up.

'Oh, nothing. Yet. But with you not around at this crucial time with the client, it could all go to crap quite quickly.'

'I thought we already agreed on you taking the meeting with Gorings?'

'I'm talking about the Preston account?'

She'd forgotten all about that. She'd only just made a start on it last month and hadn't made much headway on it.

'Take the lead on it.'

'What?'

'I don't think . . . no, I know I won't be back for a bit.'

'Landri, there hasn't been much groundwork done on this . . . unless you have any notes.'

'I do not.' She was being cheeky, she knew that. Yet, in all honesty she cared more about what lay between the pages of the notebook than anything going on at work. A first time for everything.

'When do you think you'll be back, Landri?'

'I don't know. This is your chance to shine . . . without me.' She couldn't help the dig at the end. It was the least he deserved. 'Also, can you put me through to Bannerman, please.'

Bannerman, their boss. A fair man who had been a gracious supporter, she thought, as she rose up the ranks, despite the firm's obvious bias towards middle-aged men.

They'd developed a mutual respect for one another and she'd

learned to hide her disappointment upon realization that after fifteen years at the firm, she could do his job just as well as he could. Perhaps even better.

'Landri, the whole place is turning to shit without you!' Bannerman said.

'It's been a couple of days,' she responded dryly. 'About that. I'm going to need to take a bit more time off.'

'How long are we talking?'

She wanted to say, *indefinitely*. 'HR are always telling me I need to use up my annual leave. Well, I have a month's holiday owing. I'd like to take that now.'

'That's a stretch, Landri.'

'But perfectly within company policy and what HR are telling me I should be doing.' She also thought about Bannerman taking weeks off in bulk during his children's summer holidays.

'It is, but it's a crucial time with your clients and Steve, well, let's just say he doesn't hold a candle to you. You sure you can't take less time?'

'I have given fifteen years of my life to E&S and have worked diligently with the firm's biggest clients. I have only ever taken sick days off in the last week and have never really been offline during my annual leave. I have made this firm millions in revenue and I am one of its biggest assets.' She believed none of that sentence. 'Right now, I need a break. . . I really need this.' That bit she truly meant with every fibre of her being, though.

The conversation ended with Bannerman agreeing to three weeks' annual leave and working from home for the extra week. It was something.

As soon as she hung up the phone, the relief she felt was instant. The lines in her forehead feeling like they were disappearing, her shoulders dropping.

Breathe.

Chapter Thirty-One

Listen to your husband's complaints. Do not share your own.
Mrs Adeline Copplefield,
'The Manual for Good Wives' (1888)

Landri
Present day

It finally truly dawned on her. She had a month off. Well, three weeks but a whole month before she needed to think about going back into the office and her old life. It was the longest she'd ever taken off from any job.

She'd been working since the age of seventeen, through university, all of it, and had never known a time when she had nothing on her schedule.

It felt great! Sometimes. When she wasn't feeling extremely guilty at offloading work onto others, even Steve; when she wasn't thinking about how this could adversely affect her career. Luckily, those thoughts were coming at her less and less now, overtaken by a sense of calm whenever she stepped into that glorious library and cocooned herself in that nook. It felt like another world. A Narnia-like escape from the thoughts which riddled her head and tried to thwart the decision she had made for herself.

When the email came through, confirming her leave and working from home, she felt an even bigger sense of relief rush through her. As if a burden had been lifted from her shoulders.

'Lovely day today!' called out Gwen as Landri stood outside

the house in her now favourite leggings. She felt pretty aimless and was actually feeling good about that. She'd shut the door behind her with no destination in mind.

'I'm off to the garden centre to get a few bits. Do you garden?' said Gwen.

'Erm, no. Not my thing. The one here looks all right, though. The property people get a gardener in,' she said, moving closer to Gwen.

'Not the same. My mother used to love coming into your garden, spending time with the old lady.'

'Her name was Temi,' corrected Landri. This protection felt towards her great-great-great-grandmother was growing with each turn of a notebook page and every conversation with her grandma. They had spoken on the phone twice in one week. A record considering they would usually only speak once every month if that. An encounter that always felt false and full of unanswered questions. Things were not suddenly perfect. The calls still contained those awkward moments, only now they were filled with talk of the former occupants of the house, as Landri tried to piece together its history, as well as her own.

'Yes, I'm sorry, you're right. You'd think I would know better considering I hate people referring to me as an old woman! I may not look it, but I feel twenty-two.'

'Why specifically that age?'

'My Herman and I met when I was twenty-two, married a year later. The most magical time that was. Do you have someone special in your life?'

Landri thought about the proposal. Ross. Her partner of five years whose calls she dodged with one-line text messages. The man she hadn't even thought of today.

'There is someone,' she replied vaguely.

'Maybe you'll tell me about him one day. Anyway, that garden . . .' began Gwen. 'It's where they used to meet.'

'Who?'

'My mother and Temi. Keep up!'

Landri smiled.

'Temi used to give her lemonade. Home-made. How did I forget that? Temi loved showing my mum all the pretty flowers too.'

Landri felt an abundance of warmth at this new information. Like the library, every time she stepped out into the garden there was a feeling she couldn't quite articulate. A warmth mixed in with a knowing of some sort. Important people from the past leaving an imprint in its soil.

She'd never known Temi, of course, but Landri's own mother had lived there once, if only for a short time. The nook in the library looked fairly modern and she wondered if her mum was the one who'd got it installed. A question she'd not dared ask Grandma. Plus, it could have been anyone, because before Landri's mother, there was of course Grandma's grandmother, Amelia. Then the first-born child of Temi who, according to Grandma, was a woman called Iyabo. Yet it would seem Iyabo and her bloodline were completely off the grid.

Growing up, 'family' had never been present in her life. She sometimes joked of herself being an island, but had always assumed this to be a 'Landri' thing – pushing everyone away, yadda, yada, yadda. But what if it had started earlier, with Temi?

Gwen continued and Landri was sorry to have zoned out a little.

'Funny that . . . I'd forgotten so many things and then, after we last spoke, all these details came flooding back. The conversations I used to have with my mum . . .'

Landri wasn't prepared for the single tear that careered down Gwen's face. 'It's been over thirty years since she went and I still get a tear now and again.'

'I'm sorry, Gwen.'

'She was almost ninety and I had her for a long while, but you never get over losing your mother. Cherish every moment with her.'

'I . . . my mother's gone too,' Landri stuttered.

'Oh, she must have been very young. I'm so sorry to hear that.'

'You know what, I've forgotten something inside,' said Landri quickly, the words tumbling over one another.

Gwen nodded, dabbing her eyes with a handkerchief, as Landri ran up the stairs, closing the door behind her. Once inside she closed her eyes and an image of her mother appeared, but this time it wouldn't shift. She took two deep breaths, hands curled.

Then, despite every will in her body, she was back there again.

Thirty-four years ago

She was five. Too young to understand a lot of things, but she knew her mummy wasn't coming back.

From everything Landri had learnt so far in life, when a grown-up tells you something, it's usually the truth. Yet her mummy had said 'See you later!' just the day before, and she still hadn't come walking through the door.

So, her mummy had lied – and if she could lie, then everybody else could too. So when Grandad finally said she was never coming back, maybe he was lying too?

Her grandparents stood by the kitchen sink, both turning to face her. Grandma's eyes were red and she looked even older than she usually did, like she could be Father Christmas's wife.

'Darling.' She stooped to Landri's height. 'Granny and Grandpa are talking.'

'Sowwy,' Landri said quietly. It was rude to interrupt grown-ups. Mummy told her that.

'Your Aunty Carole is coming to get you later. You remember her? Your dad's sister?'

The Manual for Good Wives

'I want to stay here, with you?' She couldn't leave her home and grandparents, because what if when Mummy came back, they too were gone? What if Mummy came back and she couldn't find her?

Landri circled her small arms around her grandma's waist. She'd held onto her countless times before but what she wasn't prepared for was the way in which Grandma peeled each of her arms away and slowly stepped back.

'I can't do this,' Grandma simply said and walked out of the kitchen. Landri looked to Grandpa who held her gaze for just a second before rushing after his wife. That was the moment Landri realized she was alone. That the only person who truly cared for her had gone.

Present day

She quickly opened the notebook, staring once again at the page which had moved her the most.

My firstborn. Left in a faraway land. Away, as I wished. This is my shame.

Whilst Landri wasn't ready to examine her own life, she would instead focus on great-great-great-grandmother Temi. The one who had abandoned her own child, judging by this entry.

That Landri could deal with.

That she could connect to.

Chapter Thirty-Two

A union as a result of a genuine affection for one another is beyond price.

Mrs Adeline Copplefield,
'The Manual for Good Wives' (1889)

Temi
1883

I continued to watch in dread as every bit of money Olu and I had saved depleted daily.

I was careful to be diligent with our outgoings but after months of cutting back, I calculated there was only enough money to feed my family moderately for around six months. The staff had left and I felt appalled at myself for not being able to offer severance pay. Olive stayed for as long as she could, but after securing employment elsewhere, also had to go. I had not paid her in three months.

I had assisted my husband in building the business, yet these skills were overlooked whenever I responded to a HELP WANTED sign at a bookkeeper's or any such office. Admittedly, I had only been turned down by three potential employers when I decided to admit defeat.

I could no longer ignore the feeling of having nowhere to run to. For one very fleeting moment the thought of returning to the old country flashed across my mind.

I could never do such a thing, though. From what Iyabo had

told me, my betrayal had never been forgotten – or forgiven. I had more chance of surviving the streets of England than even one day back in my kingdom.

I would, of course, have to stay in England, but how, I had no idea.

The girls helped with the chores, although Amelia was the more reluctant. My girls ate and sometimes I didn't. My priority was their welfare before my own. We hardly used the fire, because of the cost, and we spent many a cold evening huddled together in blankets. A closeness borne out of necessity yet no less enjoyable. I had my two girls beside me and I was as happy as I could be in our current circumstances.

I made sure to purposely avoid eye contact with the neighbours who had at times made us a subject of curiosity because of the grand way in which we lived. Now, they couldn't cross the street quickly enough.

I was proud we still had Tumbleberry, our home, even if I had sold much of its furniture. All the things we did not need really, like the ornaments, Olu's beloved carvings and jewellery he had gifted me. I'd also sold our books and many other things with deep sentimental value.

Soon there would be nothing left to sell, apart from the house itself. The house Olu and I had toiled for. A symbol of how our life had excelled since leaving everything we had ever known across the sea. Yet sometimes, most of the time, I wondered to myself: what good are bricks and mortar if everyone inside is hungry?

A rare day that Amelia allowed me into her room without protest was an uplifting moment in a week which had begun terribly. The bills were piling up and shifting one pot of money to pay another was no longer working because, frankly, there was no longer any money to shift. I didn't want the girls to know this, although Iyabo had gotten a job as a housemaid, against my wishes, and now contributed to the purchasing of food. I hated that, the thought of the child I had already failed now having to be at the beck and call of a family who viewed her as less than a dog.

Indeed, my head felt as if it were about to explode with the sheer weight of it all. So when Amelia sobbed in my arms one day, I didn't ask about her being seen with a young man without my knowledge. I did not question her on the danger of hindering her chance of securing a good husband in the near future.

'Oh, Mummy, I thought he liked me, but he had sent a note to Mimi Chester and that was it. I was of no more interest to him.'

'That's all right, darling,' I said, my nose grazing the thick strands of her hair. My little girl was growing up but was still far too young to be betrothed – even though I was already married to the chief at sixteen. Of course, I would want her to choose her own spouse, but not just yet. I wasn't ready.

She pulled away from me and flopped onto her bed, the only item of furniture which remained in her room. The mahogany wardrobe had sold for a good enough price just last month.

I watched as she fell into a tearful sleep, at first not noticing the sound coming from the front door, still not used to having to answer it myself.

I opened it to a familiar face.

'How do you do?' he said, tipping his hat. 'It has been too long.'

Not long enough, I wanted to say, as a slightly older, more pleasantly dressed Simon Wetherell stood in front of me.

I stepped back to allow him to enter the house.

Apart from it being improper for a man to be in my house at this time, his company made me feel on edge. Visually, he was more refined than I remembered, with his beautifully tailored suit and shiny shoes. Yet to me he was still that raspy-voiced, rag-wearing ruffian on the ship, who I despised.

'I have done quite well for myself, Temi.'

'It's Mrs Masters.'

'My sincere apologies,' he said with a nod of his head and, I'm sure, a hint of sarcasm. 'Mrs Masters, I know you're in financial trouble and you're probably not even able to get hold of some of the money your husband may have lying around.'

'We shared everything,' I said defensively. It had been very difficult to acquire certain funds, but this was simply because I was a woman and most things had to be in Olu's name. I was certain I had acquired everything, though.

He continued. 'Whatever the issues, it would be remiss of me to watch you and your family suffer.'

His expression took me back to *The Foundlander*. How he had made me feel that night as I scrubbed the deck.

'A woman like you should not be wearing a dress like that, it is not a garment fit for a princess.'

How I wish I had worn the one good gown I still owned – and had not had to sell – and not this, the oldest dress I possessed, with its frayed hem and discoloured fabric.

He moved closer to me, crossing an imaginary boundary I had placed between us.

I wanted to spit in this man's face, but was also aware we were alone in this room with my daughter upstairs. I would be polite, simply to remain safe in my own home.

'You are clearly in dire straits.'

I opened my mouth to speak, but what was the point? He was right.

'A woman with your lineage should not have to live in this way.'

I turned my gaze away from him.

'I know how it has been for you since your husband's premature departure from this life.'

I now looked to the wall where a painting of a thoroughbred horse once hung. Olu had bought it when we'd first moved into this house. He also said one day we would own a house big enough to stable a dozen horses.

'I can help you,' said Simon.

'Excuse me?'

'I can help you. Just say the word and I will pay for everything that is outstanding, with a tidy sum left over to ensure you and your daughters are well.'

'What must I do for this?'

He moved even closer to me and, once again, I was reminded of that night on the ship. He placed his finger on my cheek and I jerked away quickly.

'I have always admired you, you know this. Even dressed in boys' clothing on *The Foundlander*, you carried yourself with such grace. You were so . . . effervescent. Unlike anyone I had met in my village. Of course, your being a princess, I could never have a woman like you.'

I felt his hot breath.

'You are everything a man would desire in a wife. Beauty, royalty and loyalty.'

'Whatever do you mean?'

'I want you to be my wife.'

I wanted to scream!

'Before you protest, Temi, think carefully about what I am offering you. You're a widow now. All your problems would be over.'

I would have to lie with you and I would rather die.

'I thank you for your kind and generous offer, Mr Wetherell, but—'

'Think about it.'

'I do not need to.' I was coming across as too abrasive and I'd no idea what Simon was capable of. I changed my tone. 'I am very flattered indeed.'

'But?' he said with that smirk I hated.

'It would be a dishonour to my husband if I were to marry his friend.'

'Olu and I were never friends,' he spat and this made me want to launch an open hand into his face. How dare he?

I was relieved when Iyabo walked into the room, fresh from a morning's work. 'Ma, is everything all right?'

'Yes, the gentleman was just leaving.'

At the front door, he turned to me. 'Even your daughter is dressed like a common maid. Is this what you deserve? No! You deserve the best. Not to be answering your own door! How can a princess do this?'

I closed my eyes, not wanting to know how much he knew about Iyabo, my life. Had he been watching me all this time, lying in wait?

'When you are about to be thrown onto the streets, send word to me. I have left my address on the banister as there was no furniture left to place it on. My offer will still stand. I have waited long enough for you, Temi, and I can wait a while longer.'

I shut the door and slammed my back against the hard wood. I slid down the wall slowly as a wave of helplessness covered me. It was at moments like these that I sometimes felt I couldn't go on.

'Ma,' said Iyabo's voice as she ran to me, sitting on the floor beside me and then followed surprisingly by Amelia, who sat on the other side. Each embracing me from either side with Iyabo squeezing my hand, assuring me that everything was going to be all right.

The visit from Simon may have taken a lot from me in terms of hope, but it was the presence of Ellen Carmichael which restored some of it.

When I heard that American drawl I had come to miss echo

up the staircase, I immediately leaped out of my bed of wallowing and ran downstairs towards her.

'Well, well, well, wonders will never cease,' she said, the warm familiarity of her voice a callback to happier times.

When she'd visited earlier in the year, I had not been ready to truly receive her. Now with the house looking like an empty shell, my reasons were more that of embarrassment.

'Ellen . . . you have sent food baskets, visited with me and allowed Amelia to stay at your home, and yet I have not once asked of your own well-being.'

She looked refreshed in her blue velvet dress and matching hat trimmed with lace. She was a picture.

'Now, now, don't you fret. You took the situation really badly, as did I, but I have many a people around me to keep me sane. You hardly had anyone. It is understandable.'

'Thank you for your graciousness.'

'It's been a year, and I will never get over it, but I have learned to adapt. My father sent for me and the children and I assured him I'd be staying here. Now, though . . . I have reconsidered.'

'You're leaving?' My stomach lurched in anticipation of the obvious answer.

'It's for the best. Too much to remind me of Mr Carmichael here. At least in Boston I will be surrounded by memories that existed before we met. It would be good for the children to know my side of the family too. Amy will soon be coming out in society and, well, I would like her to attend a very particular debutante ball.'

Ellen leaving was a blow I had not seen coming.

'But don't you fret, Temi, dear. I have the perfect solution for you and your money woes.'

Ellen hadn't needed me to tell her of my predicament. There was no staff and I hadn't bought a new dress in months. Then there was the bare house.

'You need a husband.'

I opened my mouth to speak.

'Now, before you protest, listen. It's not proper for a woman without means to be without a man. You and I are alike.'

'We are?'

'You like the finer things in life and want the very best for your children. Am I wrong?'

I nodded reluctantly. Perhaps if she knew of Simon's visit, she would berate me for showing him the door.

'This doesn't have to be about love, but convenience . . . and maybe in time you'll feel what you felt before.'

'Did you not love Mr Carmichael?'

'Mr Carmichael and I were just fine. He gave me security and prestige and I gave him a younger body at night!'

Now I laughed. 'I'm hardly young anymore.'

'Unlike my good self, you look every inch the young woman. Use this while you can, Temi. It's the only way to climb out of these financial woes.'

She turned to me, her expression serious. 'This doesn't have to be about love,' she repeated. 'This is about survival.'

Chapter Thirty-Three

Observe sound judgement when selecting a spouse. Do not say
yes merely because you have been asked for your hand.
Mrs Adeline Copplefield,
'The Manual for Good Wives' (1889)

Landri
Three years ago

The very first night in the shiny new riverside apartment was one of the
best moments of her life.

Ross gazed at her with a smile which warmed every inch of her as
they stood side by side on the balcony overlooking the water.

'We've done it,' he said, moving behind her and wrapping her in
his arms so tightly, she believed he would never let her go. That feel-
ing of love and security. Until that point in their relationship she'd
been learning to trust he was hers forever and that he would never
leave.

'I love you, Landri. More than I have ever loved anyone and now we
have everything we want. Well, nearly everything.'

Before meeting Ross, Sadia and Claudine had been adamant that by
her mid-thirties she should be 'intentionally dating'. Sometimes when
her two closest friends discussed these matters, it felt like they were speak-
ing another language, because unlike for them, marriage never seemed
that important to her. But standing on the balcony that first night, she
started to believe marriage might not be so bad after all. That she could
certainly sign up to live with this man for the rest of her life if it meant

feeling like this. Loved. An emotion she never thought she'd ever had a right to.

The first week or so after the move, she'd noticed subtle changes, though. Ross's on and off affection became more apparent and he even accused her of being a nag when she complained, whilst distancing himself from her even more. He rarely pulled his weight around the house, even though she'd anticipated a 50/50 split of the chores.

Staring down at Ross's light blue boxers in the basket one day sparked something inside of her.

'Why am I always washing your pants?' she asked as he padded into the kitchen with a coffee cup.

'What are you talking about?' He plonked the cup into the sink where it would remain until she rinsed it.

'I don't mind putting your stuff in the wash with mine, but when have you done it for me?' She'd asked this partly in jest, but mostly with an undercurrent of annoyance at having to not only look after the house but hold down a full-time job which came with lots of unpaid overtime.

'What, so I get criticized yet again because of a few pairs of pants in a wash you were doing anyway?'

'No, that's not it . . .'

The simple comment had morphed into something bigger, and on that day, just weeks into the move, Landri found herself on the balcony with Ross again, but this time batting an exchange of words that changed everything.

'What gets me, Landri, is that no matter what I do, it's never enough, when I'm the only one who's ever been there for you.'

She nodded her head.

'Your family don't care about you. Even your grandmother couldn't wait to jump ship and move to Italy when you were a kid!'

This was true.

'I'm the only one who truly cares about you and a pair of pants is what you want to focus on.'

He was right.

'Just remember who's been here. Me. Okay?'
She nodded again.
'You'd be nothing without me.'

Present day

Landri now felt comfortably settled into a new routine.

A daily healthy breakfast thanks to that overpriced but gorgeous artisan bakery. A walk past the cricket pavilion – an activity which no longer made her think about Ross. Then settling in the garden – if the day was clear – to read a precious page of Temi's notebook.

Temi wrote:

How it is that love can turn to hate?

She didn't hate Ross. She simply didn't like the person she was with him.

I despise who this man is and what he has made me become.

Who could Temi have been writing about?

'It's so lovely to be out here. It's like I can feel her,' said Gwen, joining Landri in the garden.

'Your mum?' asked Landri. The white garden furniture was basic and hard against her bum, but sitting under the sun with a cold rooibos tea chatting to Gwen felt glorious.

'Yes, indeed.'

'I feel that way about Temi. And my mum.' She hadn't meant to reveal the last bit to a stranger, but Gwen no longer felt like one. 'When my grandma inherited this house, she never really stayed here, and when she married Grandpa they moved somewhere else before going back to Italy.'

'Italy?'

'That's where my grandma was born and her mother too.'

'Your family are full of surprises.'

'I don't think Gran wanted to be lumbered with a five-year-old when my mother died.'

'I doubt she saw it that way.'

'What do you think your mum and Temi had in common? To form such a close friendship?' Landri asked, purposely switching the subject.

'She liked having my mum around. I think Temi was just lonely.'

'Paints a bit of a different picture than the murderess!'

'So you don't think there's any truth to that?' asked Gwen.

'Not at all,' Landri said. Then recalled the collection of dark thoughts written in the notebook. 'Although the notebook ... some of the entries don't yet make sense.'

'Maybe she did away with one of them?'

'And still be walking free? You said she was an older lady when she met your mum.'

'You know what kids are like, they see a twenty-five-year-old as ancient. Maybe she wasn't an old lady after all.'

'We did the maths. Temi would have been quite advanced in years when your mother met her.'

'What about the trial your gran mentioned?'

'She was obviously free if your mum sipped lemonade and tea with her! She probably owed money or something. Didn't they lock up people who didn't pay their debts in those days?'

'I have no idea. Perhaps she murdered her hubby and they didn't have enough evidence.'

'What evidence would they need in those days to convict a woman? A Black woman at that. We need to be realistic about this.'

'You could go and look at court records.'

Landri wasn't ready to leave the house just yet.

'Or I can keep reading. There's bound to be something in the notebook.'

'You're taking your time. I thought you said you were a copy-writer, so you must write and read stuff for a living. Surely you can read faster.'

'I actually want to take it slow. I'm sick of everything feeling so fast in my life. This is the first time for as long as I can remember that I haven't been on the go 24/7. I like it. I think I actually like it.'

'Smelling the roses, are we?'

'Literally!' she said, waving her hands at the decorative rose bushes around them.

Gwen raised her eyebrows as Landri sipped her tea, a beautiful ray of sunshine flooding her face along with this glorious feeling of contentment.

Chapter Thirty-Four

A husband may behave with regard and affection during the start of marriage, but may also change as quickly as the weather.

Mrs Adeline Copplefield,
'The Manual for Good Wives' (1893)

Landri
Present day

'So, this is where you've been hiding!'

'Hello to you too,' said Landri as Sadia and then Claudine rushed past her and into the cocoon she'd happily lived in for the past eleven days.

'We've all been frantic!' said Sadia, looking sun-kissed and with a streak of colour at the side of her bob.

'I told you I was okay and just needed to get away. And I gave you my address when you insisted.'

Sadia's gaze searched the corridor, with Claudine immediately grabbing a seat on the sofa.

'So you leave a modern riverside apartment for . . . this?'

'This is my ancestral home – be careful what you say,' said Landri, only partly joking.

'I think it's lovely,' said Claudine. 'Probably a really good investment for the future.'

'That's something, I suppose,' said Sadia.

'Can't actually sell it. Ever,' said Landri.

Sadia made a face. 'We'll just have to settle for the fact you're still alive then.'

Claudine snorted. She was generally the quiet one in the friendship group. In fact, Landri was surprised to even see her there, having been trying to get her in the same room for months. Although she did make it for the proposal and had said yes to the wedding planning shindig Sadia had organized. Indeed, Claudine and most of her friends appeared to only have time for wedding and baby stuff – things they deemed important. Otherwise they were usually 'busy'.

'As I said in the texts, I'm fine.'

'Anyone could have written those texts,' said Sadia.

'I distinctly remember answering your "in case you've been kidnapped" question about my favourite ice cream flavour.'

'Indeed.' Sadia wrinkled her nose.

'I like vanilla, leave me be!'

Sadia pulled her into an embrace as Claudine looked on smiling. Whenever they all got together it was generally a good time, until the feelings of exclusion surfaced. When her two friends began discussing nurseries and 'wifey' stuff.

Both were wives and mothers. Claudine, a successful PR executive, was planning for baby number two with her husband, whilst Sadia, a human rights lawyer, had taken a career break to look after her boys Gregory Junior and Rory. The same Sadia who once said she'd rather poke her own eyes out with a toothpick than cave in to the patriarchy. They were seventeen at the time, but still . . .

They sipped wine in the garden before Sadia announced she was going back inside because of the wrinkle-forming effects of the sun.

'I went ahead and cancelled the wedding planning brunch. The girls are really upset though, right, Claudine?'

'Leave me out of this,' she warned, trudging back out to the garden. Even at university, when Landri and Sadia fought, Claudine never took sides. Once she'd locked them both in their dorm room until they came to their senses. Instead, they'd ended up getting drunk on cheap cider and drunkenly vowing to never fall out again.

That vow had lasted three weeks.

'This isn't like you. This isn't you! Ghosting everyone!'

Landri wasn't even sure she knew who she was these days and found it almost hilarious that Sadia did.

'I did not ghost anyone and what are you, twelve? Plus I'm surprised the girls noticed. I hardly hear from them anyway these days.'

'I'm not them and I expected more from you. I even paid a deposit for our planning brunch.'

'I'd been engaged for five minutes.'

'Ross told me weeks ago he was going to propose.'

'You knew? I guessed as much,' said Landri, feeling a slight disappointment at the thought of her partner and best friend conniving behind her back. Especially as Ross wasn't Sadia's biggest fan. 'I'll pay you back the money, okay?'

Sadia's eyes widened. 'This isn't about the money. None of this makes any sense. And poor Ross.'

'Poor Ross now, is it?'

What about me?

'He wasn't okay when I spoke with him last night.'

Landri felt a further weight of disappointment. Somehow, Ross had managed to win their sympathy. Not that she needed or wanted it. She'd just much rather be heard, and right now her best friend wasn't listening.

She never thought it would be Sadia disturbing her peace in this wonderful old house with its colourful, luxuriant garden. She'd been expecting some type of expansion to the joy she'd only just started to feel here. Now here was Sadia, of all people, threatening to take her back into a darker place.

'What's going on, Landri? Tell me. We're supposed to be friends. Best friends.'

'We still are, but I guess friendships change . . .'

'What's that supposed to mean?'

'Never mind.'

'No, go on.'

Landri was never one for confrontation and she had already said way too much. Their friendship may not be perfect but she valued it.

'Go on!' urged Sadia.

'Okay then, before I got that promotion and work got manic, I used to try and get us together. I'd book stuff like a dinner or a spa day and you were never interested, none of you were. So I stopped. But you can book a planning lunch on a whim and get all the girls together.'

'Firstly, I thought you were getting married, so of course I'm going to start planning. It's important!'

'That's it, isn't it? I'm the last one standing. The only one who isn't a wife.'

'What are you talking about?'

'You never have time anymore, but for a wedding, that's different. Suddenly I'm of value.' Landri had no idea where this outburst was coming from, especially when, in all honesty, she too no longer had time for 'spa days'. But that wasn't the point, and every word, each syllable felt satisfying to say.

'I have a husband and two children! Tell me where I'm supposed to find the time to go gallivanting to spas and out on shopping trips? I have a kid who's puking on a freshly mopped floor, a husband who can't find his fucking socks, and a mother-in-law who thinks my spag bol should be banned from human consumption. I don't have the time like I used to, and if you can't understand that, then . . .'

They looked at each another before bursting into snorts of laughter.

'Looks like you could have done with that spa trip after all,' said Landri, so glad the intensity of the conversation had eased.

'Oh, fuck off!' Sadia said, laughing.

'Shall we start this again?'

'Let's. But have you got any gin anywhere in this big old house?'

Landri smiled. 'We'll take a walk to the artisan shop and get you a poncey version.'

Sadia leaned over, grabbing Landri's hand. She felt zero regrets for saying what she had, because it was the start of a conversation that needed to be had.

Chapter Thirty-Five

Dampen sexual desire with foods that are bland in taste, avoiding what is excitable to the senses and warming to the nether regions.

Mrs Adeline Copplefield,
'The Manual for Good Wives' (1893)

Temi
1883

With Ellen's impending move, I was keen to spend time with her before the trip. But when she invited me over for tea one afternoon, I was surprised by the presence of a handsome man in the drawing room.

'What a pleasure,' he said, taking my hand brazenly. 'My name is Edward Cutler and I am pleased to make your acquaintance.' He spoke quietly and in that same style of American accent as Ellen.

'Likewise,' I said, taking in his beautifully tailored single-breasted jacket and confident demeanour.

'I see you've met my brother,' said Ellen as she floated in.

'Fresh from home and ready to make England my second one!' He spoke much more slowly than Ellen, each syllable carefully enunciated. I also noticed his slight moustache which decorated a delicate oblong face which I dare say was attractive.

'I will leave you ladies to converse but hope to have the pleasure of your company for dinner on another occasion.'

'It would have to be soon, as Ellen will shortly be departing.'

'You make it sound like I will be dead!' said Ellen with a laugh.

He leaned closer and in a way that was inappropriate. 'I meant just the two of us,' he said. My eyes widened. Ellen had not heard those words, but I had.

I swallowed nervously, a small fluttering in my stomach.

'Now, off you go, brother dear,' she said playfully.

Once we were alone, I found myself still thinking of Edward.

'It seems my brother is rather taken with you,' said Ellen.

I shrugged non-committally. 'Don't be silly.'

'I know Edward. He has a penchant for a beautiful lady. Usually a young and helpless damsel – which you are not.'

I wasn't sure if Ellen was being playful or cruel, but still I could not get this man out of my head whilst failing to understand how I could even allow him to enter my thoughts in the first place. Surely this was a dishonour to Olu?

As the afternoon wore on, Ellen complained of feeling poorly and needing to lie down. Sad our day together was about to be over, I allowed her butler to escort me to the door.

'Don't leave just yet!' said Edward, rushing up behind us. 'Stay. Keep me company!'

'Oh . . .'

'You would be doing me a huge favour. Mary Ellen was supposed to accompany me to my new home to offer her honest opinion on my taste in decor . . . you must take her place!'

I cleared my throat. 'A woman accompanying you in your carriage . . . who is not your wife? This is most improper.'

'I can assure you I am a gentleman, albeit a bachelor.'

'What of my reputation?'

'I can change that.'

The way he said those words felt loaded, causing a small feeling of desire to flutter in my nether regions. I needed a glass of water!

'As I understand it, you're a respectable widow, above reproach,' he said with a smile. 'A woman of your stature and taste can only assist me in the best way.' His eyes appraised my one good dress draped over my fitted bustle. The one I only wore when visiting Ellen. She hadn't made any comment on seeing the same garment over and over again and for that I was grateful.

Edward Cutler arranged for a carriage to take us quite a distance away. The journey felt longer than it should what with the shame of riding with a gentleman who was not my husband. I was grateful for my hat to hide any guilt in my expression. I willed the horse to move at a faster pace, especially in the more populated areas of refined men and their ladies walking side by side. Then the less genteel. Children with dirty faces running after one another, women in their stained dresses shouting at the tops of their voices. The type of woman I was about to be very, very soon if something did not change. I glanced at the gentleman beside me, Mr Edward Cutler, and for one brief moment believed he may be the answer to everything.

We stopped in front of a beautiful large house, pillars either side and with an expanse of freshly trimmed lawn and hedges surrounding it. The coachman helped me out of the carriage and just seconds later Mr Cutler stood by my side.

'This is a beautiful house,' I said as we stepped inside, realizing the exterior had done no justice to the grand entrance hall the size of three of my rooms. A large crystal chandelier hovered above us, lighting the elegant wall panelling and an abundance of paintings I suspected were of high value.

I had always seen Ellen's ornate surroundings as the epitome of wealth but this was on a much grander scale.

Edward showed me into a large airy room he called the gallery. More large paintings adorned the walls, tall porcelain ornaments standing proudly side by side in an ornate cabinet. A room solely for art!

The reception room with its high ceilings and elaborately moulded cornices, as well as a grand piano, was where we finally sat down.

'I hope I have not worn you out, Mrs Masters.'

I had no idea why this comment sounded suggestive. What was happening to me?

'The stairs?' he clarified.

'Oh, I am used to a good climb,' I said. If I were of a lighter hue, I am sure the colour red would have suffused my entire face!

I cleared my throat. 'I hadn't imagined the home would be furnished already.'

'There are still parts of the house in need of a woman's touch.'

'All it really needs is to be lived in.'

'I agree.' The way he said this, the expression in his eyes as they searched mine . . . I coyly looked away.

'My wish is that soon, Mrs Masters, I will have loved ones with which to fill this house. I'm sure you understand.'

I cleared my throat. 'Indeed, I do, Mr Cutler.'

'My sister tells me you were widowed at the same time as she lost dear Mr Carmichael.'

'Indeed.' It still shocked me to hear that term. Perhaps because Olu lived on in so many ways. Always present in my heart, my home, and in Amelia, who I believed had started to look less like my mother and more like him. In the three years since that terrible day, I had never been ready to claim the term widow. Yet now, in the company of an eligible gentleman, I simply had no choice.

'I'm sure an eligible bachelor like yourself would have no issues acquiring a wife—'

'In Boston there is no shortage of women eager to become Mrs Edward Cutler, but I'm what you like to call . . . selective.'

He moved close to me and I did not resist when he gently held my arms. 'Mrs Masters, may I say, you are . . . exquisite.'

I also did not protest when his finger touched my cheek.

Ignoring Simon's repugnant, clumsy attempts to woo me, it had been so long since a man had touched me like this.

'Mrs Masters, this may sound almost deranged, but please excuse me for what I am about to say . . .'

'What would you wish to say, Mr Cutler?'

'Eddie, please call me Eddie.'

'I shall call you Edward.'

'Having only known you a few wonderful hours . . .' He touched my cheek again and I felt a flutter in my heart, in spite of myself. 'I think . . . being here with you now . . . I believe that you will, one day very soon, become my wife.'

Chapter Thirty-Six

When selecting a husband it is prudent to choose one who is
securely detached from his mother.

> Mrs Adeline Copplefield,
> 'The Manual for Good Wives' (1891)

Temi
1883

'That man took my best friend Sandra Jane to a ball and said he
could not abide her snorts. That girl did not snort and was beautiful and came from one of the finest families in Boston. But, oh no,
not good enough for my brother.'

We were having dinner at Ellen's. My attire consisted of an
exquisite blood red gown Edward had sent to me, a luscious
princess-line evening dress made of jacquard woven silk and lace
by Ellen's favourite designer, Emile Pingat. It felt wonderful to
wear such a dress. Not least because I too was a princess, but also
watching him watch me in the dress he had selected felt somehow
alluring.

Also, to taste good food again felt even lovelier!

At least for now, I could forget my troubles and enjoy this
inclusion as brother and sister reminisced about their childhood.
Apparently Edward had been a cad during his younger days and
this was making me doubt how genuine his words were when
professing his love for me.

Everything had happened with such haste. Showering me with

even more gifts such as the beautiful velvet-lined jewellery box I had no use for, having sold most of my trinkets. I'd refrained from confiding in Ellen about him and wasn't even sure there was anything to confide. A few looks here and there. Gifts, compliments. Mr Edward Cutler had been saying all the right words, two weeks after our first meeting, but I craved action.

'I don't think Mrs Masters is interested in hearing of my unfavourable past. One that, I may add, I am not proud of.' The way he looked at me made me want to believe anything he said.

He quickly changed the subject to a woman named Anne. A woman not their mother, who had reared them.

'It might sound strange to you but we spent more time with her than our own mother!' said Ellen.

'Not at all, it is the same where I am from,' I said, stopping myself from speaking any further on this, just glad Edward and I had this in common, another truth to draw me closer to him. If I was honest, the threat of having to sell my home was another draw, but I also felt driven by an emotion. Lust. A sensation I had long forgotten since the demise of my husband, but one I found both shaming and enjoyable. In one moment hating this betrayal of Olu, in the next counting the moments to when I would see Edward Cutler again. When I would feel that tingling sensation at the sound of his voice.

'Anne was a lovely woman,' said Edward.

'We were so sorry when she died.'

'Did she have family?' I asked.

'She'd run away from the South and a life of slavery and we, the Cutlers of Boston, gave her a home. One of our father's better decisions!' said Edward.

'Oh, do stop criticizing Father. Let it go!'

'Let what go?' I asked, amused at this sibling exchange.

'From as long ago as I can remember, Edward here has pitted himself against our father. As if in competition.'

'This simply isn't true,' he protested, but I was more interested in this Anne lady.

'So Anne was an African?'

'Indeed,' confirmed Edward. 'I know it may seem odd to some, but I truly saw her as my mother for a time. I never saw her colour.'

Perhaps this was another confirmation that we were suited. To love someone of my complexion was not unusual to him and Ellen, as perhaps it would be for others.

In that moment, I made a decision about Edward Cutler.

There was only one choice. It didn't matter whether I was ready or not. Edward Cutler wanted me, he'd made that perfectly clear in that huge house of his and almost every day since. Edward could offer me and my children a life we could only dream of and certainly one that did not involve wearing the same garments over and over again and sometimes only being able to consume bread and water for dinner. Olu and I had entered this country with a goal to make our lives and the lives of those who came after us better, and with Edward Cutler by my side this would be possible again.

Edward and I were married six months later in a very simple ceremony with just a handful of guests who ate heartily and drank the best wine imported from France. I wore a pale blue dress with a fitted bodice over a wonderful layer of petticoats and I felt like one of the princesses in the books I had grown so fond of.

Ellen hadn't said much to me since the announcement of our engagement, blaming her preoccupation with returning to America. We both knew she did not approve of mine and Edward's union, but we were both too dignified to admit this.

Meanwhile, Iyabo appeared ecstatic at the marriage whilst Amelia had surprised me with a nonchalance I did not understand, having expected tears and recriminations. I wasn't sure if indifference would have been any better, though.

Now we were to live in that beautiful grand house, Edward allowed me to select my own staff and of course I immediately sent for Olive. Unfortunately, it was then that I learned she had died some months ago. Dear sweet Olive, who had been my confidante when I knew no one in this new country except Olu and our kindly landlady Mrs Bryers. However, the daughter she'd called 'Ellie' – Eleanor – jumped at the chance to work for me. This pleased me greatly as I had always felt indebted to her mother.

Edward insisted on an immediate honeymoon, which I had never had with my first two husbands. It wasn't a concept familiar to me, but Edward was keen to allow the first week of married life to be spent in harmony and away from the usual day to day.

I waited for Edward in the lobby of the Lighthouse Hotel as he engaged in conversation with the hotelier regarding our room. I could hear the sound of the ocean waves outside though the water was unusually calm. I would forever associate it with turbulence, anxiousness and death, but now it would be the setting for a beautiful turning point in my life.

As Edward escorted me to our room, the fluttering in my tummy was either nerves or excitement, both emotions so similar, it was hard to decipher. What I did notice, though, was the absence of any fear.

The uniformed boy opened the door to the room and I entered first, Edward behind me. He tipped the boy who nodded gratefully, shutting the heavy door behind him.

'Sea view,' said Edward in that quiet way I had become used to.

I adored the way Edward made me feel, protected and wanted. At times I convinced myself I was betraying Olu; other times I told myself he would want me to be happy and provided for. With Edward being such a wealthy man, he allowed us to keep Tumbleberry as a second home. I was grateful for this, unsure if I'd ever be ready to dispose of such a special place.

For me, what had started out as a need for survival had turned into something resembling affection. Not the type of deep love I would forever share with Olu, but something with much potential. Then there was this undeniable desire which came with it. An intensity I had never known. The need to be touched by him whenever we were alone. It certainly wasn't ladylike to feel such desires, but something inside of me hungered for him every time Edward was near me.

Now it was our wedding night.

We faced one another on the hotel bed. Edward said something about going downstairs for dinner. Was I hungry? I wantonly moved my face towards him . . . took a sharp intake of breath as I moved my lips onto his. His shock was obvious, but when he placed his hand on the back of my head and responded with delicate but strong kisses, I knew I had not done anything bad.

That night, my husband Mr Edward Cutler took me with a vigour I had shamefully thought about since the moment we had met. Our bodies moved together seamlessly, my need for much more when it was over.

'Well, Mrs Cutler, that was unexpected,' he said with a huge smile. My desire for my husband had reached a crescendo and I didn't understand such feelings. What was clear and without any doubt was that for the first time on my wedding night, I did not feel afraid.

Chapter Thirty-Seven

Widowhood is a lesson in independence one is never prepared for.

Mrs Adeline Copplefield,
'The Manual for Good Wives' (1888)

Landri
Present day

She missed her friends already, but was glad to have the house back to herself. To delve once more into the pages of Temi's notebook.

Now halfway through the notebook, this saddened her, as she believed once she reached the end there would be nothing more to hold onto. Its appearance in her life had added to the stirrings of possibilities which clearly had always existed inside of her. Possibilities she'd never dared to explore.

So what if the words were sometimes illegible due to the effects of time, or if some of the scribbles made no sense?

Ellen. Friend. Enemy? Kind.
Where are you? Have you simply perished my love? Or if you're alive, why do you not come back to me?
Each passing hour leads to not even a scattering of love.
I could turn to the savagery expected of me and kill.

She closed the notebook carefully.
Landri did not want to believe the gossip which had followed

Temi's name through the family grapevine and, it would appear, this street. Yet she couldn't ignore the tone of some of her words. They were sometimes uncomfortable. Clearly written by a woman in deep pain, desperation calling from each word.

What if reading the rest of the notebook led her to truths Landri was not ready to face? According to some of the words, it was thinly plausible that at least one of Temi's marriages had been unhappy enough to have made her think of . . . murder? Without dates it was hard to piece together when Temi had written what.

Landri needed light to balance some of the darkness she'd ingested with Temi's words.

She'd seen the shop Chimes & Things on quite a few occasions now, indeed anytime she guiltily headed towards the artisan bakery, which was far more frequently than she would have liked.

The ping of a bell heralded her arrival in the shop and she was immediately confronted with helium party balloons, oddly shaped candles, and of course a selection of different-coloured wind chimes which chimed indiscriminately in the background.

She absorbed the scent of lavender and something unidentifiable as she clocked two women talking to each other, one holding a silver and black puppy.

'Hello there?' asked an older lady, her naturally blond hair dyed with streaks of blue. She was dressed in a turquoise kaftan and appeared almost to float towards Landri.

'I'm looking for a storage box, for somewhere to store a notebook.' She moved over to a section housing a plethora of shiny goods, from fluorescent cuddly bears to pretty silver purses.

'Not something I often get asked.' Her smile was warm. 'My name is Chime, by the way.'

Of course it is, thought Landri.

'Landri,' she said with a nod. A chat seemed to accompany

everything on this street, whether it was buying a loaf of bread next door or simply walking down the street. She was getting used to it now. It was nice.

'Ruler!' said Chime.

'Excuse me?'

'That's what your name means. When I was little I used to play with a little boy called Landry.'

Landri's eyes widened. Not many people had even heard of her name. At school it was just another thing to single her out for, along with the dead mother. Growing older, she'd finally learned to love the distinct and unique name her mother had given her.

'I wonder what he's doing now. Probably got fed into the corporate jungle and makes people poor for a living,' said Chime with a smile.

'Perhaps,' said Landri, amused in spite of herself.

'Do you spell your name with a Y?'

'With an I.'

'How interesting,' said Chime. Landri already liked her.

'I have this notebook. It's quite old,' she said. 'It deserves more than to be wrapped up in old newspaper. I'd like to keep it somewhere safe.'

The door pinged as another person entered the shop.

'That sounds very intriguing . . . where did you get it?'

'I found it in my house in between some books on a bookshelf. It's a house I inherited. Never lived there before.' Landri had no idea why she was explaining all of this.

'And what's in the book . . .? I want to know more!'

'So do I. I haven't finished reading yet.'

She followed Chime over to a display of small leather and suede boxes, where a green box with a giant pink rose on the front caught her eye.

'We also have plain boxes.'

'No . . . I think it needs to have a flower on it.'
'Drawn to that one, are you?' said Chime.
'Very much so . . . and I'm not actually sure why.'

Chapter Thirty-Eight

If you seek amorous congress over and above what your hus-
band desires . . . you may be encouraged to seek medical help
and possibly be diagnosed with hysteria.

Mrs Adeline Copplefield,
'The Manual for Good Wives' (1889)

Temi
1884

I enjoyed being the lady of the manor, so to speak.

My life as Mrs Edward Cutler consisted mostly of managing a
small staff whilst making sure my husband remained happy.

Amelia now attended Bedford College for Ladies, whilst Iyabo
appeared to be happiest sitting at home with her beloved embroidery or plaiting my hair. I had not forgotten how she'd taken
employment as a maid just to keep us going through the grimmest
of times and without one word of complaint. If any feelings of
resentment towards me lingered, they never showed.

The biggest surprise of all was that Ellen was still yet to travel
back to America. Edward joked this was to keep an eye on his
conduct towards me and I would have believed this if I ever saw
her! When she and her children did come to visit, it was often to
converse with her brother, our own interactions brief and not as
they once were.

Despite this, I nursed a contentment which had been denied
me for so long.

Edward and I had never spoken about children. The thought of having another at my advanced age did not seem a reality; besides, my main reason for this marriage had been to protect the ones I already had. Yet if he required this, I would not be adverse to the possibility.

However, the truth was since our wedding night at the Lighthouse Hotel six months ago, Edward and I had made love only a handful of times. He was forever telling me how beautiful I was, so I could only feel confusion as to why he seldom touched me.

'Did your desire for me wane as soon as I accepted your marriage proposal?'

It was forward to say such a thing, but I tired of being silent. With my first marriage, I had been mute, and with Olu, whilst my voice was encouraged, I sometimes still lacked the courage to fully use it.

'Oh, my dear love, of course not.' He sat at his bureau and looked up from the paper he had been writing on. 'You are the most beautiful creature I have ever had the good fortune to set eyes on.'

'So then, why?'

'I am a very hard-working man and sometimes I simply like to rest. Do I not give you what you need?'

'Indeed you do . . .'

'As I thought,' he said, returning to his writing. 'So this need not be a discussion, my dear.'

When the time came for Ellen's departure, I felt it necessary to explain how disappointed I had been with our dwindling friendship.

'Nonsense! Our friendship has far from dwindled, it has simply changed in nature.'

'Well, yes, and with that in mind, I assumed we would have spoken more . . . as sisters-in-law.'

'Firstly, when have you ever known me to be about convention? Could you imagine us sitting together and discussing embroidery patterns?'

'No, but I have hardly seen you.'

'Temi, dear, when you marry a man like my brother, certain precepts must be adhered to. You are a Cutler wife now and should not partake in frivolous things.'

'With Mr Carmichael our friendship flourished.'

'Edward is a very traditional man and nothing like our dearly departed husbands. Let's just say he requires a more traditional wife, and that means one who doesn't spend her time frolicking with friends.'

'You're his sister and I value your wisdom on matters of the heart.'

'Therein lies the problem, Temi dear. How am I possibly to advise you on your marriage to my own brother?'

This made some semblance of sense. 'So it wasn't that you disapproved of me?'

'Not at all. In America a maidservant has been known to marry the man of the house. In my homeland, anything is possible!'

A white one, perhaps, I wanted to say.

I wasn't sure I fully believed her, but what did it matter? Soon I would never see her again and I would be alone with my dissatisfied thoughts regarding my husband.

She sent for her maid, who walked in with a folded newspaper.

'Do you read the local paper? *The Tribune?*' she asked and I thought she was deliberately changing the subject. 'There is a weekly column called "The Manual for Good Wives" and it is written by a knowledgeable gentleman by the name of Mr Wicksmith.' Ellen gestured for her maid to hand me the newspaper. 'It gives excellent advice on what it takes to make a good and fulfilling marriage.'

I began scanning the words. Whilst I still read books, it was Edward who enjoyed time alone with his newspaper.

'Page twenty-four,' she instructed.

I read out loud. Confused. '*Try Glycerine and Cucumber formulation. Best for preserving soft, smooth skin. No Lady should be without such a magical formula to remain beautiful.*'

'Not that part. Below it.'

'*A column by a T. L. Wicksmith: 'The Manual for Good Wives',*' I read.

'Follow the advice and you will be just fine.'

'How do you know this is written by a man?'

'Most of them are,' she said with a laugh.

'A man is writing about what a woman should do?'

'Well, yes. A man knows what he requires and needs from a wife, so it's perfect!'

'Have these articles helped you, Ellen?'

'Of course not! I am an outspoken Bostonian woman. And a widow besides.' Her voice quietened. 'Temi dear, you and I had very unique husbands. Ones who enjoyed this equally unique and unbridled side of us. Relished it, in fact.'

My throat felt heavy at the mention of Olu and Mr Carmichael, both united in death and both without us.

'Men like my brother … Look, he's never been married before, and as I have told you, I always thought he would go for a young bride as men of his years often do. Oh, don't look so crestfallen, you look not a day over twenty with that lovely skin of yours, whilst the rest of us are more inclined to be in need of that glycerine and cucumber formulation!'

Ellen continued to speak as I peered down at the page, at 'The Manual for Good Wives'.

Even from earliest of life, men are less accustomed than women to exercise self-control and, luckily, are less restricted in these indulgences. The role of a good wife, therefore, is to be forgiving of such traits as it is surely only natural.

'That's just this week's instalment,' she said. 'It's different every time. Read it, study it, do what you want with it, and I promise you your marriage to my brother will be just fine!'

Chapter Thirty-Nine

*Some husbands may not allow an abundance of acquaintances
for their wives. If you retain one friend – female and respect-
ably wed, of course – be sure not to disclose details of your
marriage.*

Mrs Adeline Copplefield,
'The Manual for Good Wives' (1889)

Landri
Four years ago

*'Ross!' said Sadia, looking up from the restaurant table littered with
remnants of Indian food among bottles of wine and pink confetti.*

*'Sorry to interrupt the birthday celebration!' said Ross as a simulta-
neous boo erupted from the girls.*

*'I know, I know. Happy birthday, Claudine, by the way,' he said, his
focus on Landri, sitting beside Sadia and wearing a paper hat adorned
with glitter.*

*'Can't keep away from her, can you?' said a tipsy Sadia, on her first
ever night away from the baby.*

Landri moved away from the noise and went outside with Ross.

'What's happened? Is it Grandma?'

*'No, she's fine. I was worried when you weren't answering your
phone.'*

'It's loud in there. I didn't hear it.'

*'I thought we agreed you'd pick up when I called. I do the same for
you.'*

'*I don't call when you're out.*'

'*What did you say?*'

'*Nothing. I'm sorry I didn't answer the call.*'

'*Well, it's almost twelve, so best make your excuses so we can go.*'

Landri hoped she hadn't heard him correctly. Maybe she'd downed more than the two drinks she'd assigned herself for the night.

'*Just say you have a headache. Come on.*'

'*Ross, you do know how hard it is to get these girls all together in one room?*' *She attempted to make her voice sound jokey, as if she wasn't seething inside.*

'*It's late, Landri and—*'

'*What?*' *she said impatiently.*

'*I miss you.*'

'*We live together, Ross. I hardly ever go out!*'

He leaned in. 'I can't help loving you so much, can I? I know, I know, it's pathetic!'

'*Don't say that,*' *she said, brushing his eyebrows lightly with her fingertips, her annoyance ebbing away.*

She took a deep breath. 'Okay, well, the restaurant closes soon anyway.'

'*Exactly,*' *he said. 'This way, you get a lift home too!*'

When she explained to the girls she was going, they waved her away happily. It was only Claudine who seemed upset about it.

'*It's my birthday!*' *she whined.*

'*I know, I know. We've had a good time, though, and it's almost over anyway.*'

'*Got control issues, that man of yours?*' *Claudine said, just before a loud hiccup.*

'*What did you say?*'

'*I'm just drunk!*' *she roared, followed by a fit of giggles.*

Of course, Landri had thought about that question more than once. Just as often, she'd also dismissed it.

Landri
Present day

'Aren't you going to let me in, then?'

Ross stood at the door of her haven, the place she'd called home for almost two weeks now, one that seemed to shine with perpetual sunlight and joy. Or maybe it had nothing to do with the place, and more about *her*.

'Tumbleberry? Another one of your secrets?' He stepped forward but she didn't move.

'How . . . ?'

'How did I know where to find you after you refused to even give me the address?'

'Yes.'

'That's what you want to talk about? Not the fact that I haven't seen you for two weeks after you walked out on me, the day after I proposed to you?'

She refused to let the guilt of that sink in, more concerned with why her grandma or her friends had told Ross where she was. No, her friends wouldn't do that. It had been her grandma. She'd been an idiot to believe they had gotten closer, if she could betray her trust like this.

'I told you I was safe.'

'Are you not going to let me in?'

This is what he does, she told herself. Playing on the guilt until she caved. She didn't want to let him into her new home, her safe space. She didn't want to give in again.

'Everything all right?' called a friendly and familiar voice from across the road. Gwen.

'Everything is fine!' said Landri, now forced to step aside and let Ross into her home.

*

'Is there someone else?' he asked five minutes later.

'No, no way. I'd never do that.'

'You kept this place a secret, so I'm wondering how many others you have tucked away.'

'I told you about the house. How do you think I was able to afford my part of a riverside apartment in London?'

He made a face. She flinched.

'What else can it be then?'

Maybe it was the shoulder shrug or the clueless expression on his face implying that her leaving had nothing to do with him that did it – but she was angry. If only this anger, this overdue mass of emotion, could leap to the surface and not remain inside.

'I thought you'd be pleased,' he said. 'With the engagement. Isn't it every woman's dream to get married?'

'I wouldn't know.'

'Come off it. You're pushing forty.'

'So are you.' She said this quickly, looking at his expression to check if she'd gone too far. Yet hadn't she already done that by getting away from him? 'I just think we should have had a conversation about what we wanted out of a marriage first. Finances, if we want children, housework . . .'

He raised an eyebrow. 'Housework? Seriously?'

Yes, fucking seriously! she wanted to shout, scream.

'I thought you were happy.'

'I was. Sometimes. Oh, I don't know.'

'So I'm the bad guy?' His lips pursed, eyes widened.

There he was! The Ross she'd met two weeks after moving in with him.

'You're never satisfied with anything, Landri. You push everyone away and I'm literally the last one standing. Even your gran . . .'

'You don't get to say that.' She surprised herself with how firm her words sounded. 'This is about us, not my past. Us. Now.'

He exhaled. 'Let's go home and talk then. Get it all out in the open. That's what you want, isn't it?' His arm extended in her direction. 'Come on.'

She shook her head slowly, then much faster. 'I can't, Ross.'

'What?'

'I can't.'

He dropped his arm. 'I'm sorry, Landri . . . I know you feel pressured. I just . . . I just want you home!'

'I will come back when I'm ready.'

He looked at her, his face now becoming flushed.

In the past that look would be enough to bring on the guilt and for Landri to forget her own feelings and pander to his. To hold him in her arms, rocking gently as she agreed with him when he affirmed he was the only one she would ever need.

'Landri, I'll give you till the end of the month,' he said, face now morphed into a more determined expression. 'If by then you haven't come back . . . then don't bother ever coming home.'

'What does that mean?' Her lips began to quiver and she had never hated herself more.

'It means we're done.'

She hadn't thought about the actual end of the relationship. Only that she'd needed time out, a rest, to get away.

'Actually, you know what?' he said, quickly heading for the door, 'I don't even know if I want you anymore!'

The door slammed behind him and then she remembered to breathe. Clutching her middle as she began to quietly sob. A pain so deep inside of her, she wasn't sure if it was actually for Ross.

No, it wasn't, this was something else. These tears were for someone else.

Lola Jaye

Landri
Thirty-three years ago

Six days and six sleeps since she'd last seen her mother.

The house filled with people every day. Even her father who hardly ever came to visit was around much more. The only new constant she enjoyed was Grandma's spaghetti, chilli and meatballs and freshly squeezed orange juice. Sometimes her grandma would forget to prepare the drink. On one such day, Landri walked into the kitchen to get the juicer. She'd seen the way her grandma had used it and could do it herself. Instead, she wandered into a space of rushed voices.

'Has anyone told her Clara isn't coming back yet?'

'Keep your voice down.'

'It's not fair, Antonietta! How long do you expect to keep this up?'

'How do I tell her that? I don't even understand it myself. How could Clara, my Clara . . . How could she do such a thing?'

'Did you not see that anything was wrong? You're a doctor after all.'

'So it's my fault, is it? It's my fault she drowned herself, eh? Is that what you're trying to say?'

Landri gasped.

Both heads turned to her.

'Landri!' said Grandma.

This had been the very moment her life changed once again. The moment she believed she deserved the opposite of love. Her mum's actions the first of many to reinforce this idea.

Then Ross, the moment he finally said he didn't want her anymore.

Chapter Forty

To be a good wife is an amalgamation of hard labour, a constant understanding . . . & good luck.

Mrs Adeline Copplefield,
'The Manual for Good Wives' (1890)

Temi
1885

After Ellen left, I did not experience the loneliness I had feared. The notebook Olu had lovingly gifted me was now a constant companion, as well as a vessel for my mounting feelings towards my *darling* husband Edward.

A husband who hardly spoke to me anymore. Hardly touched me.

My husband who stayed away most days without even the excuse of work. Returning home in the early hours of the morning reeking of what I could only describe as the scent of another woman. A woman not his wife.

I ignored it all for weeks before deciding the time was right to ask him outright. Or until I had simply amassed enough courage. Because to do so risked my very existence. This house, the fine garments my children and I now wore, the food in our stomachs, all were a result of my union with Edward. I had to be careful not to shake that reality in any way. I had already tasted poverty too many times and had no intention of revisiting it.

*

'You dare question me?' he said in that low voice I had once taken for sincerity and meticulous manners. 'It is not your right to ask me such a thing. It is unseemly. Do you think my mother would have asked my father such a question?'

'I simply wanted to know if you were entertaining another,' I said, watching his back as he walked up the long staircase and into a room I dared not enter without knocking.

I should not have been so brazen.

In my own room, I lay down, unable to weep. Instead, writing in the notebook feelings I could share with no one. Asking why I could not have simply stayed a widow and not subjected myself to this treatment.

Every day killing me with silence.
What have I done to make you this way?
This misery. Worth title of wife?
Loneliness is worse because you are here.
I despise you.

Herbs from the village can kill in the right concoction.

I hate you.
They poisoned my sister.
Taye.

I despise myself.

Widowed by the one I loved with my whole heart. Left with the one
I despise.

Chapter Forty-One

The wife is in charge of the running of the home but never the financial affairs.

Mrs Adeline Copplefield,
'The Manual for Good Wives' (1889)

Landri
Present day

Widowed by the one I loved with my whole heart. Left with the one I despise.

Landri closed the notebook, shaken. No longer able to simply dismiss Temi's writings as random thoughts. Here she was confessing to actually hating one of her husbands. And the reference to poison . . . what did that mean? Had she done it?

Who could know what went on in any marriage? In those days a woman, let alone a Black woman, would have nowhere to go from an abusive relationship.

She stopped.

A realization spread across her mind, followed by a tingling sensation throughout her body. She swallowed and then tears she hadn't bargained for blurred her eyes. Had she too been . . . ? No, she couldn't say it, think it.

She'd read a book once and seen a couple of dramas on TV about a man being abusive to a woman without ever physically touching her. His weapons were his words. Sometimes many words, sometimes none. Possessing this hold over her even when the woman did not realize it, and once she did, holding on even tighter. So tight that it hurt.

'No!' she said out loud at no one. That wasn't her story.

Yes, it was.

Ross wasn't controlling.

Yes, he was.

He'd thrown one of their dining chairs once, yes. Not at her. But across the room in anger.

Yes, but what if it had escalated?

If things were so bad, she would have left him before now.

Right?

She closed her eyes as if to block out the barrage of thoughts now attacking her mind. Her palms pressed to her ears. Yet the noise would not stop, could not until she admitted the truth to herself.

She could not even mouth the words, let alone say them. She wasn't ready to acknowledge them in any way. Not yet. Instead she made a pact with herself. To stay where she felt safe. And that was here. At Tumbleberry.

Chapter Forty-Two

To your husband you are a delicate flower of unending beauty.
If the rose begins to wilt, he may see it as only natural to seek
other blooms.

Mrs Adeline Copplefield,
'The Manual for Good Wives' (1888)

Temi
1885

Marriage to Edward continued to progress in much the same unsatisfying vein.

The loneliness palpable. Two strangers living in a large house in separate bedrooms who happened to sometimes cross paths. Always polite enough to greet one another in the morning over breakfast. Deep down, nestling in my own heart, the fiercest of disappointments.

I was once of the belief Edward had been my rescuer, a prince to lead me into a fairy-tale life. Instead, he'd turned into a man who around once a month asked me to come into his room and demanded marital relations whilst smelling of alcohol and another. Thankfully, I was able to resist his weak advances, alcohol preventing much physical exertion on his part, and in minutes he'd be snoring odiously on the bed as I watched. Oh, how I despised the man I had married. The reminder I lived in a beautiful house and materially wanted for nothing only went so far.

*

I stopped reading 'The Manual for Good Wives' out of frustration and decided I would be a *good enough* wife. Making sure the staff left Edward's dinner covered in the kitchen when he was absent; instructing Eleanor to make sure his clothes were pressed and ready for him in the morning. I would even allow for his indiscretions as long as it kept him away from my bed.

I fulfilled my duties as a *good enough* wife whilst he reneged on being a good husband a little bit more each day, with the late nights, lack of any attention and, most of all, his indifference towards me.

'I would like a child,' he said one morning as we sat for breakfast. I pretended not to hear him. 'Did you not hear me, Temi?' He spoke in that soft, low voice, his words stabbing me with each syllable.

'I am thirty-nine years old, Edward,' I explained.

'Our dear Anne had six children before raising Mary Ellen and myself. The last one she bore at the age of forty-five or more, if I recall.'

It took me a moment to realize he was referring to his and Ellen's former nanny.

'How could you possibly know this detail?'

'I cannot be precise but she was not of tender years when my father and she . . .'

'Your father?'

'Let's just say the child was a little on the lighter side.'

'Anne bore your father's child?' I said, as the truth registered.

'My father was a good man and he would never have done anything unless Anne was willing. It was he who was seduced.'

My heart sank as I thought of this faceless woman named Anne. A faithful employee taken advantage of by the man of the house, Edward's father. I felt a sickness rise within my throat.

'I can understand why he went with Anne, even if Mother did

not. There is something quite delectable about a coloured woman.'

I swallowed, trying not to think about whether Anne had been given a choice in the matter. I was a well-read woman. I knew what happened to those who were enslaved and those deemed 'free'. I thought of the many people captured and chained from my own kingdom. Mothers, fathers, sons and daughters never to be heard of again. The trail of grief left behind.

His eyes narrowed and I felt as if I were not even in the room. 'The way you move, the speech, the curve of your bodies. The negress in all its glory.' He turned to me. 'A woman of my own race holds no such desire for me.'

'I see,' I said, trying not to catch the fear lodged in my throat. The thought of relations with this man repulsed me and I could never allow another man to lie with me that I did not consent to. One of us would have to die first.

'With this marriage, you and I both receive what we desire. Let's be honest here, without me you and your children would have been on the street. You were a princess back in Africa and have I not treated you as one?'

I could not answer.

'Are you not able to speak, Temi?'

'I do not know what to say.'

'How about, thank you? Thank you for saving you from the gutter and giving you all of this.' His arms gesticulated towards the space around us as I could only stare at my plate of half-eaten food. Attempting to absorb all he had spoken about his desires. He sickened me and yet he was right. I owned none of this, not really. Unlike with Olu and I, nothing was shared between us. Everything belonged to Edward, so my children and I were simply lodgers – and this felt unsettling. As if our very existence had been built on a house of playing cards.

'Temi?'

'Yes, my dear husband, you are right.'

'Say it then. Say thank you.' He grabbed my arm suddenly. 'Say it. Say thank you like you should. Be grateful for what I provide.' His hand tightened its grip as he moved his chair closer to me.

'Edward, you are hurting me!'

His face had reddened, he even looked different. Like a beast desperate to be unleashed.

'Say it! Say thank you, Edward!' His voice was slightly louder now. 'Say it,' he spoke into my ear, making me jump at the ferocity of the sound.

'Th—' My mouth refused the command.

'Are you deaf?'

I shook my head defiantly. Determined he was not going to win any part of this bizarre contest. No longer that frightened little girl in the chief's sleeping quarters, I had been through too much to bow down to this.

'I'm waiting . . .' he sang eerily.

'No.' I shook my head for emphasis. He then shoved me to the ground, his hand raised as if to strike me. 'Edward!' I yelped.

Our eyes locked.

'Get out!' he roared in the loudest, fiercest voice I had ever heard from my husband. I clumsily launched myself upwards, my stomach lurching with fear, and scrambled to the door.

That night I did not sleep. Could not. My eyes were fixed on the locked door. Imagining Edward breaking it down to finish what he had started. How long could I keep him at bay? How long before he simply took what he wanted?

I had unlocked a rage behind the quiet, calm demeanour and I wanted no part of it.

I could no longer stay in this marriage. Yet with no resources, I remained trapped. Even the house which belonged to Olu and I had automatically become a part of Edward Cutler's estate, as was the law. I hadn't managed to stow away any money because

Edward controlled everything and simply gave me an allowance for housekeeping. He thought it unthinkable I work, and in the first days of our marriage and as lady of the house, I had agreed.

I would simply have nothing if I left this man.

Death is too good for him. This betrayal, more than I can bear, I wrote.

There could be only one way out.

Chapter Forty-Three

Upon your marriage, your worldly goods will become your husband's.

Mrs Adeline Copplefield,
'The Manual for Good Wives' (1889)

Landri
Present day

Her eyes moved over the words once more.

Death is too good for him. This betrayal, more than I can bear.

With only a few pages of the notebook left, Temi's thoughts were becoming even darker. Landri could only hope the last pages would vindicate Temi in some way. Show she hadn't killed her husband. Offer some resolution, whatever that looked like.

'I am way too invested in this!' Landri said out loud.

She peered out of the window and spotted Gwen walking towards her own house.

'Gwen!' she called, running outside. 'Come and join me or I'll just carry on talking to myself!'

'Oh, I do that all the time,' said Gwen.

They sipped iced rooibos tea whilst enjoying the soft breeze and watching a variety of birds explore the garden.

'Anything new in the notebook?'

'No, not really,' she lied, not ready for Gwen to pass judgement on Temi just yet.

'That young man I saw you with . . . I got the sense all was not right.'

'That was my partner, Ross.' *Ex-partner,* she wanted to say, yet the words were not ready to leave her lips.

'You don't have to explain. As long as everything is all right.'

'It will be,' she said, with more certainty than she felt. 'How long were you married for, Gwen?'

'Fifty years.'

'Happy years?'

'What a thing to ask,' she said, smiling.

'Sorry . . .'

'No, that's okay. It's not something I have ever been asked before. People assume that, good or bad, you just get on with it. I suppose in my generation that is true. For some. Not everyone. My husband was a good man, though.'

'What did he do?'

'An engineer. Worked hard and long hours. But me and the children wanted for nothing and I kept a good home.'

'You probably think I'm odd. Almost forty, no hubby.'

'Kids do things differently these days. My children weren't married until their thirties. When I was a girl, you did it quickly, especially if you were in the family way.'

'Were you in the family way, Gwen?' said Landri with a wink.

'Cheeky! No way. My mother would have killed me!'

Their laughter slowly quietened into a silence, one which Landri felt compelled to fill.

'My mother died when I was five.'

Gwen moved forward in her chair. 'Oh, my love.'

'It's fine,' replied Landri, waving the words away.

Gwen shook her head. 'No, it isn't, my love. She was your

mum and that can never be fine. You poor baby. I knew she must have been young when she died. But you . . . only five.'

Gwen quickly grabbed her hand and at first this felt alien, odd and perhaps even unwanted. But Gwen just held on tighter, smoothing the top with her thumb and bringing with it a trust for this woman who two weeks ago Landri hadn't even met. This lovely woman with a grey bouffant hairstyle, acknowledging her mum and acknowledging how she felt.

'Her name was Clara. She was beautiful and loving. She liked cherry-flavoured ice poles. I don't know why I remember that.' She turned to Gwen, her eyes not focusing. 'One day she walked into the sea and kept going until she was no longer there.'

Gwen's eyebrows wrinkled. 'Oh, my love, are you saying . . . ?'

'She ended her life. Yes.'

Perhaps it was seeing Ross and then reading those notebook entries which had left her feeling vulnerable, because opening up to Gwen about her mother had not been planned.

She was glad it had happened, though.

Her mother, Clara, was the first person on this earth to love her and yet five years later she had gone.

'I carry this around with me everywhere I go,' said Gwen, pulling out from her black leather purse a grainy black-and-white picture. A little girl in a puff-sleeved dress with ankle socks and Mary Jane shoes. 'This is my mother, Muriel. She was born in 1903. She would have been a bit younger than this when she met Temi for the first time.'

'She's a cutie,' said Landri.

'When she grew up, she broke a lot of hearts, my dad's included.'

'You must miss her.'

'Every day.' A silence ensued and this time Landri didn't break it immediately. Because to do so was to run away from feelings which needed to be brought to the surface. Like memories of her own mother. Because to keep these precious memories buried would mean erasing the parts of her which had nothing to do with her mother's final act.

Like Temi, her mother would never be erased again.

Chapter Forty-Four

For a wife to work is to declare to others her husband incompetent and without ability to provide for his household.

Mrs Adeline Copplefield,
'The Manual for Good Wives' (1889)

Temi
1886

I decided the easiest way to live was to focus on my children.

Iyabo insisted she did not wish to seek a husband and at the age of twenty-four was happy to move into the realm of spinsterhood. This was worrying for me simply because I did not have a personal fortune to leave her. Without a husband, how was she to live? I couldn't help feeling my unsatisfactory interactions with Edward may have decided this for her, whilst she insisted this was not the case. In just a few short months, she'd witnessed the love I shared with Olu and had seen the difference. As for Amelia, our paths hardly crossed as she spent most days in her room or out with her friends. The house was big enough for such solitude from one another.

'Where are you going?' I asked one day as Amelia headed towards the door. She was turning into a beautiful young woman and resembling her father more and more each day. How I missed him.

'Ask the coachman, you always do.'

'I have a right to know where the carriage I pay for is taking you.'

'Don't you mean that Edward pays for?'

She spoke his name with such disdain.

'I will not have you speak to me in this way, Amelia. I am your mother.'

She exhaled quickly.

'You will stay at home today,' I said.

She moved closer to me. 'Mother, I am now eighteen years old and I am old enough to be married and out of this house.'

'Until you are married, you will obey my rules.'

'Duly noted,' she said, before turning on her heel and walking in the direction of the front door anyway. My words had no power anymore. Like my husband, my daughter had stopped listening to me a very long time ago.

The next time I saw Amelia, she had eloped and was married to a man I had only just met. An Italian doctor called Davide. I almost needed my smelling salts when I heard the news and it was Iyabo who held me as my entire body shook with rage.

'You . . . you have married without our consent? Without discussion first?'

The newlyweds stood in front of us, as if everything spoken so far hadn't just broken my heart into tiny little pieces.

Amelia shrugged her shoulders.

'So this is why you refused Edward's generous offer of a coming out ball.'

'Yes, Mother.'

'Are you in the family way?'

She rolled her eyes. 'No, Mother.'

'No, Mrs Cutler,' said the young man by her side. 'We are simply in love with one another.'

The way my daughter looked at him reminded me of the way I used to look at her father and, in that moment, I didn't care that Edward was away, I just wanted Olu here with me, helping me deal with this.

'What of your dreams, Amelia?' She had confided in me, in a rare moment, a desire to study medicine now that women were able to gain degrees.

'Davide has agreed to me starting my medical training. He is a progressive husband!' She turned to him and giggled. I had not heard that laugh in so long.

'I don't understand . . .'

'What's there to understand? We're in love, married, and I am about to embark on a new adventure. You have no need to worry about me now. I'm no longer your problem.'

'You have never been a problem!'

Davide shifted closer to Amelia, their bond astounding. Amelia was a wife.

'I intend to follow in the footsteps of my heroine, Sarah Parker Remond.'

'Who?'

'Oh, Mother, is that not why you sent me to Bedford College for Ladies? She was the first woman of our hue to attend there.'

'I did not know this . . .' I said absently, trying to engage, but my mind was elsewhere.

'She is quite a legendary figure there! How can you know nothing of such a woman? She was the only Black woman signatory to the women-only petition requesting the right of women to vote. I simply adore her!'

'Indeed, she does sound remarkable.'

'She studied at the hospital of Santa Maria Nuovo, and so shall I.'

'I've never heard of this hospital.'

'That's because it's in Italy.'

'I beg your pardon?' I said, hoping I had misheard my child.

'Florence, to be precise. I'll be moving to Italy with my husband and his mother in four weeks. It's what we both want. A fresh start for us both.'

Iyabo moved closer to me again, held my hand and squeezed. Support. Love. I needed it all in that moment.

'Children come and go,' said Edward. 'Isn't it just part of life?'

I was aghast at this insensitivity when Edward finally returned two days later. He asserted that Amelia marrying a doctor and moving to a prominent European country such as Italy should have made me proud.

I didn't bother to ask where he'd been for two days.

I no longer cared.

The day I was to say goodbye to Amelia, I still hoped for a change of mind.

'Mother, I hope you can be happy for me.'

How could I not be? Like Juliet in one of my favourite stories, she had fallen in love. With an Italian too, although it would be in Florence, instead of Verona. How could I not be happy she had found a love just like I had once?

I could only hope hers would have a better ending than mine and that of Juliet.

'Not that you have asked for it, but you have my blessing all the same,' I said with a smile, and she allowed me to embrace her.

When we said goodbye, I hoped it would not be the last time I saw her. The only positive about this situation was that, whatever happened with Edward and I, she would be well looked after. Indeed, I was proud of her. My daughter was on her way to becoming a doctor following in the footsteps of the mighty Sarah Parker Remond, who after some reading, I managed to find out was a staunch anti-slavery campaigner, bravely taking her message all over the world and serving on the committee for the Ladies' London Emancipation Society.

This was the type of woman my daughter looked up to. Not

one who stayed in a cold marriage, relying on the love of a man who chose to withhold it.

After Amelia had left, Iyabo continued to be a great source of comfort. In the garden she would sit and embroider whilst I picked the flowers which had bloomed so beautifully in the sun.

Amelia wrote regularly, remaining somewhat distant in her letters, but at least she was safe. My little girl was safe.

The day my life took another unwelcome, unexpected turn, I had been shopping in a small shoe shop which sold exquisite leather designs only those with the deepest pockets could afford. I settled on a pair of pointy toe lace-up boots – one pair for me and another for Iyabo. We would usually shop together but she'd complained of a headache and I felt sure the boots would cheer her up.

I returned home to find Eleanor waiting by the gate.

'Why are you standing outside?' I asked as she climbed into the carriage to retrieve my purchases.

'I am not due to start work until this evening, madam, but wanted to wait for you in case you needed help.'

'That's very kind of you but these bags are heavy. Get someone to help you,' I said. 'Actually, I don't recall giving you the morning off. Did I?'

'No, madam, Mr Cutler said everyone should go home for the rest of the day and that I should leave and return for the evening. That's why I was outside,' said Eleanor.

'He hadn't discussed this with me,' I said absently, aware my husband rarely discussed anything with me. I believe Edward still thought himself to be a bachelor.

We left the purchases downstairs and I walked up the grand staircase, the house feeling uncharacteristically quiet. I headed towards my own room first, then thought to see if Edward was home. The moment my hand gripped the door handle, a feeling of foreboding came over me – as if opening his door would mean the end of life as I knew it. I heard the giggling immediately. I wasn't stupid. I knew Edward had a mistress, or several in fact, and had long since rationalized I could live with it. What he had never done was brought anyone into the home before, and this new level of disrespect felt earth-shattering.

Yet what choice did I have?

I removed my hand, rationalizing the need to discuss this with him at another date.

It was when I turned to leave that I heard it. That laugh. That incessant guffaw, belonging to my daughter Iyabo.

PART THREE

Chapter Forty-Five

If a husband prefers to seek his pleasures outside of the home,
this should be executed discreetly.

Mrs Adeline Copplefield,
'The Manual for Good Wives' (1893)

Temi
1886

Long ago in my kingdom, when my father forced me to marry a man I could never love, I had felt alone. When Olu died and my daughter wanted nothing to do with me, I had felt alone. There had been many periods of loneliness in my life – prolonged or brief – but this was the first time I had felt so completely and utterly alone and, worst of all, hopeless.

They were all gone. Amelia in Italy, Olu washed up at sea in an unknown land, Iyabo . . . and now Edward. A man I am appalled to have ever called my husband. Glad he was now out of my life, even if the circumstances leading to this had been sordid and wrong.

Up until the moment I discovered his dalliance with my daughter, I had willed him out of my life. Regretted on so many occasions that I had married a selfish man such as Edward. I had wanted him gone for good. Dead.

Now it had happened, some would say it had been at my hands.

I say, let them prove this. Let them try! I'd done nothing but be a faithful and dutiful wife up until the moment I could take no more. Leading me to where I never wanted to visit.

Let no one judge my actions!

After I'd heard him cavorting with Iyabo, I had waited until the next day before confronting him. In the morning, I'd instructed the coachman to take me somewhere, a long journey that would give me the necessary time to think not only about what I had just seen, but also about what to do next. An anger had gripped my belly, easing the further away the horses took us. The street Olu and I had first lived in was reassuring to revisit – from the comfort of the carriage, of course. The unkempt pavements and small children running about the place caused a well of emotion to build inside of me.

'Are you sure this is where you want us to stop, madam?' said the coachman.

'No . . . actually, I would like you to take me to the woods. I shall direct you if my memory serves me correctly.'

'Yes, madam.'

It was hours later, when I returned home, that I finally felt able to face my husband, armed with nothing but a bunch of freshly picked flowers. That evening I assisted cook in preparing his meal, just like the wives back in the old country would do for my father, even when they had staff. Thankfully, Iyabo had made herself scarce by staying in her room, protesting she wasn't hungry.

I had watched as he chewed each morsel of his favourite, the treacle tart. A most fitting name I would say.

'Are you enjoying your dessert?' I asked.

'It is lovely, Temi dear. You know I have a sweet tooth.'

'I made it myself.'

'Which is why it is that much more delicious.'

I had stared as he chewed and then scraped his spoon uncouthly over his plate, having consumed all of it. Every lovingly prepared morsel.

'How could you?' I'd said.

He'd looked up, still chewing the last of the tart.

'My daughter? Of all the women you could have, you chose Iyabo?' My tears were dry, a rage mounting inside of me instead.

He'd sat back in his chair. 'It is a relief that you know.'

'Why her, Edward, why?'

'You should ask yourself why your new husband could never compete with the old.'

'What?'

'Your *lost love*.' The way he spoke those words made me want to strike him right there with my bare fists.

'This has nothing to do with him. How dare you?'

'I advise you to lower your voice, woman.'

His words were still low, yet sharp. Biting. I had never hated him more than in that moment.

'I want you out of this house!' I'd said, just as Iyabo joined us in the room. I had been careful not to engage with her much that day, but she had clearly overheard the conversation. The brazenness with which she held onto his hand shocked me more than hearing their delighted groans the day before. This simple act of affection, with no regard for me at all.

'This is my house – you forget this, Temi. So I will not be leaving.'

I had already come up with a solution, having had the entire day with my thoughts and my notebook. I told him I would leave them to do whatever, but I wanted Tumbleberry. I simply wanted my home back and a fair settlement.

'We have not been married that long, Temi, so what you are asking for . . .'

'I simply require Tumbleberry and if it has been sold, I will take the proceeds. Nothing more, nothing less.'

'It remains, yes, but has been consolidated into the business. *My* business.'

I could not look at Iyabo, who'd simply remained seated.

'I don't think you understand, Temi dear. I'm not as rich as you think. I have debts. You should know about those.'

'I just want what is mine.'

'I have spent a great deal on you, Amelia's school, and the upkeep of this house. It has taken its toll on the Cutler finances. So you see, my dear, this isn't as straightforward as you think.'

I could not think of a word to say.

'I'm feeling awfully hot . . . slightly unwell,' he'd said suddenly, loosening his collar.

'What is the matter?' asked Iyabo, placing her palm onto his forehead.

'Please excuse me,' he'd said, stumbling slightly as he stood. Leaving Iyabo and myself alone.

'Why?' I'd finally been able to look her in the face, which appeared to be void of any remorse. 'Of all the men . . .'

Her response was shocking and deeply hurtful, her voice a succession of hisses. 'It is what you deserve.'

'I thought . . . You've been so good to me . . . I thought we were beyond . . . this.'

'I shall never forgive what you did to me, *Ma*. You never wanted me as a baby and then you give me to that woman! I cannot forgive you. I shall never!' Her accent had shifted between that of the old country and British, her venom audible in both.

'So this . . . this was all revenge?'

She did not answer at first. Then I repeated the question.

'At first, yes,' she'd said quietly.

'And then . . . ?'

'I only wanted to see if he could desire me. That is all. Then . . . then . . .'

'What? Did he take things too far?'

'What? No!' she insisted but I was unsure whether to believe her.

'You don't have to stay, Iyabo!'

'What are you saying?' Her eyes glistened.

Desperation laced my voice. 'I don't care what you have done, but you don't have to stay with him. He is a violent man. Please . . . you must listen to me . . .'

She wiped at her eyes. 'No, he is a good man. He said he will take care of me.'

'Edward only cares for himself, he . . .'

Edward had entered the room before I could finish, his face now ashen.

'Please, Iyabo,' I said, grabbing her hand as a single tear careered down her cheek.

'Leave us!' she hissed, more for his benefit, I thought, pulling her hand away abruptly as Edward slowly and unsteadily walked over. He said nothing and looked really unwell. I could only wonder whether he would simply do us both the gentlemanly favour and die.

Chapter Forty-Six

It is wise to spend less time greatly focused on the wedding day
& to instead contemplate the marriage.

Mrs Adeline Copplefield,
'The Manual for Good Wives' (1888)

Landri
Present day

Landri had four pages of the notebook left to go.

Now there was a need to preserve and protect not only its precious contents but the outer layers too, all of it. This was more than just her great-great-great-grandmother's notebook, *this was history.*

It was inside the Shilling and Jones property management office that she was able to access a photocopier, showing up on the pretence of finding out how the tenant search was going.

As she stood by the copier, her stomach lurched with Mr Shilling's response.

'I think we have a long-term renter interested again!'

'You do?'

'Better still, it didn't come through the app so it's going to be very long-term. They are currently in the process of providing us with the necessary documents.'

'Oh,' she said. The thought of leaving that house unthinkable and not a little scary.

'Good news, isn't it?'

She nodded in false agreement.

'They are not looking to move for another month and by then all the documents will be in.'

'How long are they looking to rent for?'

'At least a year. Wonderful news, as it saves the hassle of different people moving in and out. Which is what we like when it comes to Tumbleberry. Such a special house.'

'Mr Shilling, thanks for letting me use the copier.' She placed the notebook back in its flower box and into her bag.

'Do you not need it anymore?'

She shook her head. There was no way she could force the notebook face down onto the screen, it would probably fall apart. What was she thinking? She would simply stick to the pictures she had taken on her phone. For now. Until she could find another way of preserving this precious find.

As she walked back to the house, all she could think about was having to leave in a month. Of course it had never been a long-term solution, but the thought of leaving saddened her. She liked her life at Tumbleberry. She liked being around all that history and her ancestors. It was like she could feel them, their presence, and their journey. She'd also experienced a sense of belonging she'd never had before and wasn't sure she was ready to let it all go.

'So this is your life now. A pensioner in her eighties for a best friend, trips to the local bakery and tending to your shrubs,' said Sadia as they sat in a smart local cafe across the road from Chimes & Things. 'And not in a good way!'

'Sounds idyllic to me,' said Landri.

'I mean, it's nice enough, but it isn't you.'

'So what is me?'

'Living in an apartment facing the river with a hot man.'

Landri smiled as she gazed through the window.

'The girls are still worried about you. The text group is blowing up every day.'

'I wouldn't know, I have it on mute.'

'Rude!'

'You'll live.'

'What about work?' asked Sadia.

'Steve's covering for me.'

'For three weeks. You don't have much of that left.'

'Sadia, you're really killing the vibe here.'

'Sorry,' she said as the server placed their order on the table.

'I've been writing again,' said Landri.

'You write for a living.'

'No, I mean, I don't know, I'm just dabbling.'

Hearing herself say such thoughts out loud validated it – and also meant she had to follow through with what had been brewing in her head for days now.

This terrified her.

'What, some raunchy romance novel?'

'No . . . I think I want to write about Temi.'

'She does sound amazing! Bumping off her husband, or husbands plural.'

'No, not that. I'm not even sure that happened. Anyway, innocent until proven otherwise.'

'Indeed! Oh, and talking of which, I'm going back to work very soon.'

'Why didn't you tell me?'

'I would have if you hadn't subjected us to your pre-mid-life crisis and run off to the back of beyond!'

'I'm so pleased for you!'

'Just part-time at first. The world has changed so much in four years.'

I've changed so much in two weeks, thought Landri.

'Tell me about this book,' said Sadia.

'I didn't say it was a book.'

Whilst glad she was now accountable to Sadia to at least produce something, she wasn't actually sure what that something
would be. The idea would come to her, though; the moment her
mind and heart freed themselves from the clutter amassed over
the years and allowed something more creative to land in its place.

It would come.

Chapter Forty-Seven

Patience, self-sacrifice and an acceptance of your fate are attractive characteristics in a wife.

Mrs Adeline Copplefield,
'The Manual for Good Wives' (1893)

Temi
1887

My life without Edward in it felt aimless, without structure and without hope.

Living in a nondescript guesthouse, alone with my thoughts. And as the months passed, I began to consider what the world would look like without me in it. Who would mourn me? Not many. Iyabo and my family in the old country had mourned me long ago. My demise would mean little to Amelia who was busy embracing all that life had to offer in Italy. Perhaps death would serve as a chance to be with Olu again. Could death guarantee this?

Thinking of my own demise did not mean I would ever take my life, there just seemed to be this bizarre comfort in thinking it.

I had not left the bed for days now. I simply cried, slept and rose out of it to urinate in the outside toilet. My hair remained unkempt, another reminder of Iyabo's absence. My daughter who now lay with my husband. Refusing to leave with me that horrid day.

The luxury of spending so much time in bed meant moments for extra thought. My anger at my daughter's betrayal now resembled something like pity. Edward was the only one deserving of my scorn, clearly following in his father's footsteps with his penchant for taking advantage of *African ladies*. Hadn't he done the same to me? The only difference being he had married me – an act he saw as honourable but which only allowed him to strip me bare and leave me with nothing. To take me from being a 'lady' to someone he felt more comfortable with me being.

A nothing. A nobody.

I sometimes gazed at the half empty wardrobe, home to my beautiful dresses hanging inside. Recalling the joy each piece once gave me. Fleeting joy, but joy nevertheless. Eleanor pleaded with me when I told her to go home and that, once again, I could no longer pay her. 'I don't need paying. I just want to see you are all right, madam.'

'As much as I am grateful for your loyalty, I do not require the extra burden of guilt in wondering how you are to feed yourself. You must seek employment elsewhere.'

I hated it when she left. It was just me again.

For now, this was my life. And to think about a future felt terrifying.

Until I had to. And that moment arrived sooner than I would have liked.

'You're a month behind with your rent so you'll have to go,' said the landlady.

'My husband, Mr Cutler, has been paying—'

'Well, he's no longer doing so. I'm happy to allow you to stay on another week or two, but if you don't have employment . . .'

'Yes, of course.' The shambolic guesthouse Edward had agreed to pay for had, I thought, been a humiliation too far. Now it had reached an even lower level. Oh, how I wished I had crushed those berries into his treacle tart that day. I had gone to the woods with the sole purpose of carefully picking a bunch of Lords-and-ladies berries. I had never forgotten Olive's tutorial on what it could cause in the wrong hands. And I had wanted my hands to be doing all of the wrongdoing. However, when it came down to the moment of truth, I knew in my heart that I, Temi Masters, was no murderess.

Yet now, soon to be homeless, Temi Masters wished she could invent a time machine to transport her back to that moment. Then I would have watched as he choked on the remnants of a treacle tart! Begging for mercy, an apology etched into his final gasps of breath!

'Mrs Cutler?' said the landlady.

'Mrs Masters,' I corrected. I was now a divorced woman and the shame of that was outweighed by the joy of shedding the Cutler name.

'Mrs Masters, I wouldn't normally do this, but I do have a friend in need of an employee.'

I looked on questioningly. I was excellent at bookkeeping and of course I could write well, I thought. 'I would be happy to meet with them.'

'Excellent. I think they need a couple of domestic servants, so if you know of anyone else?'

'Excuse me?'

'Do you know anyone else I can send?'

I cleared my throat and dusted down the front of my dress. 'I appreciate your efforts, it's just . . . well, I practically ran the business with my husband and . . . well . . .'

'Mrs Cutler, unless you—'

'Mrs Masters,' I corrected.

'Unless you can think of any other ideas, I will have to ask you to vacate the premises as soon as is possible.'

A feeling of panic began to rise up inside me. This had been my address for the last three months and the one I'd sent to Amelia. If I left, how would she find me?

She turned her back.

'Wait . . . please do give me the address of your . . . friend and I will enquire,' I said.

'That is a good decision, Mrs Cutler.'

'I've been expecting you,' said Mrs Dornton. I walked through a doorway which led to the back of the house, where a maid was beating a rug and a cook plucking a chicken. The stench of raw meat and cigarette smoke gripped me immediately, my stomach churning.

None of the workers glanced my way, and for that I was grateful.

'You will mainly help with the domestic chores. Anything which needs to be done.'

I stopped listening, trying to take in the atmosphere of hopelessness, the silence, the stench. This reminded me of the house I had shared with Edward where I had only ever seen the back once. An area never the domain of the mistress of the house and certainly not for me.

'I . . . I've changed my mind. I cannot do this.'

'Not good enough, is it?'

'This is not my reasoning.'

'Indeed it is. I see your garments cost quite a bit. A woman fallen on hard times and now the likes of us is not good enough for you. Even a coloured woman!'

'I'm sorry to have wasted your time,' I said, rushing away.

'Not that way, the back way for the servants!' she called behind me.

I sat on the edge of my bed, the notebook staring back at me. My final gift from the love of my life, Olu.

I picked it up. Once, I used to bring it to my nose, not for the scent of leather but to see if it smelled of my husband. Any such scent (if it had existed) would be long gone by now, but it gave me comfort to try. Except for now. It simply reminded me of all I had lost, once again.

'Why did you leave me?' I said, talking to the notebook. With no grave to attend, I supposed this notebook served as a symbol of a memorial.

What would Olu think of my current predicament?

Once again, I could not afford tears – literally. I was days away from being thrown onto the streets and I needed to find the strength to carry on. Again.

There was no time for weakness and no space to weep. Strength was what I needed, even if I felt devoid of it.

That night, I wrote in my notebook.

Strength.
Hope?
Exhaustion.

I dipped the pen in the inkwell and continued to write. The release I felt when each word hit the page was invigorating. This simple practice continued to assist me in ways I could never repay. This gift from Olu, prompting me to pay Edward Cutler one last visit.

Chapter Forty-Eight

*Appear flattered and enamoured by what your husband does
for you. This shall excite him enough to repeat it.*

Mrs Adeline Copplefield,
'The Manual for Good Wives' (1893)

Temi
1887

It should have felt peculiar to have to knock on the door of a
house I had once lived in. Yet this vast, ornate building had
never felt like my home anyway. Not like Tumbleberry, where I
had birthed Amelia, the scene of so many happy moments with
Olu.

But Olu was gone, and the house we had built together
remained. Spoiled daily by the existence of a man who had no
right to it.

It was after the first knock I realized the door was open. Where
were the staff? I was reminded of the time Edward told our staff
to go home whilst he . . .

The scream interrupted any reminiscing. It was coming from
upstairs and sounded full of terror and, worse still, had come from
the mouth of Iyabo!

Something inside of me snapped, releasing a surge of energy I
had no idea I could possess. Rushing up the staircase, almost trip-
ping over my hem, I followed the voice now overpowered by
Edward's.

I pushed open his bedroom door and the scene I encountered would stay with me forever.

Edward kneeling, hunched over Iyabo's limp body, and for a moment, I thought she was dead. At the sound of my 'Stop it!' her arms began flailing as both his hands gripped tightly around her neck. My mind was blank, my vision tunnelling as I lunged for him, pulling his weight off of her. This brute strength I had conjured up, getting him away from her, making him stumble backwards. Then I reached for my child.

'What has he done to you?' The question sounded so redundant considering what I had just witnessed. Edward strangling Iyabo!

She nodded furiously, her hand gently rubbing her throat.

What happened next did so quickly.

A force from behind, Iyabo's eyes widening with a scream, Edward pushing me to the ground, my head hitting the floor, him straddling me. His hands now around my neck, squeezing, squeezing. The life draining from my body, feeling so very weakened.

Is this how it ends for me?

Then a sound.

The sound of Edward's head as it connected sharply with a figurine of an elephant, just before it fell from Iyabo's grip.

Now I was the one to rub at my throat, my focus now clear again. Turning to look at Edward, his body limp on the floor.

There was silence and then that surge again. Allowing me to reel off a set of instructions, which included 'You must leave, Iyabo, go!'

'I . . . I . . .' she stuttered.

'I will say I did this.'

She turned to Edward's crumpled body, but I pulled her back to me and gave her the name of my lodging house. 'Listen. You were never here!'

I would send for the authorities and take what was coming to me. I had failed my child from the moment she'd been born and now was the time to put that right.

I sat down beside Edward's inert body as Iyabo did as I instructed. To pack up as many clothes as she could, take my keys and go! I would alert the authorities soon. I simply needed my breath to return to normal; for the last few minutes to sink in and make some semblance of sense.

I felt a sense of relief once I heard the front door bang shut. My daughter was safe.

'You!' said a quiet, angry voice. Edward, stirring on the floor, his eyes wide open and alert. He was alive! I wasn't sure whether to be pleased or not.

'You . . . you will hang for this!' he hissed, his hand touching the side of his bloodied head.

'You tried to kill my daughter.'

'Who's going to believe a couple of n—'

'Don't you dare!' I warned, crouching down to him. That surge again. 'You're going to do what I say from now on.' I shifted closer to him, pulling him up to a seated position. We were now face to face, our eyes level. 'If you tell anyone about this, I will reveal to the world how two *'negresses'* – isn't that what you call us? – floored you, and if that isn't humiliation enough, I have documents.'

'What documents?'

'Papers . . . proof of, let's just say, the fraudulent way you like to do business with your colleagues.'

'You don't know what you're talking about.'

'Oh, I took some insurance with me when you threw me out of my own home. I didn't want to stoop as low as blackmail, but after witnessing what you just tried to do . . . I am free of any guilt.' This was a lie of sorts. I had known of Edward's unsavoury business dealings, as I saw how he kept the books, sneaking into his study to check that our finances were satisfactory. I had not seen fit to take proof as insurance at the time, so there were no papers, except the one I had on my person. The very reason I had come back to this house.

'It would only take one anonymous word to some of your associates like Keanon & Son.'

'What would you like me to sign?' he said with a barrage of weak coughs. I had not one ounce of sympathy for this man.

'I took the liberty of bringing along the deed for Tumbleberry for you to sign over to me.'

I stepped aside as he slowly got up. If the bash on the head had taken something from him, it was that quiet, yet potent strength. Now he appeared less of a threat. Still, I couldn't be sure he wouldn't strike me, even in his lessened state. So I remained on guard. I remained ready.

We relocated to the study where he sat at his bureau.

'I want you to give me all the cash you have here at the house.'

'A thief now, are we?' he said.

'Call it rent for the time you spent holding onto *my* house.'

'It will be worth it to be rid of you once and for all.'

'Likewise,' I said, smiling as he signed the papers I'd had drawn up with the last of my money. I was no pushover and knew what needed to be done. I'd been a wife who'd once assisted her husband in business. I was not without knowledge. Mr Edward Cutler had underestimated me.

Everything began to feel surreal and in a good way.

Going 'home' that night to Iyabo. Holding one another the entire night in silence. The following days spent still trying to persuade her to stay, even though she was adamant she missed home and wanted to return.

'Why would you want to return to Aunty Kike after she—?'

'She was a good mother and I miss her.'

'I thought you said . . . ?'

'I lied. I am sorry but I was angry with you.'

I blinked back my tears. Perhaps for believing my beloved Aunty Kike could be so cruel but mostly because this meant she had, after all, been the better mother. She was the one who had given Iyabo the selfless love she'd always deserved.

'I did not want you to feel good about it.'

'About what?' I asked.

'About leaving me.'

Every word she said made sense.

'Forgive me?' she muttered as I held her close to me.

'I have nothing to forgive. It is you I hope forgives me, my sweet, darling daughter.'

Packed with gifts for Aunty Kike, my mother.
Waving away another.
Ship. Iyabo. Home.
Another grief to bear.

Chapter Forty-Nine

As a wife, your home is your domain, and a place in which to banish any thoughts of academic advancement.

Mrs Adeline Copplefield,
'The Manual for Good Wives' (1891)

Landri
Twenty-eight years ago

Landri had a favourite teacher at secondary school: Mrs Hines. During break time she'd sometimes stay behind and chat with Mrs Hines about nothing much in particular, just happy not to be among the others in the playground, standing around by herself. Sometimes Mrs Hines would share an apple with her and talk about her cat who Landri longed to meet; other times about how things were at home. Landri was aware the teachers felt sorry for her. Living with her grandparents, mother dead. But that was okay because Mrs Hines was nice to talk to.

'What would you like to be when you grow up?' she asked. No one had ever asked her that before.

'I like writing stories.'

'Oh, Landri, come on!'

'What?'

'Now that might be a fun hobby, but you can't build a career on it,' said Mrs Hines, as Landri cleaned the blackboard. She loved that particular task, the feeling of wiping away the white chalk strangely comforting.

'How about something else?'

'*Like what?*'

'*How about something sporty? You do very well on the netball team, don't you? And running,*' added Mrs Hines.

'*I don't really enjoy it. Gran thinks I should be a doctor like her.*'

'*Your gran's a doctor? Are you sure?*'

'*Yes. But I'm rubbish at science stuff!*'

'*We don't use terms like that. You are not rubbish at science. We use kind words to describe ourselves.*'

'*I've never been that great at science,*' corrected Landri. '*But I really enjoy writing and making up sentences . . . I really like English class. So . . . I think I'd be better as a writer.*'

'*Oh dear,*' she said with a sigh. '*Let's start again, shall we? Let's look at something more sensible . . . more realistic . . .*'

Present day

Yet through it all, she'd managed to gain excellent qualifications at both school and university, which brought her to a job that allowed her to write whilst also playing it safe. Yet even in that, she never felt enough. Whether it was an interviewer whose eyes widened when she walked into the room, or a major client handing her his empty coffee cup, this constant feeling of not being enough was ever present, not just at home, but everywhere.

Yet now, and perhaps because of Temi's notebook, she was starting to believe she might actually be good enough, worthwhile even.

'Thank you, Temi,' she whispered after reading and re-reading the final page of the notebook.

Landri had never felt more alert, awake and alive. Her mind buzzed with words, sentences, a fizz running throughout her body.

Even a walk past the golf course only served to increase what was brewing in her head. This lovely, excitable dance of ideas begging to come to the surface, a bit like when she'd think up an amazing slogan for a product, but ten times more powerful.

Whilst sad to have reached the end of the notebook, Landri felt only excitement at the possibilities the rest of her life could bring.

Her current job was a great role and had served her well, but now she hungered for something different. To expand her knowledge on subjects that excited and enthralled her. To put pen to paper. To create. To write.

That need, that longing which followed her as a lonely child, was no more. She was now ready to show the world what she, Landri Sommers, was made of.

Chapter Fifty

A widow can be bound up in one of two emotions: heartbreak or relief.

Mrs Adeline Copplefield,
The Manual for Good Wives (1893)

Temi
1887

One of my new activities as I sat in the only room I could afford to heat in my beloved Tumbleberry was to check obituaries.

Far from it being a macabre pastime of mine, I was simply searching to see if Edward's name ever appeared. I had not seen him since that well deserved 'knock on the head', so couldn't be sure if he had one day died from those injuries or had simply just . . . died.

One day, a name did stand out and thankfully (or not) it wasn't Edward's.

OBITUARY

T. L. Wicksmith of Gallington, a writer at this very publication, 55 years old, died yesterday at his home. Struck by a falling tile from a rooftop. He leaves a widow.

I recalled the conversation with Ellen. Her acceptance of a man writing that column for *The Tribune*. His name ambiguous and open to interpretation.

In one moment, this maddened me all over again, and in the next, I had slipped on my coat which had seen better days and was headed out of my front door.

I walked towards a building I really had no business even entering – according to some. Yet my own self-belief was stronger, enhanced by the fact I had nothing left to sell, hardly any money about my person and everyone I loved was nowhere in my vicinity.

I had nothing left to lose.

Along the crowded street, clutching four pieces of paper, I passed the ladies dressed in smart coats draped over large bustles, their men dutifully walking beside them, the putrid smell of fresh horse manure, along with the somewhat comforting sounds of the carriages attached to said horses. My hands fixed on my dress to hasten my walk, past the blacksmiths, the draper's storefront still decorated with flags and bunting left over from the queen's jubilee celebrations. My gaze averted as I passed the police station. I still couldn't be sure if one day they wouldn't come for me and arrest me for what my daughter and I had done.

One could never be sure.

I hurried along, past a beautiful duck pond I hadn't known existed, children throwing bread towards grateful birds. When I arrived at my destination, I could only follow my gaze up the steps and to the huge sign that read The Tribune. My breath was heavy with exertion and excitement as I climbed each step and walked through those doors.

Inside, a lady directed me to the editor's office without question, perhaps noticing the fine clothing – my one good dress – a mask not telling the whole story. That whilst I was indeed the owner of a house, I did not possess the means for its upkeep or even for food.

Someone apparently without the food problem was Mr Crabtree, a tall man with a growing stomach, which protruded teasingly from under his jacket.

'If you have a story of interest, madam, you can visit with a number of reporters who will assist you,' he said dismissively.

'I am here to see you, Mr Crabtree, senior editor of *The Tribune*.' I took in the large desk littered with paraphernalia I couldn't imagine him using in one day. Stacks of papers, various fountain pens.

A look of intrigue spread across his face. 'May I have the pleasure of knowing your name?'

'My name is Mrs Temi Masters.'

'What an interesting name. A pleasure to make your acquaintance, Mrs Masters. What can I do for you?'

'It's more, I suppose, of what I can do for *you*.'

He raised an eyebrow.

'After hearing of the loss of your advice giver, Mr Wicksmith, well . . . I believe I can offer my services to this publication.'

He cleared his throat. 'Are you referring to "The Manual for Good Wives"?'

'That is correct, Mr Crabtree.'

'Madam, this is a respected publication.'

'Indeed, and I am here to offer my services, to you, to this publication as a writer.' It had taken all of my audacity to even place myself in the same sentence as *writer*. Of course I wasn't a writer. I had never trained and had published nothing. Yet this was about survival. I had diligently read what the former advice columnist had imparted and was certain I could do better. Indeed, I felt confident of that. There existed pages of my own writing in my possession thanks to the notebook. I just needed this one chance to show Mr Crabtree what I could do.

'This is highly unusual, Mrs Masters.'

I placed my four pieces of paper on the untidy desk. 'I have produced samples of my writing here. I believe, as a woman myself, I can relate to your female readership on a much deeper level, don't you think?'

He cleared his throat again. He did this a lot.

'Well, I . . .'

'Mr Crabtree, please just . . . Do take a look at the writings I have produced.'

Scanning the first sheet, his eyes flickered, his lips moving together as if silently chewing.

'What do you think?' I said confidently, whilst inside fighting a mass of insecurity.

The knock at the door startled me.

'Mr Crabtree, can I be of assistance?' said the secretary, looking towards me as she spoke.

'No, dear Penny, everything is under control. Thank you.'

She closed the door slowly, her eyes fixed on me.

'Well, Miss . . .'

'Mrs Masters.'

'Of course. I beg your pardon. Mrs Masters, this is very . . .'

I didn't mean to hold my breath. It had not been easy to reveal this part of myself to anyone, let alone a stranger. The writing was personal and if he hated it, then by extension, he was hating me. Perhaps the dearly departed Mr Wicksmith was right and we women were prone to hysteria!

'Mrs Masters, this writing . . . it is remarkable.'

My lips quivered slightly. 'In a good way?'

'In a magnificent way. Well done.'

I exhaled. 'So is this something *The Tribune* would like to publish?'

I no longer cared about the advice columnist role. Just the thrill of having my work published had now taken over. My work, being read by others!

'Calm down, dear,' said Mr Crabtree. He cleared his throat again. 'Whilst this is certainly the type of work we would like to publish and you are an immensely talented woman . . .'

'Thank you,' I said gratefully, missing his hesitant tone.

'Hmmm.' He scratched the end of his nose. 'We are always looking for good storytellers and at least once a month we do feature a short story.'

'What of the advice columnist vacancy?' I said, now believing that yes, I *did* want that role. It would appear my confidence was growing by the second.

'Oh, Mrs Masters, you would have to apply for such a role. It is one that is hotly contended.'

'I can only imagine. How do I apply?'

His smile did not appear genuine. 'Mrs Masters, and I mean this with no disrespect, but the readers of that section are women.'

'As am I.'

'Let's just say, their experiences would differ from yours.'

'Are we not all women?'

'Indeed, but . . .'

'Whilst I am painfully aware of what you are trying to imply, Mr Crabtree, you would be surprised at just how similar my life as a married woman is to that of others.'

'My readers are used to advice from a certain . . . a certain . . .'

'With all due respect, Mr Crabtree, would it be presumptuous of me to assume that my experience as a woman would be more *believable* than that of your former writer, Mr Wicksmith?'

'Mr Wicksmith being a man is irrelevant. He was an excellent advice giver and our readers respected him as such.'

'Mr Crabtree, I can offer your readers a much wider perspective on love, marriage and family life.'

'I do not doubt that.'

'I was happily married until recently. I am a wonderful mother and I keep a pristine and impressive home.' All lies, of course, but I'd experienced them all at one time in my life. Feelings recorded not only in the notebook, but in my heart.

'Mrs Masters, you are a delightful woman, of that I am sure.'

'Thank you.'

He released a huge sigh and moved a hand through his hair. 'Miss Masters.'

'Mrs Masters.'

'Mrs Masters, I beg your pardon. Mrs Masters, I shall be blunt. I don't believe our readers would be interested in anything you have to say. I am sorry to have to say this to you.'

'Why do you say this to me, Mr Crabtree?'

His eyes averted my gaze. 'I do not believe my readers would be concerned with stories of emancipation like some of the Black writers who have made a name for themselves.'

'I was not aware that tales of slavery would be the domain I would choose to concentrate on. I have, as you can imagine, many stories. Next point.'

His eyes widened. 'Our readership would not be concerned with the thoughts of someone who is, say, domestic help.'

'I hire domestic help, Mr Crabtree, I have never been one. In fact I was born into a life where I was waited on hand and food, with servants assigned to me even as a tiny baby. '

His face was rapidly turning red. 'My readers will not be interested in musings about Africa.'

'I have lived in Britain for almost twenty-five years. My *musings* will reflect that. Anything else?'

'Mrs Masters, you are making my refusal very difficult for me to communicate.'

'So it is a refusal, is it? Even though I have answered each one of your concerns succinctly? Even though I fit all the criteria you are seeking in a writer?'

'Not all the criteria,' he mumbled.

My patience was thinning. 'Thank you for your time,' I said, before turning on my heel.

'You will find the same with all the newspapers. Except, of course, if you try a Black publication, of which I'm sure there are many who would appreciate your excellent talent.'

I turned to face him, my lips pursed. 'Is that so?'

'*The Tribune* could not possibly employ a lady such as yourself in this role. I'm sorry to be the bearer of bad news.'

I turned away. 'Good day.'

As my hand touched the doorknob, he spoke.

'Mrs Masters, your work.'

'Keep it,' I said, opening the door and walking out.

That night in my room, the temperature particularly cold, I sat on my bed, the notebook staring back at me. I mulled over Mr Crabtree's words. Indeed, the Black publications would be more accommodating, but they would not pay half as much as *The Tribune*. That newspaper was in a class of its own and it was there I needed to be, if I were to have any chance of ensuring the upkeep of Tumbleberry and, frankly, living the life I had become accustomed to.

There, I was being honest. I wanted more than just to get by and I make no apologies for this.

I picked up my pen and wrote.

Chapter Fifty-One

A woman must always know her place.

Mrs Adeline Copplefield,
'The Manual for Good Wives' (1893)

Landri
Present day

She couldn't remember feeling this fired up in years.

Landri wanted – needed – to tell the story of her great-great-great-grandmother in some way, yet she didn't know where to start because there was so much to her. Princess, wife, business-woman and mother. She could just concentrate on bringing the notebook to life, of course. String the collection of love stories together and produce her own interpretation of *black love*. But, no, this had to be about Temi, irrespective of a man.

This has to be about Temi Masters.

What about her life travelling from West Africa and her survival in this new and strange country called Great Britain? About how she survived. Oh, how she survived!

Could she write a full-length book? No, because that would demand a discipline she wasn't too sure she possessed just yet. An article, maybe – but she wasn't a journalist.

Stop with the excuses, Landri, said a voice. Her own voice.

Temi wasn't one to let anything get in her way, so why should she?

Landri had almost reached a dead end with her thoughts.

Almost, because something kept niggling away at her. Telling her that what she needed existed in the writings of Temi Masters. It was already there and all she needed to do was find it.

Chapter Fifty-Two

For many ladies, a husband is the only way of securing a future which does not involve unrelenting poverty.

Mrs Adeline Copplefield,
'The Manual for Good Wives' (1888)

Temi
1887

I must have written pages and pages, yet this time not in my notebook. These words and sentences were about someone else. Someone I had once been and would never be again. Someone I liked, despised and sometimes pitied.

The more I wrote, the more enthused I was to write more. A silent force drove me forward as I recorded my thoughts on line after line, page after page.

I wrote about my three different experiences of marriage and motherhood.

The disappointing choices I had made and what had led me to now.

The tears were plentiful as I wrote, but so was the laughter and the joy.

I wrote it all without stopping, felt like I was holding my breath; and when I'd finished writing an abundance of pages, I felt spent, happy.

If writing could do this for me, what could my words do for others?

I placed the papers to one side. Then I started writing once again. This version, a little different and written on the finest paper I owned. Once finished, I folded the three pieces of paper into an envelope addressed to *The Tribune* and posted it with an abundance of expectation.

Now, all I had to do was wait.

Chapter Fifty-Three

Marriage is always the goal.

Mrs Adeline Copplefield,
'The Manual for Good Wives' (1888)

Landri
Present day

'I've remembered something!' screeched Gwen as she stood at the door.

'You'd better come in, then. I have loads to tell you too!'

Gwen followed Landri into the kitchen. 'This cannot wait!'

'What is it?' asked Landri.

'Your great-great-great-grandmother Temi was a writer!'

Landri's brows knotted as she sat down slowly. 'Are you sure? I mean, I would have known that. A book is bragging rights after all, and my grandma would have said . . .'

'How do you think she afforded such a big house like this in those times? No husband, or benefactor?'

'Inheritance? I don't know!'

'You know when someone's been gone for as long as my mum, you tend to forget the individual conversations you had. Or you don't want to remember them because it's all too painful. Anyway, my mum used to speak of Temi a lot – it seems she had a profound effect on her, though she was only a girl at the time. Anyway, more and more of what Mum said is coming back to me now, thanks to you.'

'I mean, she does write beautifully in her notebook and perhaps those notes were the origins of a book.'

'Good point.'

'No, no, that can't be it. I don't think there were many Black writers in this country during Victorian times, let alone Black women. If there were, we would have known about it.'

'Oh, because history is never whitewashed, is it?' Then came the wink.

Landri pulled out her phone, annoyed to have to switch it on as she rarely did these days.

'Who are you calling?'

'The Wi-Fi isn't very good here so I'm using my phone data.'

Gwen stared at her blankly.

'Never mind. I'm searching for a list of Black female writers of that time in the UK. When I put Temi's name in before, nothing came up. Maybe she used a different one.'

Landri peered at the search engine, ignoring the multiple beeps alerting her to unread messages.

'Lillian Thomas Fox, Mary Ann Shadd Cary, Ida B. Wells. These are mostly African American women.' She thought about her grandma. Their strained relationship over the years doing nothing to cloud the pride she felt whenever she thought of her achievements as a doctor in Italy. Following in the footsteps of her own mother and grandmother.

She placed the phone to one side. 'I think you're mistaken, Gwen. There isn't much I know about this family, but a book—'

'Call your grandmother,' said Gwen.

'I could get used to this,' said Grandma. Landri's usual response would have been defensive, but now she could chuckle. Pleased they talked more now, even if the subject was mainly Temi.

'Currently I am cooking risotto and hoping it doesn't stick to the pan.'

'I'll go then . . .' said Landri.

'I didn't say you should go. I can stir and talk.'

'What are you having it with?'

'Plantains on the side and an olive salad. Must have something from the old country!'

Grandma was thrilled when she'd found a nearby grocer selling African and Caribbean foods. Over the years she'd been able to incorporate them with the Italian dishes she also very much loved.

'Gran, about Temi. Do you know if she was also a writer or a journalist?'

'A what? Of course not!' When her tone shot up an octave, so did the Italian accent. 'Whoever told you this has it wrong. You need to be looking more at what my mother and her own mother Amelia achieved. They were pioneers who followed in the footsteps of the great Sarah Parker Remond. Look her up! A great line of women doctors in our family.'

And there it was. What she knew had been coming.

'Until it got to Mum,' said Landri. She hadn't wanted to go there but knew she had to. 'Gran, were you ashamed she never followed in your footsteps?'

The line was silent and Landri feared she'd gone too far.

'I was never ashamed of my daughter.' Her voice cracked and although Landri didn't want to upset her, certain things needed to be said. They never spoke about her. Never.

'She was my only child and I wanted the best for her. Me and her father. She just . . . she just got together with that *musician*, your father, and that was it.'

'She came from a line of high achievers but her biggest one was having me!'

'It was, Landri. And you are precious.'

Landri squeezed her eyes shut, the words not penetrating.

'I loved Clara, your mum. There is nothing harder than losing a child.'

'Why do you think . . . ?' began Landri, the words lodged in her throat like bile. She hadn't planned on talking about her mother, but now they were.

'The risotto is burning!' said Grandma.

Both of them hung up quickly. An unsurprising end to the conversation.

Just because Landri was ready to talk about her mother, it didn't mean her grandma would ever be. She'd never been the most affectionate or *in touch with her feelings* type of grandmother anyway. And that was all right. Landri could wait for that conversation.

In the meantime, this new information about Temi needed further investigation.

She stared once again at the notebook containing precious records of a time long ago. This gift she had found wrapped in old newspaper.

Hang on.

The newspaper! The notebook had been wrapped in old newspaper she'd since kept in the drawer and inside the leather box.

She ran upstairs and carefully unfolded the large pages of a newspaper called *The Tribune*, dated 1893. Four sheets in total. An advertisement for soap to 'keep you young and beautiful'; a report about an escaped convict. History at her very fingertips and, although interesting, nothing stood out in relation to Temi.

Then it did. A name.

One she had seen before, written in the notebook.

Chapter Fifty-Four

Do not show you are more well-read than your husband. He
already knows and does not wish to be reminded of it.

Mrs Adeline Copplefield,
'The Manual for Good Wives' (1893)

Temi
1887

My audacity paid off.

I was informed by a letter from *The Tribune* that my article on
the 'trials and tribulations of seeking a secure marriage proposal'
had pleasantly surprised the editor. I was to submit an article a
week and would need to come into the offices to receive my documents and sign a contract as Mrs Adeline Copplefield, writer of
'The Manual for Good Wives'.

I had done it!

It wasn't hard to come up with the surname Copplefield,
inspired by the character David Copperfield, the protagonist of
one of the first books I read from cover to cover. It was the name
Adeline which had the deeper meaning. In the old country, *Ade*
means crown and also forms a part of one of my names, *Adekunbe*.
A name which hinted to that other part of me, my royal lineage,
which since moving to England had been all but ignored. Also,
line sounded a lot like *lie* . . . to signify, I supposed, that what I
wrote was not my true belief. As what I truly believed would
hardly be fit for human consumption!

So there we have it. *Ade-line*: an amalgamation of my two worlds.

The joy of achieving such a feat was short-lived upon realizing I would have to personally attend *The Tribune*'s offices. The same place where Mr Crabtree had made it quite clear I would never be welcomed as a writer.

Indeed, *Temi Masters* wasn't welcome. Mrs Adeline Copplefield, on the other hand . . .

I paid a visit to Eleanor, who had stayed in touch since leaving my employment. She promised to go to the offices and collect the contract on my behalf – but not before begging to come back to my employment.

'At this moment, I do not have the funds to pay you, but once I begin to earn a comfortable wage, I will of course call on you again.'

'Don't matter about that, Mrs Masters. I hate where I work now and would rather work for you with no pay than go back there.'

'That is rather silly, Eleanor,' I said, more than touched by her loyalty.

She was becoming more and more like Olive, who I still missed to this very day. Of course I wanted to hire her back immediately.

'Let us see what occurs after today,' I said. Securing regular work and thus being able to rehire Eleanor depended very much on what happened when she collected the contract from Mr Crabtree.

Would my plan be foiled? Could I actually get away with this deception?

Soon, we would both find out.

Eleanor returned with the contract, which I read over, signed and handed back to her to return to Mr Crabtree at *The Tribune*.

I waited expectantly and when she returned again, Eleanor shrugged her shoulders and said, 'They were happy. Didn't say much, really.'

Her words sounded so nonchalant and non-committal, yet they were the best thing I had heard in so long.

For me, they were the beginning of everything.

Chapter Fifty-Five

To a husband, there can be something quite alarming about a strong-willed wife who insists on using her own mind. Proceed carefully so as not to alarm him to death!

Mrs Adeline Copplefield,
'The Manual for Good Wives' (1893)

Temi
1887

It had been some time since I'd achieved this level of fulfilment.

I should have known such feelings would have come from the strokes of a pen. Olu had known all those years ago when he had gifted me the notebook. I should have known by the utmost joy reading the written word had given me, even as a young girl. I was a writer. Putting pen to paper for others, for strangers, to read!

At times I still could not believe in this wonderful turn of events, but Mr Crabtree appeared happy with my words, sentences and good humour for 'The Manual for Good Wives', judging by the edits he sent back via Eleanor each week. I enjoyed every moment of the process, having never before realized just how creative I could be with my words and imagination.

As well as much-needed finance, it also gifted me the best way to finally take control of my life, whilst writing about a fantasy one and getting paid for it!

My first article focused on the subject of a single woman in search of a good gentleman to marry.

Do not be overcome with elation, but do exercise patience when you are left with a number of calling cards from an interested gentleman . . .

Of course, I managed to convince myself no one would actually read what I wrote and that *The Tribune* would see sense and press for my immediate dismissal. What actually happened was I received a letter via Eleanor after she'd handed over my third article. It stated a keenness for more articles, and they were happy to give me free rein on the subject matter as long as they adhered to standards set in 'The Manual for Good Wives'.

That I could do. I simply had to think about what my old friend Mary Ellen Carmichael would want to read or what she'd find amusing.

I may have missed her a smidgen. Her letters had all but stopped after my parting from her brother, yet writing this 'manual', I was reminded of her fondly.

Mr Crabtree sent my first cheque through Eleanor. A substantial amount that, if it continued in this vein, would allow me to climb back to a position I much preferred. To hire Eleanor part time, purchase more comfortable cotton sheets. To perhaps, one day soon, refurbish my home with the quality furnishings it had once been used to.

This brought me much happiness. Yet there would always exist a void no amount of money could fill. The loss of my children. The knowledge that my first instinct would have been to spend my good fortune on them.

The Manual for Good Wives

1888

Each week, a fresh piece of advice.

> *You have chosen a gentleman. The gentleman has also found your*
> *company to be agreeable. The gentleman, having sought permission*
> *from your father to court you, via a letter, has made his intentions*
> *very clear. Soon, the prize of marriage will be yours.*

Mrs Adeline Copplefield was now responsible for my being able
to eat whatever I wanted and to live without fear. To hold my head
up high with the knowledge that my bills had been paid on time
and in advance. To walk with the confidence that no one would be
knocking on my door uninvited, asking to be paid. It mattered not
that my house was furnished with the bare minimum and I could
only afford to heat one room for two hours a day. None of that
mattered because everything I had was because of *me*. Or rather,
Adeline Copplefield.

It was a thrill to write to Amelia and tell her of my good
fortune as a writer. Amelia who had sent one letter in the past
six months. A letter I cherished with all my heart. Iyabo had
been more charitable with two letters, detailing the happiness
she had found in teaching local children and how Aunty Kike
had marvelled at the small gift I had sent with her. How they
had danced together with my mother at the mere mention of
me.

> *As courtship can occur over a short space of time, such moments may*
> *be enriched with what the gentleman believes the lady desires to hear*
> *and see. Hence, a long courtship is advisable.*

Apart from writing, tending to my garden became my biggest
joy. At times, I would amalgamate the two, when the perfect

mixture of warm and cool weather graced the skies. Sitting in the garden and writing amongst my favourite lavender and, of course, my roses.

> *. . . When seeking a husband, look between the crevices for matters of depravity, lest you regret this in the future . . .*
>
> *'If that thy bent of love be honourable, Thy purpose marriage, send me word tomorrow.' Romeo & Juliet. Act 2, Scene 2.*
>
> *Unlike with Juliet, it is unthinkable for a woman to propose to a man, but subtle hints are permissible!*

When Eleanor informed me of the boy she was courting, Tommy who worked at the fishmongers, I encouraged her to read Adeline's column.

She was the only person who knew Adeline's true identity and I trusted her with this information. She and her late mother Olive had been privy to so much of my life already, and this I welcomed, because such a secret needed to be shared with more than just my notebook.

Chapter Fifty-Six

A husband trusts you with an ability to partake in all manner
of important decisions, such as what is served for dinner.
Remember to be thankful of this, good ladies.

Mrs Adeline Copplefield,
'The Manual for Good Wives' (1893)

Landri
Present day

Landri stared at the large and mostly crinkle-free pages of *The Tribune* dated 1893. It now felt like the most delicate of tissue paper with the power to disintegrate at any moment. She did wonder if she should be wearing blue plastic gloves like those historians wore when handling some ancient artefact. Too late, because she was impatient, already scanning the words of a Mrs Adeline Copplefield in a column entitled 'The Manual for Good Wives'.

As a gentleman will have expectations for what he deems a good wife, should you not harbour the same expectations of what you require in a husband?

The answer, dear ladies, is a resounding yes! As a married woman you are deemed unfit to partake in many of the liberties afforded a husband. The ability to sign deeds to your own home, make a will or have access to any earnings you may have accumulated will be foreign to you. Most notably, your children as well as yourself will belong entirely to your husband. It is imperative a choice of husband be made wisely, as to obtain a separation and then divorce is extremely difficult, even if you are subject to violence or adultery. Despite the 1857 Matrimonial Causes Act, many of you do not have the means to be afforded both the indignity and luxury of a divorce.

As an ardent reader of fiction I have enjoyed yet thoroughly assessed Jane Eyre by Charlotte Brontë, in which a husband determines his wife, Bertha, to be insane, thus helping himself to all of her worldly goods. He alone rules on the heinous decision to hide her away and disposes of her as he wishes. Such is the husband's power.

Dear ladies, I am not advocating to not seek marriage. Pursue with fervour, but above all, with common sense.

Mrs Adeline Copplefield

Landri opened the notebook again. The name was clear. Adeline. More than once. On three separate pages towards the end of the notebook.

Ade Crown Royalty

Temi.
Unhappiness

What I write, how I live. Conflict.
Ade line
Copplefield
Writer
Who is Temitope?

Who is Adeline?

A child.
Daughter of a king.
Duty fulfilled.
No longer I.
Adeline Copplefield, an untruth, but at ease.
Temi.
Hardship.

'Temi was Adeline! Temi Masters was Mrs Adeline Copplefield!' she said again to an open-mouthed Gwen. 'She wrote both names in the notebook. I can't believe I missed the clues all along. I mean, of course I scanned the newspaper when I first found it, I knew it was old, but to be honest I was more wrapped up in the notebook.'

They both gasped simultaneously. Again.

'It's like she wanted whoever found the notebook to also know she was Adeline Copplefield, a writer! A writer of a column. I still can't get my head around this.'

'It's almost unbelievable,' agreed Gwen.

'Gwen, my great-great-great-grandmother wrote a column for a successful newspaper, anonymously. You saw the article, there's no way anyone would have guessed it was her.'

'Or that she was a Black woman.'

'That too!'

'What now? I mean, we can't give up on this.'

'No way. This just gives us more to work from. I can type the name Adeline Copplefield into the search engine and see what comes up.'

Minutes later, they both stared at the laptop screen, surrounded by crystals and paper butterflies. Ironically, it was Chimes & Things which had the best Wi-Fi, with Chime allowing Landri unlimited use, as long as she filled her in on her findings, which Landri and Gwen gladly did.

'There's still nothing online about her, even when I put in both names. It's like Temi and Adeline have both been erased from history,' said Landri.

'She wouldn't have wanted that. Maybe that's why she entrusted this huge secret to a little girl. My mother,' said Gwen.

'What a secret! I mean, a Black woman telling white women how to treat their husbands?' said Landri.

The three women looked at one another and burst into fits of laughter .

'Your great-great-great-grandmother sounds like such a radical babe!' said Chime.

'I'm so proud of her.'

Landri tapped in more words and the screen illuminated instructions on how to obtain old court records, which would involve a trip to the National Archives.

'When can we go to this archives place?' said Gwen as Chime left to attend to a customer. 'We need to see what we can find out using both names.'

'To see if she was on trial for murdering one of her husbands?'

'No, I'm with you on that. There's just no way she would have been let out to become an older lady if that were the case. There has to be something else.'

'Do you think she got in trouble for impersonating a white woman?'

'I don't know about that . . .'

'Hopefully I'll be able to find out.' Landri felt protective towards this woman she'd never met. Connected by a blood line, which had been shredded, diluted, and at times hadn't meant that much to her.

'Fancy a trip, Gwen?'

Landri had enjoyed three weeks cocooned in the house of her great-great-great-grandmother. Enjoyed the friendship of two

women and sitting in that beautiful garden Temi had once tended
to. Now it was almost time to leave that oasis, at least for an
afternoon.

'Try and stop me!' said Gwen.

'What have I missed?' said Chime, rushing back.

Chapter Fifty-Seven

A good wife never complains. A large comfortable pillow in
which to emit your screams is advised.

Mrs Adeline Copplefield,
'The Manual for Good Wives' (1888)

Temi
1888

I had been writing undetected for *The Tribune* for six months.

During that time, 'The Manual for Good Wives' had remained consistently much loved by readers. I had experimented – with prior warning, of course – by branching out to women who had never married. I had expected Mr Crabtree to instantly disagree when I had sent my sample via Eleanor, but he agreed to print it as an appendix and the response from readers was excellent.

Ladies who remain unmarried are viewed with an air of pity. Yet a
spinster need not be this misfortunate being! Whatever has led to the
predicament of being unmarried is of her own concern and not that
of her neighbours.

Whilst it is easy to feel lonesome as old friends marry and produce
offspring, to have not married can give way to pursuing a higher
education and even working for a living. Work can provide fulfil-
ment which can engage you for most of the day, as well as provide
you with an income so that you have no need of a husband.

The success of my articles was always going to lead to Mr Crabtree insisting we meet, and when that day came, I was far from ready.

'Oh, Eleanor, what a conundrum I find myself in.'

'Do you mean a pickle?'

'Yes, that too,' I said with a sigh.

'It's just best to wait and see what happens. Especially when there's nothing much you can do about it now.'

'You're right, Eleanor dear.' I squeezed her hand gently.

'Can I get you anything else, madam?'

'No . . . In fact, you may have the rest of the night off.'

Her lips began to quiver.

'Don't worry, I will still pay you for the night. Go on home and spend time with your loved ones.'

Her smile widened. 'Mum always said you were a good'un.'

'As was she.'

Once Eleanor left, I picked out an outfit from my wardrobe. Luckily I had been able to purchase the odd gown almost as smart as what I had been used to. I would wear the blue velvet with white gloves. The strong colour always allowed me to feel a confidence I probably did not possess and would be perfect for when I met with Mr Crabtree and revealed my true identity.

The steps leading to *The Tribune* office were slightly more intimidating than I remembered. This time, a gentleman held the door open for me and, walking through it, I felt all eyes were on me. They weren't, of course. Just a throng of busy people, tapping keys on a writing machine called a typewriter or mulling about clutching pens.

It was Mr Crabtree's nosey secretary who recognized me first.

'I am sorry, but his eleven o'clock is taken with another appointment. You'll have to . . .'

'Never mind, dear. I will take it from here,' said a male voice.

Mr Crabtree smiled as I moved towards the door he held open for me.

'I was well aware it was you,' he said as soon as the door closed. 'I recognized the writing from the papers you left.'

Immediately he said those words, I began to relax.

Chapter Fifty-Eight

*Being concerned with what exists outside of the home, how-
ever tempting, is simply not becoming of a wife.*

Mrs Adeline Copplefield,
'The Manual for Good Wives' (1889)

Landri
Present day

Although Landri had simply wanted to jump in a cab and head to
the National Archives, it wasn't going to be that simple.

There was an appointment system, meaning she wouldn't be
seen for three working days.

'Don't worry, it's only a few days,' said Gwen. 'In the meantime,
you can help me pick out an outfit for the trip.'

'It's only to an archive office!'

'So what? I don't get to go on as many adventures as you young
people. Let me have my moment!'

Both women giggled merrily as Gwen twirled and curtsied in
each outfit pulled from her wardrobe.

'You have so many clothes.'

'Most of which I should donate or chuck away. I just can't bring
myself to. My Herman bought most of them for me.'

'Ross showered me with gifts once,' said Landri absently. Yet
she suspected their situations were very different. Ross had done
the gifts, compliments, all of it, just to get her to a place of total
reliance before turning into the person he really was. She'd read

an article about it once, dismissed it . . . but now, she saw it with blinding clarity.

Gwen settled on a lovely vintage grey and brown suit gifted from Herman on their tenth wedding anniversary.

'He was such a romantic,' she said, twirling in front of the mirror.

'With great taste!'

'He married me, didn't he?' They both chuckled. 'I just hope my children don't sell them off when I go.'

'You're not going anywhere yet,' said Landri. 'You look amazing and are much more active than I am.'

Gwen sat down and sighed heavily. 'Oh, we all go eventually. Just some of us have the privilege of living longer, as you know.'

Landri loved how Gwen never shied away from mentioning or referring to her mother, Clara, holding up her memory in a way she had never experienced. Gwen often made references to how she looked like her after Landri had shown her a picture. It had been taken just a month before she was gone, Clara smiling towards the camera as her little girl giggled beside her. Her eyes perhaps hiding what she truly felt in that particular moment.

'You've been such a tonic to me,' said Gwen. 'This whole adventure about Temi Masters has forced me to remember things about my mother I thought I'd forgotten. It feels like I'm getting to know her all over again. Thank you for that gift.'

Landri could relate. Nowadays, she'd find herself thinking about her grandma much more often too, and with an empathy and understanding once missing. Landri would make it a point to continue to call her more often, even when her questions about Temi subsided, and not just on birthdays and Christmas. Simply ringing to say hello. Finally able to take her grandma as she was. A woman who had lost so much over the years, including a much-loved husband and a daughter she never expected to outlive. A grandmother who may never want to talk about her daughter's death, or her feelings, yet could teach Landri the perfect recipe for seafood plantain risotto or arancini or how to make the perfect jollof rice. Maybe that was all she could expect and she simply needed to be okay with that. Her dad had lost interest years ago and her grandma was the only relative present in her life. This in itself was sad considering there were great-aunts and uncles still living and a multitude of cousins scattered all over the world, including Nigeria, the United States, Italy, and here in the UK. Perhaps one day she'd ask Grandma for more stories and, eventually, introductions. Perhaps one day, she would contact her aunty Carole and get her father's number. In the meantime though, she was determined to find out all she could about Temi Masters – and perhaps once that was done, the rest would follow.

Chapter Fifty-Nine

Do not be over-familiar with a gentleman when walking together; merely accept his hand out of assistance.

Mrs Adeline Copplefield,
'The Manual for Good Wives' (1888)

Temi
1888

Mr Crabtree graciously agreed to keep our 'secret', due in part to *The Tribune*'s readership rising by twenty percent since my debut, as well as the plentiful readers' letters. Dozens were arriving each week, and most were very flattering and full of compliments about my writing and 'worthy and useful advice'. A basket of flowers also arrived once, from a grateful wife: *I would never have chosen wisely if not for your words of advice. You have my eternal thanks, Mrs Copplefield.*

'Our readers appear to be in agreement that you are a breath of fresh air, and I would have to agree,' said Mr Crabtree during one of our clandestine meetings away from the office. It was becoming too risky to meet there, especially with that nosey secretary.

'I believe your young secretary Penelope is rather sweet on you,' I said brazenly as we sipped tea in a very smart teahouse. The bone china felt exquisite against my fingers as I brought the cup to my lips.

'Now, Mrs Masters, Penny is my secretary.'

'If I can be most bold, why have you never married, Mr Crabtree?'

'Are you about to offer me advice, Mrs Copplefield?'

We both laughed, albeit nervously. Assuming the role of another person still felt tinged with danger, treacherous even, even if it was for the greater good. Because apart from the monetary rewards, it was mostly knowing I was helping others which fuelled me. If by reading between the lines, so to speak, one woman could see she was more than what was expected of her in this society, I'd have achieved something.

'In answer to your question,' he said, shaking me out of my thoughts, 'I have never met a woman as remarkable as you.'

I wasn't sure what to say to that, so instead took a sip of my delicious tea.

1889

It felt unfamiliar yet manageable to have a man occupy my life who was not my husband. A friend who happened to be male. Yet Mr Crabtree became just that. Of course, he was also my employer, but the secret nature of this appeared to bind us closer together.

I continued to deliver articles for *The Tribune*, which in the last year continued to increase its circulation. The letters were plentiful and advertisers were keen to do business with this thriving newspaper. My remuneration had also increased and along with such success came calls for my photograph to be included with articles. Mr Crabtree hit on the excellent and useful idea of keeping me anonymous as it added an element of mystery.

Amelia finally answered one of my letters and invited me to Italy – a trip which I desperately wanted to take. Yet the thought of boarding a ship ever again filled me with a dread that felt physical. Every fibre of my being rejected any thought of ever stepping onto one again. A ship had brought Olu and I to this country, yet had also taken him away. In some respects it had done the same with Amelia and Iyabo.

I wrote back, asking if she would mind coming here, disappointed at my own weakness.

I needed to confide in someone about this and I felt Mr Crabtree would not understand, so I opened up my notebook and put pen to paper.

I cannot forget the sounds.
Deafening sounds. Calls to 'get on board'.
Smells. Confined.
Sickness.
Hopelessness.
Simon.

The Foundlander.
Olu. Gone.

I stopped writing. The memories were still there. Vivid.

I could never board a ship again.

A decision which all but meant I would most likely never see either of my daughters again.

Chapter Sixty

You are subordinate but no less his equal.

Mrs Adeline Copplefield,
'The Manual for Good Wives' (1893)

Temi
1891

'Mrs Masters, I didn't expect to see you.' Mr Crabtree waved towards Penelope as he shut the door behind me.

I stood by his desk with a determined gaze.

'Please, Mrs Masters,' he said, gesturing to the seat.

I sat down, peeling off my white silk gloves. 'Mr Crabtree, are you happy with my work?'

'It is exemplary as always.'

'Has circulation of the newspaper improved again this year?'

'For the third year in a row since you began writing for us, yes.'

'Yet you choose to compensate me at a rate much less than Mr Regis, who also has a weekly column.'

'Why, yes, but the subject matter is completely different.'

'Now, now, Mr Crabtree. We all know it is I who has increased the fortunes of this newspaper. So I can only guess that this discrepancy is because Mr Regis is a man. A white man at that.'

'Come now, Mrs Masters.'

Eleanor was friends with Mr Regis's wife's maid, and between them they had conspired to retrieve certain documents, telling me all I needed to know.

'Are you going to sit there and deny this, Mr Crabtree?'

'No, I am not,' he said wearily. He'd known me long enough to know he could not win this argument.

I continued. 'As appalling as that sounds, I will accept it, as I have no choice as a woman. What I will not accept is being paid less than your female writer Joan Dibden. She writes considerably less, and is hardly responsible for the growth of this newspaper as I have been.'

'I see . . .'

'Am I right to believe that even your own pay packet has increased considerably with the growth of *The Tribune*?'

His face turned an embarrassed crimson. 'Yes.'

'It is only fair I am compensated also.'

There was a pause. This I had expected. I had no evidence of Joan Dibden's wage packet, just an assumption which turned out to be correct.

He cleared his throat. 'Mrs Masters, I must say I am simply heartbroken you would speak to me in this manner. I allowed you to carry on working when, let's be honest, many would have fired you. All at considerable risk to my own reputation.'

'You continued to hire me because of my excellent writing – were those not your words? Oh, and my glorious use of the English language and how I was able to inform your lady readers of the importance of their roles in society, whilst adding my own experiences which you were sure women of all ages and standing could identify with. Did you not say this?'

'Yes,' he said tiredly.

'So what is it to be?'

His silence told me all I needed to know.

'Very well.' I stood up. 'I will not be submitting this week's manuscript and henceforth will be taking my work elsewhere.'

'Mrs Masters, let us not be hasty, especially when we both know it will be difficult for you to secure work as—'

'Then I would rather the writings burn than make their way in your direction. Good day.' I turned on my heel. Of course, there was nowhere I could present my work, but in that moment I did not care. I had invested some money in minor ventures, careful never to find myself in a penniless predicament again, and whilst the returns would not keep me in the style I had come accustomed to, I could start again. I had done so many times before. I was Temi Masters. I could do it – even if sometimes, just sometimes, I was tired of having to always pick myself up and start again.

'Mrs Masters,' he said, just as I reached the door. 'Where will you go?' His voice was sympathetic, gone the ill-judged bravado of earlier.

'This does not concern you, Mr Crabtree.'

'I will change the terms of our agreement to reflect a pay rise.'

I faced him. 'Go on.'

'I cannot pay you the same as Mr Regis.'

'I understand that. I will take the same pay as Joan Dibden.'

'Of that, you have my word,' he said.

As I walked out of the door, I whispered to myself: 'Well done.'

That afternoon, I felt infused with something quite rare. I felt seen, truly seen, and this felt fabulous, albeit unfamiliar.

Walking out into my garden, I looked up to not a cloud in the sky, then down to marvel at the new blooms which had sprung up seemingly overnight. The roses, so vibrant and full of life.

'You would be so proud of me, Olu,' I whispered. 'I wish you were here with me.'

The joyous feeling continued, turning into a confidence which allowed me to finally do something I had been thinking about ever since reading of women who were starting to demand more in society. Brave and challenging women.

Lola Jaye

I headed to the local branch of the National Society for Women's Suffrage – but only after shrugging off Eleanor's comment that they were nothing more than a 'bunch of ladies who hated men'.

The small sign confirmed I was in the correct location and, once inside, I was delighted to see a room filled with women. All women. One on an actual typewriter, the likes of which I had only seen at *The Tribune* offices.

'Can I help you?' said the woman looking up from the typewriter.

'I am looking for the Women's Suffrage, please.'

'That's us. We're just a small branch.'

'Wonderful . . . I would love to offer my services.'

Her face broke into a smile. 'We need all the help we can get.'

I smiled.

'We just lost our domestic, so this is great timing, Miss . . . ?'

'Mrs Masters. Domestic?'

'Isn't that what you are applying for?'

'Not at all.'

'Oh dear.'

'I was thinking . . . Oh, I don't know . . .' My confidence was wavering. 'Fundraising perhaps. . . . Writing your newsletter. Yes, that or . . . or doing some editing.'

'I'm not sure we need—'

'We need all the help we can get,' said a voice from behind me. Effectively placing an end to this excruciating exchange.

'I'm Meredith,' she said.

'Nice to meet you, Meredith,' I said, turning to the tall woman in a flowing skirt and matching hat. Her smile was friendly and I at last felt at ease.

'I think Gladys forgets we never turn away any offer of assistance. We are here for *all* women.'

I followed her into a small office. 'No one is assigned just one task, as we all step in when needed. I'm sure you will be an invaluable part of our small gathering of ladies.'

I sat down.

'There are many coloured ladies who help with the movement.'

'There are?'

'I am not sure of your age, but did you contribute to the petition back in 1866?'

'No, but I have heard of it. A triumph!'

'Yes, indeed. Its most noted coloured signatory is a Sarah Parker Remond.'

'The American lady who spoke about slavery?' I said absently, recalling Amelia's current association with her. The most recent letter had detailed being under her mentorship in Italy. My little girl. I could not have been prouder. 'By all accounts she is a remarkable woman.'

'What we have here is a smaller branch than our counterparts across the country, but we hope to do some collaborative work with the larger chapters.'

'Power in numbers.'

'Precisely. It's probably a few years off but we hope to do a procession with ladies from the colonies . . . maybe Indian or African.'

'That sounds wonderful!' I said. This was all I needed to pledge my commitment to the cause.

What followed was a twice-weekly attendance, perfect as it only took two days a week to write my letters for *The Tribune* and I had also picked up a few hours of bookkeeping for some of the small businesses in the area. It had started with the fishmongers where Eleanor's beau Tommy worked, both of them vouching for my hard work and efficiency. Indeed, like with *The Tribune*, she was able to be discreet, allowing them all to think I was a man delivering such a stellar service. This brought in much needed extra money, allowing me to afford once again the trappings I enjoyed. Like a gardener. Overseeing my beloved garden with him just one of the many delights I was able to enjoy again.

My life feeling full once again.

I wrote to tell my daughters of my new role as a writer and they both responded with what appeared to be pride.

This filled me with nothing but happiness.

'Many of us here feel rather helpless with not being able to help our foreign counterparts,' said Gladys, who had taken to me over the weeks, it seemed. 'Just look at how well you're doing here!'

'Indeed,' I said, scanning a leaflet advertising the next meeting. This would be the first one I would attend and members of the other branches would also be in attendance. I was excited.

'It's our moral duty to help everyone,' she said.

I was the first to acknowledge that whilst I had experienced a few challenges since arriving in England, others had faced many more and continued to do so. 'I believe securing the vote for these women would be a fabulous stake in a country they now call their own. As do I,' I said.

'The vote?' said Gladys.

'Isn't this part of our ethos?'

'I think Meredith will explain it better,' she said, just as Meredith entered the room.

'Securing the vote is vital . . . yes, but for British women,' confirmed Meredith.

It took me a moment to decipher what she actually meant.

'Once we get the right to vote we have more power to help those who are needy and need us. In this respect, everybody wins,' she continued.

I tried to ignore the smirk on Gladys's face. This, I expected of her. What alarmed me more was Meredith's attitude.

From that moment, I began to experience myriad emotions

whenever I entered the office. Elation in finding an organization which I thought would be working for the betterment of all women, then deflation upon realizing my naivety.

I wanted to thrive at the organization, but at what cost? Was my staying more to do with wanting Amelia to be as proud of me as she was of Sarah Parker Remond, her heroine?

It became clear I could no longer stay when, six weeks into my post, a permanent domestic was found. A Black lady named Georgette.

I made my apologies via a letter of resignation and never returned to my local branch of the National Society for Women's Suffrage. It felt rude or perhaps cowardly of me not to outline my real reasons in the letter, but I did not possess the energy to try to explain.

Chapter Sixty-One

It is sensible not to receive gentleman callers when you are alone at the house.

Mrs Adeline Copplefield,
'The Manual for Good Wives' (1888)

Temi
1892

Amelia was with child!

Her latest letter confirmed this and my joy was infectious.

'Oh, Eleanor, I am to be a grandmother!'

I held out my hands and she clutched them and we danced and danced around the library I had recently refurnished along with an abundance of new books. Of course, this level of outward emotion was uncharacteristic of me, but it was not every day I became a grandmother!

As for Amelia, I wished more and more that I was in closer proximity, especially during this time. My only consolation being that, as a doctor and working in a hospital, she would be surrounded by an abundance of medical knowledge at such a dangerous time.

I still enjoyed Mr Crabtree's company at afternoon tea from time to time. He had invited me to his home on numerous occasions, which I declined for obvious reasons.

'I mean no disrespect to your reputation, Mrs Masters, but the less we are seen in public together, the better, don't you think? You know, considering our current shenanigans!' He appeared to enjoy the illicitness of what we were doing with the fictional Mrs Adeline Copplefield. For someone like Mr Crabtree it was possibly the most exciting and duplicitous thing he had ever done. As for me, entering this country as a married woman, disguised as a boy, was much more of a story. But he needn't know any of that! Indeed, Mr Crabtree knew hardly anything about me despite the years we had worked together.

'You do not speak of your children, Mrs Masters.'

'What would you like to know?'

'What do they do?'

'Do you mean, who have they married and if not are they in servitude?'

'No, I—'

'Amelia, my youngest child, is a married woman and a doctor in Italy.'

'That is splendid. Italy too!'

'What do you mean?'

'Your love of Shakespeare, as seen in some of your columns.'

'Yes, indeed,' I said.

'It must be so hard for you, what with your daughter being so far away.'

I sipped at my tea, thinking of Amelia giving birth without me being there. In the old country, she would be surrounded by a collection of hand-picked women, ready to welcome the new addition to the kingdom as well as having a succession of traditional practices to follow. It was hard to admit that, thanks to me, the traditions and practices of my people were lost to my own child. At the same time, I was no longer willing to hold onto the guilt of that, because leaving my home had been a necessary act I could never regret. Besides, Iyabo was now in the position to fully immerse herself in such cultures – minus the forced marriage aspect, I would hope.

'Mrs Masters?'

'Oh yes, my apologies. What were you saying, Mr Crabtree?'

'You mentioned having two daughters. What of your firstborn?'

'My, my, Mr Crabtree, you do remember every detail.'

'About you, Mrs Masters, yes. You are a most fascinating woman.'

'Iyabo is her name and she is teaching across the seas in the country of our birth and living with my wider family.'

'Your wider family is in Africa, is that right?'

'My family is somewhat scattered.' I was beginning to feel a little hot around the neck. Speaking about my daughters was one thing, but my family in the old country was a place I no longer wished to revisit.

'I suppose this is why you write with such heartfelt words.'

'I have experience, Mr Crabtree. Of the sort you will never read in my columns. What I present to you is a somewhat sanitized version.'

He raised his eyebrows. I had said too much.

'You are a wonderful woman, Mrs Masters. Well-read and, dare I say it . . . rather handsome.'

'Oh, Mr Crabtree, you know our relationship will always be business-related. Even you inviting me to your home is inappropriate, as I would be mistaken for a woman of ill repute.'

'I have yet to care what others think. In fact . . . I would be honoured if we were to become more than . . .'

My jaw tensed. 'This is highly inappropriate, Mr Crabtree. We are friends, nothing more.'

His forehead furrowed. 'I never wish to offend you, Mrs Masters.'

'Good.' I exhaled. Of course, he had not offended me, I was simply feeling exposed, having spoken about Amelia and Iyabo in such detail.

*

My library began to grow with its sizeable number of delicious books just waiting to be devoured. Eleanor had expressed interest in some of the titles and I continued to be impressed at how well she could read and the joy she took in it.

'Mum always used to say how much you and your late husband liked to read. Said no daughter of hers wouldn't read!'

This comment touched me more than she would ever know. Olive, sweet Olive.

I continued to write more and more. Imagining the possibility of enough material to one day fill a novel. Having already become a successful writer for a newspaper, to go on and write a book or even a play, like Shakespeare, was perhaps taking things a tad far. Yet possible. I could do it. How unfortunate, then, that writing under my own name would not allow any of it to come to fruition. If there was one fact I was certain of, it was that I could never publish anything under my own name and identity.

1893

Spring finally arrived and I was able to tend to the shrubs in my beautiful garden after drafting articles in the morning. To be out there felt like being at one with nature. The fullness of the spring breeze enveloped me, as I spoke with Olu – in my mind and some-times out loud, knowing he would never respond. Yet managing to find comfort in our 'encounter'.

When a letter arrived from Amelia saying she'd given birth to a daughter and named her Antonietta, I felt a sadness at not having Olu here to share this wonderful news and then regret for not agreeing to the offer of a trip. Amelia had needed me and, once again, I had let her down. I could only hope and also believe she would be a better mother than I ever had.

That night I fell into a heavy sleep and was awakened during the early hours by a loud shriek.

'Madam!'

My heart rate quickened. Something was terribly wrong.

'Madam!'

'What is it, Eleanor?' Rarely did she enter my bedchamber unannounced and never at such an hour. My mind leapt to Amelia and Iyabo. Sweat began to form on my skin.

'Is it my daughters? Are they hurt?'

'No, Madam, it's Mr Crabtree,' she said. 'He's at the door.'

'Mrs Masters, we have a problem,' he said. 'You are in deep, deep trouble.'

I flickered my eyelids and tilted my head as if I did not understand him. But I did. I had been waiting for this day, hoping it would never come, yet knowing one day it would.

'Is . . . is it the police. Am I to be arrested?'

Mr Crabtree closed both eyes and exhaled.

Chapter Sixty-Two

*Should a wife not expect respectful care and tenderness from
her husband?*

Mrs Adeline Copplefield,
'The Manual for Good Wives' (1893)

Landri
Present day

The line to enter the building was longer than Landri had
expected. Who knew the archives centre would be so popular?

'Are you all right with standing for so long?' she asked
Gwen.

'Oh, don't you worry about me, I'm fine. I told you, I don't
get out much and I'm keen to know more about this relative of
yours!'

'You and me both.'

Once inside, it had taken five minutes. Just five minutes to
enter the name 'Mrs Adeline Copplefield' into the court system
records and find a match.

'Gwen, I don't believe it. It's here! She's here!'

Gwen shifted in closer. Both women watched the screen, their
mouths slightly open in anticipation.

'You were right, Landri.'

Then a gasp from both women when they noticed the
photograph.

*

They'd been silent since leaving the archive offices. Landri, unable to stop thinking of the words she'd seen printed about Temi beside the grainy photograph of her great-great-great-grandmother.

Liar!
A wicked perpetrator of shameless acts which have inflicted immeasurable harm . . .

She had stared at that one image, a profile view of a beautiful Black woman, her face upturned. Her features unmistakeably different from those around her. Alone, dignified . . . and unapologetic.

Landri had never felt more proud.

They'd planned to head off to Kew Gardens, which was nearby, but that wasn't going to happen now. Now they could only remain silent with their thoughts as they sat on the terrace of a bustling cafe.

The words *wicked woman* had also sung from the archived document detailing Temi's arrest and subsequent jailing. She had been locked up. That part had been true.

'It's a travesty,' said Gwen, her hand moving across the table to grab Landri's.

'Oh, Gwen, she'd been through so much already. Travelling to a new country that didn't exactly want people like her, losing her husband, separated from her children . . . Only to end up in prison. I'm sure there's even more we know nothing about. The stuff she didn't write. She deserved better, Gwen.'

Landri continued, 'I often think about how burdened she must already have been with the disappointment and trauma her relatives and ancestors felt. I'm no psychologist but it must have an impact, don't you think?'

Gwen shook her head slowly. 'Whether it was waking up to your children missing because they've been taken on a slave ship or simply being a woman.'

'Slavery wasn't something I was taught about in school. I mean, I watched the *Roots* reboot . . .'

'I saw the original.'

The women were silent once again. This was becoming a much-needed habit. There was so much to process. A lifetime, a generation of feelings to process.

'What do we do with all that pain?' said Gwen. 'What did *she* do?'

Chapter Sixty-Three

Your husband is always right, even when the opposite is true.
Mrs Adeline Copplefield,
'The Manual for Good Wives' (1889)

Temi
1893

Eleanor's hot tea did nothing to calm my nerves as I sat with Mr Crabtree in my home.

'You must, how shall I put it, lie low, Mrs Masters. You mentioned you have a daughter in Italy. Go there . . . at least until the dust settles.'

'I shall do as you have suggested. I will disappear for some time. It is the only way.'

'Good,' he said, standing up. 'You must be protected, Mrs Masters, just in case Penelope does what she has threatened.'

I was touched at his concern for me.

'I must ask, what did you mean when you asked about the police?'

'Oh, nothing, Mr Crabtree. What I would like to know is what will you do if Penelope speaks?'

'This is not good news for my reputation as an editor, but I believe in time, like many of our newspaper stories, it will be forgotten soon enough.'

As he headed towards the door, I asked him another question. 'Do you think Penelope will tell?'

He turned to face me again. 'Quite the little investigator, it seems. At least she came to me first. Said she knew everything about our arrangement and she simply wanted it to stop.'

The little witch!

'She is willing to keep quiet as long as you step down.'

'She is blackmailing you?'

'Not only that, she'd like a raise in salary and a few other . . . things.'

'Like?'

'It is quite unseemly to discuss such matters, Mrs Masters.'

'I think we are both beyond that now. What else did she say?'

He cleared his throat. 'Protested to the fact I never glanced at her the way I do you . . . There, that is enough now, Mrs Masters!'

I smiled, even though this was no time for it. 'So Penelope is also jealous.' The absurdity of this woman! Being jealous of a relationship which simply did not exist would have been amusing to me if it was not endangering my way of life.

'None of this need be of concern, Mrs Masters. You just get away to Italy and leave me to contain this. Please leave a forwarding address if possible.'

'What about my column?'

'We have a few of your articles to keep us going, but I am unsure of what to do next. I have thought of nothing since Penelope revealed her dastardly plans. Just you take care, Mrs Masters,' he said and was gone.

The significance of what was unravelling finally started to become clear. More than ever, the pull of seeing Amelia and my granddaughter felt so very strong, and yet . . . and yet I could not bring myself to enquire about a journey to Italy. Even now, in this desperate situation, my fear of ships remained. If only someone had invented something with the ability to transport me there without the sea. I had read about Da Vinci's ornithopter, with Mr Crabtree excitedly speaking about the flying machine that would be available in a few years' time. Mr Crabtree always spoke of inventions when we met and at times I did wonder if these ramblings was why he had never married.

I decided to stay 'out of sight' as Mr Crabtree had suggested, but it was in the only place I felt safe.

Tumbleberry, my home.

I made sure never to be seen in public and Eleanor kindly fetched anything I needed. With such pleasant weather, I received all the fresh air needed from my garden as I lovingly tended to my flowers.

I would do all of this until the danger passed and I could get back to being Mrs Adeline Copplefield.

However, I felt a shift coming. And when it arrived, even I could not have foreseen the enormity of what happened next.

They came for me in the middle of the night.

I had expected pitchforks by candlelight, but they perhaps refrained from what they thought I deserved and simply told me to follow them to the police station.

Even though I had feared one day being escorted to such a place, now it had happened, I could not have been more shocked and horrified. The putrid smell, the squalor, the screams of women begging to be let out. I did not belong here.

I did not belong here.

By now, Eleanor was on her way to Mr Crabtree's house with news of my arrest. Mr Crabtree, the only person in the world who could possibly help me. There was no time for regrets or sentimentalities, because within the hour I was sitting inside a cell wondering if I would ever see my daughters again.

Deep in such thoughts, I was not aware of the officer speaking to me.

'Did you hear what I said?'

'No,' I said, my eyes blurry with tears.

'You have been charged with fraud.'

'Fraud? Anything . . . else?'

'If you'd like me to add more, I will. Unless you have something to confess?' He exposed a crooked set of yellow teeth.

'No, nothing,' I said quickly, swiping at my tear-stained face. Inhaling and exhaling over and over again, as relief flooded my body.

As he read out the charges, I closed my eyes and tried to think. I'd paid all of my bills, debts and any outstanding taxes. I had never defrauded a person in my life. I thought of Olu and I changing our names all those years ago . . .

I opened my eyes to a different voice.

'There's somebody here to see you,' said another officer.

A rush of shame came over me as Mr Crabtree appeared behind the bars.

'Is this necessary?' he said to the officer.

'Well, she has been arrested,' he said, shrugging his shoulders.

'This is preposterous, Mrs Masters, I promise you I will ensure your freedom with immediate effect!'

'Thank you,' I muttered in between fresh tears. Remaining stoic had been my badge of honour. A reminder I did not need anyone but myself. Yet that was a lie. At that moment I needed Mr Crabtree and I was going to let him help me.

'Am I free?' I said an hour later when I was released from my cell.

'I am afraid not, Mrs Masters. Pending further enquiry, they have released you into my custody for a sum.'

'How much—?'

'Do not concern yourself with that, Mrs Masters. I will have the housekeeper make up a bedroom.'

'Can we please go to my home?' I said.

'Of course,' he said.

*

It felt wonderful to be within my own walls again. Eleanor greeted me with a barrage of tears and I assured her this had all been a misunderstanding.

I needed to bathe after spending the night in that stinking cell, but would do no such thing with Mr Crabtree in my home.

'They say you have been impersonating Mrs Adeline Copplefield and did so to gain monies illegally,' explained Mr Crabtree.

'I have a pseudonym like any other writer.'

'Exactly. This is clearly an embellishment put together by Penelope. I have no idea why she would do this! She said she wouldn't!'

I had never seen or heard Mr Crabtree display such anger but was pleased he did so.

'Mr Crabtree, do you . . . do you think I will go to prison for fraud?'

He took too long to answer.

Chapter Sixty-Four

A good wife is silent in her ways, humble in speech.

Mrs Adeline Copplefield,
'The Manual for Good Wives' (1888)

Temi
1893

Just for a moment I wondered: is this what it felt like, moments from death?

My body rooted to the floor, unable to move, startled by crowds of men. Their hands balled into angry fists, spittle flying from their lips as they shouted my name, along with chants such as 'Liar!' and worse: 'String her up!'

There were reporters too. One of whom had set up one of those new camera contraptions at me, ready to catch me in its gaze.

'Got anything to say for yourself?' said the man in scuffed shoes and an ill-fitting jacket. 'You should be ashamed!'

'It appears you have already made up your mind,' I said calmly. My voice edged with the last of its strength, almost resigned to the fate that awaited me.

'Don't say anything,' said a gruff voice beside me, a hand gripping my elbow.

'Don't you care about what you've done? You're a disgrace!' repeated the man with those shoes. A step closer and he'd almost be touching my face with that bulbous nose, attacking me with his frightful use of the Queen's English.

I widened my eyes expectantly, tilted my head upwards. I would be defiant until the very end.

'Harlot!' said a voice from the left.

'She deserves locking up!' said another from the right.

'Hussy!'

Each voice from the throats of men who I suspected had done much worse than I in their lives, even if just in their thoughts. Yet I was the one offered up for judgement. I was the one whose course in life stood on the verge of being altered.

The steps up to the building were vast before me. I had travelled so far in life only to end up here.

'Don't you have any remorse for the pain you caused?' asked another voice. This one sounded a tad kinder, minus the edge of hate.

I looked towards him, smiling ironically. 'Pain?'

What did they know of pain?

What did any of them know of *my* pain?

A strong hand gripped my wrist tightly, forcing me to follow. Normally, I follow no one, because I wasn't a woman to be tamed any more. This time, however, following was possibly for the best, considering the self-righteous mob now clamouring for my blood.

'Lying witch!' said a thunderous voice, just as I took my first steps into that courtroom.

The courtroom gallery was full of people and, at first, I couldn't understand why. I was not a woman of any standing. I mean, in my mind, yes, but in reality, not so. It made no sense as to why so many people would attend my court hearing.

When I'd had a chance to ask why, Mr Crabtree had cleared his throat multiple times before revealing it had to do with me being an African woman. This confused me as I had over the years read in *The Tribune* of a small number of men and a woman who looked not unlike me being arrested, so I was not that much of an anomaly.

'They were for the more usual crimes of common theft . . . This . . . this case is rather unique, Mrs Masters.'

I felt an immediate sense of loss as Mr Crabtree left me alone to face my judgement. With the unwelcome assistance of the bailiff I made my way to the dock. Trying but failing to ignore the hordes of people packed into the public gallery and the strangeness of the man sketching in the corner. An onset of nausea as the judge, in a dark robe and a wig I found both confusing and ridiculous, stepped onto the podium.

'Gentlemen of the jury, you are called upon here today for the most curious case of fraud. That a woman such as this impersonated a person that was not and could never be her. Duping the good public with her advice to be read by the innocent minds of British debutantes and genteel ladies of society—'

I scoffed – internally, of course – because I had done nothing wrong. Fraud indeed!

'You have chosen to represent yourself, Mrs Masters.'

'Yes . . . Your Honour,' I said tentatively.

'What do you plead, Mrs Masters, guilty or not guilty?'

'Not guilty. Of course.'

'I understand you don't deny you are the author of these columns in *The Tribune*?'

'I am the author, yes. But if I am guilty, it is only of sharing my literary gifts with others. Helping people, women, as much as I can. If these are the charges, then I am guilty!'

Roars of discontent followed from the gallery whilst the judge rolled his eyes. I turned to look behind me, noticing Eleanor in the gallery, her face red from crying, sitting beside Mr Crabtree. This warmed me.

'Order in the courtroom!' bellowed the judge.

'I would like to add something more, if I may, Your Honour?'
I said.

'Proceed.'

'This is all a misunderstanding . . . a witch hunt—'

'The court will decide what is deemed a witch hunt, Mrs
Masters.'

'I hope I fare better than the women before me who have been
arrested for the most trivial of matters.'

'Would you say the crime you have been accused of is trivial?'

Although I could not see Mr Crabtree, I felt his exasperation,
willing me not to make things worse for myself. Yet I wanted a
voice and to be heard: not as Mrs Adeline Copplefield but as Mrs
Temi Masters.

'Nothing I do is trivial, Your Honour.'

He cleared his throat. 'Let us resume,' he said.

There was a unique humiliation which came with standing in
a courtroom in front of men in wigs asking questions, whilst a
mob of people who did not know you cast their own judgements.
For me, it was the constant questioning about my life, some of
which I didn't want to answer. Not because I had anything in
particular to hide. In some ways, if you looked closely enough, I
had already placed a lot of my life in the public domain through
Adeline – but this had been on my own terms. These questions, I
had no control over. Others were very difficult to answer because,
simply put, I'd never had the courage to ask *myself* such questions
before.

'Would you say you have a motherly instinct, Mrs Masters?'
The barrister hardly looked me in the eye.

'I don't understand the question.'

'You have two children, we are to understand, and both are
estranged from you.'

'They no longer reside in England but we are not estranged,'
I protested. 'We write to each other, Your Honour.' Around six

letters a year to Amelia, who would typically respond to two. 'Out of the two, it is my eldest daughter Iyabo who is more fluent with the pen, which is ironic really, as Amelia received the best education. Bedford College for Ladies, do you know it?' I have no idea why I felt the need to goad the judge in this way.

'Let's not nitpick. You have two daughters you have not seen for some years.'

I swallowed. I had not expected any of this. Had Mr Crabtree betrayed my trust and spoken of this? No. I trusted him. He was a good man.

'Am I also right in saying you abandoned your first child in Africa?'

'I left her with her family. Her father.'

'This is very improper for a mother to do willingly, Mrs Masters.'

I closed my eyes, took a harsh intake of breath. The images of my two girls swimming in my head. The innocent little baby I had turned away from as soon as I felt her kick in my stomach.

Then that image of her ... cavorting with Edward, him hunched over her, his hands around her neck.

'Sometimes things occur which you do not make plans for. Does this mean I am an immoral person and not of good standing? Just like the many ladies who seek the services of a governess or send their children away to school, this does not make them bad. What of a husband, does he shoulder equal blame? Where are your children, sir? Who raised them?'

'That's enough of that!' interrupted the judge, his own face now an angry shade of beetroot. 'You will stick to the line of questioning, Mrs Masters!'

I exhaled, hoping that particular line of questioning was over. I could not afford to falter now. I had to remain strong. Yet as I walked down from the stand as a break in proceedings was announced, I simply wanted to crumple into someone's arms. The only arms available were that of Mr Louis Crabtree. I smiled at him instead.

I felt pangs of hunger, but needed not a morsel of food to pass my lips. The only taste I craved was justice. The evidence against me was flimsy at least. The court had taught me the lesson they thought I deserved and I'd go back to my hole never to return to the limelight again. There would be no more musings in newspapers. I had gotten too big for my breeches, so to speak. I would give them what they wanted. I just wanted to go home.

'They have no real evidence of wrongdoing and as long as you promise to give up the writing, I predict you will be free to go home very soon,' confirmed Mr Crabtree. 'Only, may I be so bold as to offer one piece of advice?'

'Of course, Mr Crabtree. Advice is welcome at this stage.'

'Perhaps . . . perhaps refrain from talking to the judge in that way . . . ?'

'What way?'

He averted his eyes and I knew.

'Are you saying I should not defend myself when allegations are thrown at me?'

'Well, there are ways to do that, Mrs Masters.'

'Naively and demurely?' I said, recalling passages from a number of my columns. *A woman should be seen and not heard during such matters that concern her.*

Of course.

I stepped once again into the dock, refusing to feel like a common criminal, ignoring the roars and groans from the gallery. None of these people knew the real me, only what they saw or had read.

'Mrs Masters,' began the judge. The beginning of an acquittal, I hoped, and perhaps even an apology for time wasted.

He began to speak and my mind drifted to what awaited me at my home, my cocoon, my favourite place to be.

It was the loud gasps in the courtroom which jolted me from my perhaps unrealistic daydream.

'Well, Mrs Masters?' said the judge as I absorbed what he had just said. What had made the crowd break into a frenzy. 'What do you have to say for yourself, Mrs Masters, about this new evidence which has come to light?'

The courtroom was alive with gasps and mutterings.

'Your Honour?'

'How do you plead on this further charge of bigamy?'

'Bigamy? I thought this was about fraud.' I turned to Mr Crabtree and his expression was one of complete and utter surprise. I felt a need to vomit and clutched my stomach in an unladylike fashion.

'What do you plead, Mrs Masters? We do not have all day.'

Laughter from the gallery. This could not be happening. Of course, I would utter my denial as vehemently as I could. That whilst yes, I had been married before, I was no bigamist. I would be careful not to mention the chief as there was no evidence of this marriage and, well, in my mind it had never happened anyway.

'Mrs Masters!'

'Not guilty!'

This could not be happening. Perhaps this was a dream after all, a nightmare. It was only later when I saw a figure climb up to the stand that I realized this was indeed real, because this man who had once haunted my real life now stood in the witness box.

'Say your name for the benefit of the court,' said the judge.

'Mr Wetherell. Mr Simon Wetherell.'

Chapter Sixty-Five

Married persons should abstain in public from prominent displays of affection. If he insists, bat him away, reminding him of the purity and wholesomeness he insisted were the traits of a good wife.

Mrs Adeline Copplefield,
'The Manual for Good Wives' (1891)

Landri
Present day

It had been a bittersweet day. Discovering Temi's records, seeing her name in black and white, acknowledged. And that photograph. To finally be able to put a face to the name. Priceless.

Yet the negativity attached to it all could never sit right with Landri.

Pioneer, trailblazing, audacious – these were more fitting terms for Temi Masters, and not the bile she had seen printed.

She couldn't wait to share what she'd found with her grandma, but first, after seeing an exhausted Gwen home, she decided to make a detour.

The door to Chimes & Things pinged as she walked into that now familiar smell of lemongrass and lavender and the musical sounds of wind chimes.

'You look happy,' said Chime, her hair this time streaked with pink. 'It looks good on you.'

'I found out something today, about Temi.'

'The shop's empty at the mo, tell me everything!'

So she did. And the more she spoke, the more Temi's story steeped further inside of her, as if meshing with that heavy part of her being. Relating deeply to this woman who had lived long before she had cried her first cry. This woman who had risked everything just to pursue her dreams. As if willing Landri across the centuries to do the same and to never settle for the life offered by Ross. Telling her it was all right to have new dreams when you were pushing forty. That it was possible to do anything, regardless of the obstacles.

'She just gets better and better,' said Chime, as a customer walked in.

'I feel so inspired and I want . . . I want to definitely start making notes. To make sure everything I've found out isn't lost again.'

'Wait there,' said Chime.

She returned minutes later with an oblong-shaped item wrapped in shiny silver paper decorated with stars.

'A birthday gift,' she said.

'I literally mentioned it was my birthday next week, like, once.'

'I never forget.'

She hardly knew this woman, and such kindness made her feel strangely emotional.

'No cheating. Open it on your birthday.'

That evening, Landri sat at the kitchen table, talking into the old telephone.

'I can't believe it!' said Grandma. A television was blaring in the background.

'Gran, can you turn the TV down? I can hardly hear you.'

'I am going deaf, you know! Hold on,' she said with a laugh. 'All this information, it is extraordinary. I can't believe it.'

'She wrote a sort of column for a newspaper. A Victorian Carrie Bradshaw!'

'Who's she?'

'Never mind, Gran.'

'She had to hide her identity?'

'For her own safety.'

The silence at the other end of the line alarmed her. 'Gran?'

'Sorry,' her voice quavered.

'Are you okay?'

'I just could not imagine what it would have been like for her. It was difficult enough for my grandmother Amelia being a Black lady doctor in Italy all those years ago. I recall some of the stories my mother would tell me.'

'Great-grandmother Antonietta, who you were named after?'

'That's right. I wish you had met her.'

'I feel like I've met them all through Temi, the woman who started it all.'

'Indeed. Without her we would not be here. You, your mother . . .' A sigh from Grandma. 'Thank you for finding this out.'

'It wasn't hard. Once I found the notebook, well, it was easy. Plus, Gwen's been a massive help.'

'It's like she, Temi, wanted you to find out.'

The conversation had been like no other. It marked another turning point for Landri, because Grandma had now mentioned her mother Clara for a second time.

And that meant everything.

Chapter Sixty-Six

When searching for a potential husband, your first two con-
cerns should be: What are his moral qualities? Is he able to
keep you in the style to which you are accustomed?

Mrs Adeline Copplefield,
'The Manual for Good Wives' (1888)

Temi
1893

'You have testified, Mr Wetherell, that Mrs Masters here is a
bigamist?'

'Yes, indeed. She flaunted the knowledge of her first husband
shamelessly to me. Committing adultery with poor Mr Masters
without his knowledge! And then using her shameless charms on
a Mr Edward Cutler.'

I wanted to reach over and slap him hard for having the audacity to say my precious husband's name. I hated him more for that
than the lies. I could only close my eyes as the reminder of those
days on the ship were brought to light by Simon. His version, of
course.

'Once again and just to clarify, Mr Wetherell, you know without doubt that this man is still living? The first husband?'

'No, sir, Your Honour. I am only aware that he was living at the
time of her bogus and fraudulent wedding to Olu Masters when
they arrived in England.'

'Thank you, Mr Wetherell. You may step down,' said the prosecutor, smiling at Simon. 'Gentlemen of the jury, as you have heard, this woman not only duped a learned gentleman to write for a very prominent newspaper, but also disguised herself as a boy on a ship to gain passage to this country, and once here tricked another poor, unsuspecting man into marrying her. Then, when he was sadly lost at sea, got her claws into another poor, unsuspecting gentleman, a white man named Mr Edward Cutler, who we have been unable to locate as he now resides in the United States.'

That part, at least, was a relief.

'What type of woman is this? Certainly one of ill repute and low moral standing.'

I swallowed.

'One could say a common harlot!'

The accompanying murmurs did not affect me as much as the smirk on Simon's face. Finally, after all these years, he had gotten his revenge.

The sickness in my stomach reappeared with more vigour as I attempted to defend myself and deny the charge of bigamy, even though I couldn't imagine there to be any real evidence considering the lack of paperwork regarding the chief. Just the word of a man against a woman – and yet even I knew how powerful that was.

Luckily for me, though, not powerful enough when the man determined to ensure my destruction was a Black man.

Or so I hoped.

'There is one more witness who will provide clarity to these charges and give a clearer picture of Mrs Masters's cunning character,' said the judge.

I held my breath. If Edward Cutler were to appear right now, my life would certainly be over.

'Mr Louis Crabtree, editor of *The Tribune*.'

My eyes widened in disbelief. The one person who I'd thought to be on my side had now sided with the opposition.

My life *was* over.

Chapter Sixty-Seven

Marriage is an opportunity to release yourself from parental restrictions but you may then find yourself constrained by newer ones.

Mrs Adeline Copplefield,
'The Manual for Good Wives' (1893)

Landri
Present day

She peered at the very last page of the notebook for what was possibly the tenth time.

It contained only one line.

A sentence of eleven words. A line full of hope and disbelief all in one.

As if it had been written many years after the rest of the notebook, it seemed to stand alone. Prominent but separate. And the more she read it, the more powerful it felt. The words now seared into her. Leading her to make a promise not only to Temi, but also to *herself*.

Landri had a lot to think about. Her annual leave was coming to an end and she would soon be forced to concentrate on her future instead of the past of someone she had never met.

She pottered into the library again, grabbed another book. This one was a newer-looking edition of *Romeo and Juliet*. She'd hated being forced to read the play at school, the weird language confusing and at times just plain annoying. But she'd give it a shot again. Temi had mentioned it in the notebook a couple of times and, well, everyone was always going on about it, so there must be something to it.

She slotted herself into the now familiar nook, her mind going back to the last line Temi had written and then she smiled. Flooded by a warmth she hoped would never leave her. And the hope.

Romeo and Juliet lasted about ten minutes before she decided to switch her phone on. The contraption which had once ruled her life was now something she looked at occasionally, her awakened love of books having taken over. It was when she decided to give the phone a 'clean' by uninstalling many of the apps she hadn't used since entering Tumbleberry that she found one she had never actually installed.

She stared at her phone as feelings of intrusion and violation threatened to overwhelm her. Instead of allowing them to fester, she decided to give Gwen and Chime a call. They were over within the hour and, in a moment of 'oversharing', Landri told them about Ross. Sitting in the garden, she poured her heart out to two women she had only recently met and not her oldest friends, Sadia and Claudine.

These two women who had unwittingly joined her on this short journey to finding Temi Masters and in the process finding herself. It felt right and, at the end of it, she was spent.

'If it's what she wants to do, then who are we to judge?' said Chime to Gwen.

'I suppose so,' said Gwen.

Landri had thought only shame would be present inside of her when she revealed the ins and outs of her relationship with Ross. Of course, she left out some parts of the relationship that would always remain between her and her conscience, but for the most part, Landri had been honest enough. Shedding tears and laughter and hoping there would be no judgement of her or even Ross. But the warmth and acceptance with which these two women held her, literally held her, told Landri she had chosen the right people to confide in. 'Thank you for listening,' she said through teary eyes.

'Thank you for trusting us,' said Gwen.

Chapter Sixty-Eight

Love begins when the man says it is so.

Mrs Adeline Copplefield,
'The Manual for Good Wives' (1890)

Temi
1893

'I would just like to say what a grim miscarriage of justice this is,' said Mr Crabtree.

'You will answer the questions posed, Mr Crabtree.'

Mr Crabtree truthfully answered the questions surrounding my 'bigamous' marriage. That of course he knew nothing of a previous marriage in Africa and that I had never disclosed as much to him.

My relief must have showed on my face. I should never have doubted him. Never have thought that because he was yet another man whose advances I had rebuffed, that he would ever avenge me in such a thoughtless and unkind way. He was still my friend.

'But she abandoned a child in Africa. Is it not fair to say she would have been married? Or are you implying this child was conceived out of wedlock?'

'With all due respect, Mrs Masters is an employee and, as such, I had no knowledge of the ins and outs of her life.'

'How odd, Mr Crabtree. I would want to know the type of woman I am employing,' said the prosecuting barrister.

'Mrs Masters has always been a dignified and hard-working lady and far from the words used to describe her character. That was my only concern.'

'Is she not also a liar? Is this not so?' said the barrister.

Mr Crabtree cleared his throat. Loudly.

'I put it to you, Mr Crabtree, that this woman initially lied to you, duping you into taking her on as a learned writer for *The Tribune* publication.'

The murmurs in the courtroom grew louder. This was it. The moment everything would come crashing down on me. Mr Crabtree was a good man, a truthful man and one of honour. I could not and would not expect him to lie on oath for me. He had already skewered the truth, so to speak, when questioned about my first marriage. Lying was not his way and if it had been, I suspect this wouldn't have been such a close friendship.

The irony.

'So, Mr Crabtree, can you please confirm for the court that you were indeed initially duped by Mrs Temi Masters. Because by doing so, you will show the court her true character, lending weight to the serious charge of bigamy.'

Mr Crabtree cleared his throat. This was the moment my life and all I had tried to build would come crashing down. His testimony would send me to prison, for how long I did not know. I would lose everything.

I was finished.

Mr Crabtree spoke so quietly in response, I barely heard him.

'Can you repeat what you have just told the court, Mr Crabtree?' said the judge.

'I said, I knew full well of Mrs Masters's identity. I knew and I still employed her as a writer on *The Tribune*. She did not dupe me in the slightest.'

The court fell into a frenzy of surprise and raised voices as the judge banged his gavel. 'Order in this court!'

I attempted to make eye contact with Mr Crabtree but he was gazing towards the floor.

The judge, clearly disappointed, continued. 'What you are saying is that you colluded with Mrs Masters in this deception? That an African *woman* would be in charge of advising our good ladies?'

'Yes, I did, Your Honour. There was no deception on her part or mine. Mrs Masters is merely continuing a long line of writers to use a pseudonym. Even so, I knew and took her on regardless, because of her excellent writing and knowledge.'

The court erupted, as did my gratitude for Mr Crabtree. Risking himself for me. Even so, I dared not think about a positive outcome.

Yet I was wrong.

Despite everything which had been said to discredit me, Mr Crabtree's testimony, my own defence and the lack of evidence regarding bigamy, I was given a not guilty verdict.

Not guilty of all charges.

I should have been overjoyed, yet remained clouded by disbelief. I had truly believed I was going to spend many years in prison.

My breathing remained heavy and I even allowed Mr Crabtree to clutch my hand. An act I would never usually have dared allow. Eleanor cried tears of joy as Tommy congratulated me profusely. I saw in their faces a love for me I had perhaps not allowed myself to see before and I appreciated every ounce of it. Every drop.

Mr Crabtree fetched me a glass of water and I assured him I was all right and this was partly true because, finally, I was allowing the belief that I was indeed free to seep in.

Simon was waiting by the side of the courtroom building. Only a handful of the press remained. The rest I suspected had trotted off in disappointment at not getting to witness the punishment of yet another woman.

'Well done,' said Simon with a sneer. 'When I heard of your arrest I thought finally you would be punished. Yet you escape once again. This time your white benefactor coming to your rescue. What is it with you and men?'

'What is it with you and your obvious obsession with me, Simon?'

'Obsession?'

'You have tried to destroy me since the moment we first met on the ship. Why?'

'I have never tried to destroy you, Temi. Just protect you. I even offered you protection after Olu's demise, yet nothing.'

'Just tell me why?'

'Perhaps ask yourself why you have always believed yourself to be too good for me.'

'I beg your pardon?'

'Olu, Edward Cutler and this other white man. All of them perfect suitors for you, but not me? Why? What could be wrong with me?'

'So this has been about never allowing you to possess me? That is all this has been about?'

'I simply wanted you to look at me the way you did them. It was bad enough being constantly treated as second-class by the masses, but you . . . you did it too! Never allowing me to be more than an acquaintance to you. We were from the same land and yet this meant nothing to you . . .'

'Oh, you were never even an acquaintance, Simon. An irritant, yes. A thorn in my side, yes. Never, ever an acquaintance. We may have hailed from the same land, but that is where the similarity ends. I owe you nothing!'

His lips straightened as I moved closer towards him. 'You, like everyone else, have always wanted to own me, and yet what no one seems to understand is that I will never be owned!'

My eyes travelled up and down his frame with disdain, the

tailored suit and shiny brogues. 'Not by you, the chief, my father, Edward, not anyone!'

I turned on my heel, a well of rage, sadness and exhaustion bubbling up inside of me. As I walked away from Simon, the remains of the crowd and the shadow of the courtroom, it hit me, a beautiful halo of sunlight inviting me forward.

Chapter Sixty-Nine

A successful endeavour as a wife is to be a good wife.
Mrs Adeline Copplefield,
'The Manual for Good Wives' (1890)

Landri
Present day

The morning of her fortieth birthday felt surreal.

Years ago, when she'd thought about this milestone, Landri had assumed she'd be married by now, perhaps with a child in tow and definitely a dog. Instead she was sitting alone in a house looking at an ancient notebook – and hadn't felt this happy in a long time.

Only one thing niggled her. An emotion she hadn't expected to feel.

Ross. After speaking with Gwen and Chime about what had gone on between them, she had begun to miss his presence. Or him. Or the thought of him. She wasn't quite sure. On her birthday he'd always make such a fuss of her. Her last one had started with breakfast in bed – American pancakes, bacon and maple syrup (more Ross's favourite than hers) – and Landri had just been so grateful he'd made the effort.

He'd told her to wear 'something nice' as they were headed to her favourite restaurant.

'Oh, is that what you're wearing?' he'd said.

'Why, doesn't it look okay?'

'It's fine.'

She remembered the heat rising inside of her. The mounds of insecurity.

'It is a bit tight,' he'd said.

'Yeah, I know. Getting on a bit and I need to start wearing more smocks,' she'd joked.

'No, not at all. I think a woman of any age can wear what she wants. If she has the figure.'

That memory used to sadden her, pull her closer into herself. Now she simply felt relief. Which was why missing him made no sense to her.

Grandma was the first to call as always. Wishing her a happy birthday and promising to call later as she was well aware Landri had a party to prepare for.

Much to Sadia's disappointment Landri had refused a big night out, instead inviting a few of her close friends and their families to join her at Tumbleberry.

The weather was pleasant enough, and sunny. The kitchen table outside was adorned with jugs of Chime's home-made elderflower and rhubarb concoction, as well as a couple of bottles of Prosecco for Sadia's benefit. Inside, the aroma of Gwen's freshly prepared salt fish fritters and patties travelled throughout the house. Grandma had talked through the recipe for the jollof rice which Landri hoped would taste as good as what she used to eat as a child. She doubted it judging by the mushy mess staring at her from the steaming pot.

'How's godchild number one doing?' said Landri, stooping to four-year-old Rory's height.

Standing behind him, Sadia warned, 'Rory is being a little stinker and I may need to take him home.'

'You're going nowhere!' said Landri, ruffling his hair, much to Rory's delight. Greg was in the corner with Gregory Junior, talking to Chime. People were mingling, chatting, laughing. She felt full, complete. Her old and new life meshed into one.

When the doorbell rang again, she jumped. There were no more invited guests due.

A delivery man holding a huge bunch of flowers stood at the door. The card inside simply said: *Happy Birthday. I still want you. I want you back, Ross.*

'Aww that's sweet!' enthused Sadia.

Landri placed the flowers by the sink, refusing to think about it for now, and pulled Sadia by the hands. 'Let's dance!' she said.

'To this crap?'

'Shhh, Chime put the playlist together. Calls it mood music.'

'Just a load of slow-sounding instruments with no words. Yeah, great!'

'The playlist is called Landri's New Beginning. We can sway.'

'Whilst that's sweet and all, can we please just put on some Cardi B?'

'No, we cannot!'

That night as the last of the guests ebbed away, Grandma called as promised. An extended call which opened up an emotional floodgate, because for the first time in her life, Landri could hear her grandma crying on the other end of the phone.

'I wish I was with you, my darling. This is a special day.'

'Oh Gran, it's no biggie, really.'

'It is big, forty is a big one!' she chastised playfully. Then her voice lowered. 'I wish your mother was here to see you. She'd be so proud of the woman you've become.'

There it was again. Another mention of her mum.

'Do you think so?' whispered Landri with the uncertainty of a child.

'Definitely. She loved you very, very much.'

Landri had never heard her grandma say as much. Sometimes

she had doubted it, because if she had, how could she have done what she did? That was her childlike mind deciphering something she could never fully understand. Yet the adult side of her, although more logical, had felt it too.

'Oh, Grandma . . .' said Landri, her tears hot and instant.

That evening Landri and her grandma were finally able to embrace a new beginning, finally able to cry together – for the person, the mother and the daughter, they'd both lost.

And it felt healing.

Landri woke up full of the joys of the night before – and without the hangover she suspected Sadia would have.

Then she listened to the voicemail message twice.

'Hi Landri, just to let you know, everything's cleared with the long-term renter I told you about. They want to move in during the next thirty days, so please call us back and we can take it from there.'

The thought of a set of strangers taking over this lovely house – Temi's home – filled her with dread. The fact it had always been rented out was not the point. She'd found a real home here, as well as her own history, and the thought of it being used as nothing more than a rental property again filled her with sadness.

Everything had changed.

'Would you want to stay here?' asked Gwen.

'No . . . I mean, I'd eventually need to be closer to town.'

'For work. I understand.'

Actually, none of what she was saying made much sense. She was near enough to town for the house to not be a commuting nightmare, especially with being able to work from home a few days a week. There was really no reason why she couldn't move in.

'It's a lovely family home. You know, if you were to get married in the future.'

She glanced at her hand. Her finger was bare but she could still almost feel the weight of the ring Ross had slipped onto it during that fateful dinner party.

With the glow of the previous evening gone, Landri had some real decisions to make about the house and her future.

The flowers from Ross were now in a pretty vase on the kitchen table, taking up so much space. A simple message to alert her to the fact he was still there. Still affecting her thoughts and decisions.

She remembered the gift from Chime she'd yet to open.

As she carefully unwrapped it, she clocked what it was immediately. A bright yellow vegan leather (as noted on the back) notebook. Inside, lined pages, each with a star at the top of the page.

On the first page was written a note:

Gorgeous Landri,
 Keep reaching for the stars.
 Tell your own story!
 Chime.

Chapter Seventy

Seeking happiness solely through marriage is expected, yet it is wise to also seek pleasures in other worthy pursuits such as embroidery & needlework.

Mrs Adeline Copplefield,
'The Manual for Good Wives' (1889)

Temi
1893

It had been a week since my victory.

Mr Crabtree had kept his distance, I suppose it was his way of dealing with his inner shame at lying. So, when Eleanor showed him into the drawing room, I felt relieved.

'Thank you for receiving me,' he said.

'I have not had a chance to thank you for what you did. From what I know of you as a person of excellent character, what you said could not have been easy, Mr Crabtree.'

'My reputation is of utmost importance to me, as you know.'

'Yet you risked it all . . . for me.'

'I would do it all again!'

I smiled in surprise.

'Let us be frank. Your freedom was at stake, whereas . . . because of my standing . . . a slight dent in reputation, which would soon be forgotten, was all that was at risk. It is better I take the fall, so to speak, as the consequences would not have been the same. Indeed, I was merely given a reprimand, as you know.'

'What of your employment at *The Tribune*? This means everything to you.'

'Not everything, Mrs Masters,' he corrected. 'I was marched into the offices of the board of directors and, let's just say, as soon as I pointed out the fortunes and astronomical readership increase since my appointment, as well as the rich history of pseudonyms in our industry . . . well, they relented.'

I wasn't going to add that the readership had increased massively since my column. This was not the time.

'So your job is safe, Mr Crabtree?'

'In fact, I negotiated a paid sabbatical for three months and then I will return as if nothing has occurred.'

'I am very pleased for you, Mr Crabtree. You are an honourable man.'

'Thank you, Mrs Masters.'

'So what will you do in those months?'

'Live! It is time for me to cease being alone. Whilst there remain teeth in my mouth, I should at least try to acquire a wife!'

We both chuckled at this. Mr Crabtree was not generally one for jokes.

'I would like to share my life with somebody and I suppose what the incident with Penelope has shown me is that . . . well, women are still interested in me.'

'Why wouldn't they be?' I said before I could take it back. It had now opened up a question I already knew the answer to.

'Mrs Masters, as I have said before, you are a handsome woman and, well . . . you know my feelings towards you.'

'And you know what my answer will be.'

'Indeed,' he said. 'Please do not blame my persistence. I simply wanted to ensure that door was firmly closed before embarking on my quest to find a Mrs Crabtree.'

'I do understand. Just make sure it's not that dreadful Penelope!'

We both laughed and, in that moment, I knew that Mr Crabtree would be a friend for life.

One good thing to come from the dastardly charges was that Amelia had sent a letter expressing concern and stating she would be travelling to England with baby Antonietta and her husband Davide. They had yet to decide on a date, but I waited with anticipation. My concern for their welfare on a ship was eclipsed by the thought of seeing my daughter again and finally meeting my granddaughter.

Eleanor and I worked together in keeping my beautiful home just as I liked it. I hardly ever received guests yet rarely felt lonely. My writing gave me both the pleasure and company I needed.

Sometimes I would write little words and sentences to Olu; other times, simply jot down how I felt in that moment. Or I would describe the joy in getting to know one's self – something I wish I could have included in 'The Manual for Good Wives'. To truly be comfortable with who I now happened to be was a gift I wished could be afforded to all women.

Just before Mr Crabtree's enforced sabbatical, he appointed a new writer to fill the gap Adeline Copplefield's absence had obviously created. He assured me this was a woman and I had no need to doubt his integrity just because he had lied for me on the stand!

Perhaps I had come to the realization that lying or 'fibbing' was at times a necessary evil. Hadn't I done just that in my columns? Writing things I did not inwardly agree with?

I was consoled only by the fact that during the latter years, I could at times sneak in parts of myself I hoped my women readers were able to see.

*

My garden grew more and more beautiful as spring grew into summer. These were my favourite times of year. Not least because it allowed my plants and flowers to bloom, but because the hot, searing sun reminded me of a place I often refused to acknowledge. The land where I had taken my first breath. The land in which I had laughed and cried. The land where my kin, my family and my ancestors had lived and where my daughter lived still.

Home.

The sun reminded me of home.

Chapter Seventy-One

*A woman must have a blemish-free reputation to secure mar-
riage. A man is expected to sow his wild oats if he prefers. This
he will generally prefer.*

Mrs Adeline Copplefield,
'The Manual for Good Wives' (1893)

Landri
Present day

She remembered nothing of her mother's funeral, only what she
knew of the circumstances of her death. She'd wondered more
than once whether this was why she'd convinced Ross to purchase
a place by the river, even though it was more expensive than
others in the building.

It had been a joy and a privilege to breathe in the air and listen
to the gentle lapping at the river's edge. Perhaps this had been her
way of keeping Clara close without even realizing it, for she knew
the river would eventually join the ocean. Perhaps in some way
this was the same water which had brought Temi Masters into her
life, the notebook and all it now represented to her. What a
thought!

Now Landri and Gwen were stood on a pebbly beach clutching a bag of tall-stemmed lavender and bright orange roses.
Strong winds threatened to blow her off her feet as she stood
facing the sea. They were there to say goodbye. Again.

With her mother's ashes scattered in her grandma's garden in

Italy, Landri had never felt a part of that healing process. But this felt right. The water she had perhaps once seen as an enemy that had taken her mother now able to be viewed differently.

The beach was practically empty this early in the morning, with just the sound of seagulls screaming their dissatisfaction overhead.

Landri closed her eyes and thought of the mother she'd not seen since she was a little girl. The voice she could hardly remember. Unsure if her recollections of Clara were from the photographs bequeathed by her grandma or from her own memories.

'Are you all right, my love?' said Gwen, clutching her hand. Landri had never been used to so much affection and at first had shied away from it, believing it would be taken away. But Gwen had been consistent.

She handed Gwen a few stems of lavender and a large, vibrant orange rose.

'Mum, just like with Temi, I will not allow you to be erased. You lived. You existed. You will always be my mum,' she whispered.

Gwen rubbed at her own eyes with a tissue as Landri continued. 'We also honour Gwen's mother Muriel and all those who came before us. The pioneers who struggled to make a difference so that we could be . . . us.'

Landri carefully threw a stem of lavender into the water, watching as the weak tide moved it further and further away. Then followed with an orange rose.

'I'm sorry, Mum, for judging you. I never understood why you did . . . and I suppose a part of me never will. But I haven't got the right to hold anything against you. You did what you could with what you had, Mum, and I love you. Always will.' The tears streaming down her face blurred her vision as she pulled more flowers out of the bag and placed them in the water, watching as they bobbed up and down on the waves, moving further and further away. In that moment, if felt as if her mother was moving away from her all over again. She was five years old, on the floor of the kitchen, waiting for her mother to come home.

But she was no longer alone. She had her grandma, Sadia, Claudine, and a group of friends who may not see her as much as she liked, but were still there during key moments. She now also had Chime and of course Gwen, who offered her a maternal love she'd never thought she needed.

Landri would be supported by a tribe of women she would make sure to lean into. And to love.

To truly love.

Gwen squeezed her hand. 'Remember what you said about pain passing down generations?'

Landri nodded. 'Whether all that pain defines us?'

Gwen smiled. 'What about the joy, my love? If we accept that pain passes through the generations, maybe joy can be passed down too. Just a thought.'

'I never thought about it like that.'

'Look at how ambitious you are, just like all the women who came before you. Look at how lovely you are too, so warm and caring.'

Landri's smile was wide as she took in Gwen's words.

What about the joy? The joy!

Chapter Seventy-Two

If a woman is born to dream of marriage, should she dare to dream of anything more?

Mrs Adeline Copplefield,
'The Manual for Good Wives' (1893)

Landri
Present day

It had been six months since she'd first discovered the notebook.

The house which once belonged to Temi and Olu Masters had a large glossy orange ribbon stuck to its front door. The name Tumbleberry had been spruced up with a fresh lick of paint. Now a small crowd gathered outside. Everyone who had been at Landri's birthday party, along with local dignitaries including a Paralympian and the mayor, was in attendance for this very special occasion.

Landri dismissed the message icon that flashed on the screen of her silent phone. That would have to wait, she had a speech to make.

She held onto her two pieces of paper but decided to ignore them. She would speak from her heart.

'I come from a historic African dynasty which began long before Temi's birth in western Africa and what is now known as Nigeria. When Princess Adekunbe Temitope travelled across the sea with my great-great-great-grandfather, Olu, the love of her life, their stories took a different turn to what had been mapped out for them. You see, they decided to make their own story and live within the pages of a life that, frankly, was extraordinary for such a period of time. But it was on their terms.'

Gwen smiled warmly at her.

'They came to this country with nothing, both becoming successful in a short space of time. What's so extraordinary about that? Well, these were two Africans, a Black married couple living in Victorian England. They were genteel, if you like. Of a certain standing, respected, and this was something quite unusual for that time.'

Everyone appeared to be listening intently. To her.

'Temi Masters is a woman who knew suffering, unimaginable loss and more than once probably felt defeated. Yet she still managed to find hope at the end of the darkest of tunnels. She persevered, she sometimes wavered, but still she carried on, not knowing what existed at that end of that very long tunnel.

'As a widow in Victorian society, she managed to carve her way out of the darkness. And as a Black woman she achieved the impossible dream of becoming a writer, by pretending she was indeed white. Who does that? My great-great-great-grandmother, that's who.'

Applause and a couple of 'whoop! whoop!'s from Sadia, Claudine and Chime.

'Despite or because of the hard and tragic turns her life sometimes took, Temi had an understanding of life that, instead of hardening her, simply fuelled an empathy for others and a need to help. Especially women. This is the Temi Masters I have grown to know and admire and who has inspired me not only to write about her but to open this centre in her memory, in her home and in her name.'

Landri gazed around the silent crowd, surprised at the well of emotion building inside of her.

'This, her beloved home Tumbleberry, was somewhere she found peace. A safe haven where she could write before sending her work out into a hostile world. Writing not only a column, but articles and short stories read as far away as America. Writings about injustices and the weight of simply being a woman.'

She swallowed as she clocked the look of surprise on her friends' faces. She would explain later.

'She also wanted others to find that peace.' Landri smiled, her voice breaking.

'You've got this!' called Sadia, clutching Gregory Junior in the crook of her arm.

'Someone dear to me recently said that, as well as trauma, we must also celebrate the joy. I'm hoping, inside this house, women can heal from trauma and see this as a space of joy.'

A round of applause.

'I do believe my great-great-great-grandmother Temi Masters would be thrilled with what her home has now become: the Temi Masters Centre for Women.'

Applause.

'Temi Masters stipulated in her will that this building always be passed down the female line of her family. I wanted to go further and ensure that her home be used for the betterment of women beyond her blood family, a home available to all the women who need it.'

More applause.

'So, I dedicate this to Princess Adekunbe Temitope Masters. A pioneer, a writer, as well as an all-round brave and kickass woman! My inspiration, without me ever realizing it . . . until now!'

Claudine handed a large pair of orange-coloured scissors to Gwen.

'Now, this street's oldest living resident will cut the ribbon and declare the Temi Masters Centre for Women open,' said Landri as Gwen walked slowly towards the door.

'I now declare this wonderful centre open!' said Gwen, with a quick snip.

More applause erupted as Claudine and Sadia embraced Landri in a group hug and the guests poured into the building, among them Chime, Gwen's son and her two daughters.

A small reception in the garden followed with more speeches, congratulations and applause. The day was an overwhelming success.

'I can't believe you pulled it off!' said Sadia.

'Not without you guys!'

'All in a day's work!'

'You've only just gone back to work and already you're giving me free legal advice, Sadia, I really appreciate it.'

'Any time.'

'Claudine, you've been a whiz with the PR side.'

'Team effort,' said Claudine.

'My cut-throat corporate advertising friend running a non-profit. I did not see this coming,' said Sadia.

'Errm no, I have hired a wonderful professional who will over-see all of that. I'm what you call a silent partner.'

'Yeah, best stick to the copywriting!'

'I may or may not ever go back. We'll see. I mean, it's been lovely having this six-month sabbatical and living off my savings, but it's almost coming to an end and I'm still 50/50.'

'You've got weeks left. Plenty of time,' said Claudine.

'I wasn't going to say anything,' said Landri, picking up Gregory Junior. 'It's not definite yet, but that little article I posted online . . . Well, after all the traction it got, a major and I mean *major* publication got in touch and wants to do a piece on Temi!'

'No way!' said Sadia.

'Full-page spread and everything. National syndication as well.'

'Okay, this is huge,' said Claudine.

'They've been doing some digging and found out loads more stuff. Monique the editor is really excited.'

'You mentioned something about her writing about injustices?' asked Claudine.

'Yes. The notebook and the Adeline Copplefield articles are just the tip of the iceberg. All will be revealed when it's all signed off.'

Gregory Junior wriggled playfully in her arms.

'They've also found a few more of her columns for *The Tribune* and sent them to me. I haven't stopped reading them . . . It's like the stuff she wrote totally contradicted her own life, even though towards the end – around 1893 – she started to get a bit cheeky. I've no idea how she got it past editorial.'

'That's why she's so fabulous,' said Claudine. 'We have to have a girls' night and read those columns.'

'With drinks and pizza?' said Sadia.

'But of course!' said Landri.

'"The Manual for Good Wives" . . . I think Gregory will probably want me to read some of that.'

'Gregory already thinks you're perfect,' said Landri.

'That's true.'

'Anyway, they've also looked more into the stuff about her being accused of . . . you know, the bigamy and fraud, all of it. They're really fascinated with how she achieved so much as a Black woman in Victorian times and yet no one had ever heard of her. Then there's the angle of the notebook. Everyone's fascinated by it. They even spoke about getting it authenticated, as if isn't real or something!'

'Don't worry about that. Legally they need to cross off the T's and all that,' said Sadia.

'I just want more people to know about her. There was so much more to Temi than what we know. So much more.'

'Now they will, thanks to you and this whole centre which has her name. Think of all the women she's going to help even after all this time,' said Claudine.

'I am so proud of you!' said Sadia.

'Me too,' added Claudine.

Sadia flicked a piece of fluff from Landri's shoulder. 'Yeah. Sorry for being a bit weird when you first ran off like a lunatic after Ross proposed. I suppose I just hadn't understood it at the time.'

'You still don't, right?'

Sadia shook her head.

'I'll tell you both one day. All of it.'

'Not now. Today we celebrate Temi,' said Claudine.

'And you!' added Sadia.

'I still can't believe the bloody mayor is here!' exclaimed Sadia.

'I know! I just wish Gran was too.'

'Well, she is,' said Sadia pointing to Landri's open laptop over in the kitchen. Her grandma on the screen, holding a large baguette as the mayor stooped down to listen.

'Not sure what's going on there!' laughed Claudine.

That night, when everyone had left and it was just her in the house, Landri finally returned the missed call which had accompanied the email. She held her breath briefly.

'Hello,' she said tentatively into the phone.

Landri still had to pinch herself that a senior editor from one of the world's largest syndicated magazines had her number in her phone; Monique, senior editor of *Vogue* in the States.

Vogue!

'I couldn't just send this in an email without talking to you, so I called you as soon as I got out of bed. Then I remembered you were opening the shelter. How did it go?'

'It was amazing. What have you found out?' Landri said excitedly.

'Okay, so Temi Masters had a few more secrets than what we first thought. After somehow getting her home back from her third husband, Edward, she started writing for a number of publications under the name T. Masters. We found various articles, like one where she covered the first Pan African conference in London, in 1900, which was part organized by a Black woman named Alice Kinloch. Temi also helped with speeches and admin. She had a very important role, it seems.'

'I've never heard of Alice Kinloch or that there was a Pan African conference in London at that time.'

'Uh huh, and it was attended by some very prominent people in the African American community, like W. E. B. DuBois, as well as Anna H. Jones and Anna J. Cooper, two women who like Alice you may not have heard of.'

'I've only ever heard of W. E. B. DuBois.'

'You know, it's always the name of the men that gets recorded, if at all.

But it looks like Temi had really found a place to express her true views, not only in the UK but the States and probably in other parts of the world too. As you know, her daughter Amelia became a doctor in Italy under the mentorship of another prominent Black woman, named Sarah Parker Remond.'

'This is a lot to take in . . .'

'Writing for small Black publications was not going to bring in riches, so she supplemented it by opening up a small bookkeeping business which did really well, which is how I suppose she was also able to keep that lovely home. She still enjoyed the nicer things in life.

'We think she wrote something for *The Christian Recorder* over here too, which happens to be the oldest African American continuously published newspaper in the country. It's an amazing part of our history here. It used to publish ads to help reunite Black families after emancipation.'

'That's incredible! Oh, when you say continuously published, do you mean—'

'It's still around today, yes!'

'Unbelievable!' She really needed to stop sounding like an excitable child.

'Sure is, and I have a meeting with various members of their team and we are going in! We're also on the verge of verifying that letter I told you about, "The Black woman and the Suffragette movement", simply signed as An African Lady in Great Britain. We are ninety-nine per cent sure it's her. Just need to make it one hundred!'

'Did she ever go there? To the States?'

'No, looks like it was always by letter. As far as we know, after coming there from West Africa, now modern-day Nigeria, Temi never left the UK.'

Landri wished she could howl with delight, but she needed to remain professional, especially as Monique was technically her boss after agreeing to allow her to write the article – with the help of an editorial team.

'It looks like your ancestor was a very resourceful woman and clearly didn't need a husband to make sure she continued living the life she wanted. We think she will be a fascinating feature for our magazine, not only because she was a Victorian-era Black woman, disguised as a white woman, but also *what* she wrote for women, especially in her later months at *The Tribune*. As you can see from what I'd sent, you some of the later columns had a sort of hidden feminist message.'

'For sure.'

'She was a character, your great-great-grandmother and we at *Vogue* can't wait to feature her!'

Just weeks later, Landri's life felt almost unrecognizable. The manager Lucy had started at the centre and together they'd found a host of volunteers. Unsurprisingly enough, Landri never once missed the office, doubtful she'd ever go back full-time. Perhaps she'd freelance as a copywriter whilst pursuing other things . . . like writing or whatever they happened to be. Bannerman had already been in touch offering such a package. She just knew that being overworked and undervalued would never be part of her life again.

PRINCESS, WRITER, SURVIVOR:
THE UNKNOWN STORY OF TEMI MASTERS.

Landri felt a swell of emotion knowing the article she'd written had reached a wider audience through print and digital and with a major publication behind it. Smaller publications had also run the story and a morning television show had requested an interview. Landri had always preferred being behind the scenes and the thought of being on a TV screen both frightened and excited her, yet it brought to the surface a confidence she never knew she had.

The original notebook now sat proudly in a glass display cabinet at the Black Cultural Archives in London. So far, she'd refused any offers of the notebook 'going on tour', not quite ready to share it with everyone just yet. She would reconsider this in the future though, where the first stop would undoubtedly be Nigeria. The home of her ancestors.

A distant relative named Ronke had gotten in touch after seeing the publicity surrounding the notebook. She was a descendant of Temi's first daughter Iyabo and lived in Lancashire with close links to the Nigerian side of the family.

They arranged coffee for the following week, with Ronke promising a large and welcoming extended family just waiting to meet her.

Temi had left a magnificent gift in the form of the notebook, and now everyone would learn about the gift that was Temi Masters.

A child.
Daughter of a king.
Duty fulfilled.
No longer I.
Mrs Adeline Copplefield, an untruth, but at ease.
Temi.
Hardship.

From the moment Landri had opened the notebook, her life had changed. She'd soaked up each word, crying and laughing along the way, feeling a sense of fullness once she had finished. As if the notebook had somehow filled in the missing pieces and made the past whole again.

Landri was not the same person she once was. However, there was one more thing she needed to do.

To be a part of something Temi Masters had already experienced with her beloved Olu.

Chapter Seventy-Three

Is it wise to believe fairy tales exist or prudent to simply accept the opposite?

Mrs Adeline Copplefield,
'The Manual for Good Wives' (1893)

Landri

There was a tight nip in the air as she pulled the white bobble hat over her ears and the collar of her coat up around her neck. Looking up at the gated entrance to the large building which used to be her home, she actually felt nothing out of the ordinary.

She was early. She would simply wait.

This meant time to think about everything she had achieved over the past months. Feeling a swell of love and awe for Temi. This woman she had never met and yet who'd grabbed whatever opportunity she had and run with it, without fear.

What excuse did she have?

She looked up and there he was, standing before her.

Ross.

He leaned against the railings which caged the river Thames, the wind blowing wisps of his dark hair.

His smile still excited her and she recalled the way it had made her feel the first time they met and the love which had followed. A type of love she'd never felt before. One which had made her believe living without it was unthinkable.

'I was surprised to get your call,' he said as they sat down on a bench facing the water. 'You could have come upstairs, you know. It's still your home.'

'I know,' she said.

She'd felt his absence at her birthday and then the opening of the centre, because for the previous five years he'd been there for all the important moments.

'You look good,' he said.

'Thanks.'

'Where are you living now?' he asked.

'I'm renting a room across the road from the centre, with my friend Gwen,' she responded.

'When you have a perfectly big enough apartment here.'

She'd agreed to keep paying her part of the mortgage even though she couldn't actually afford it. But it was her investment and part of her future.

'I know it's been months but I still miss you, Landri,' he said.

'I miss you too.'

He exhaled. 'Being apart from you . . . It's made me reassess a lot of things about myself.'

'Me too.'

He turned to her. 'I need you, Landri. Come back. Please.'

She'd seen this side of him before. Apologetic. Open to discussion rather than an argument. She would melt under his soft gaze, allow him to take her in his arms and promise her that no one would ever hurt her. That as long as he was around, she was safe. Never allowing her to see that perhaps *he* was the one she should fear.

This was their pattern.

The most important question now was: *did she love herself?*

The answer had once been a firm no, believing herself to be unlovable. Yet now with this new journey she was still travelling, the answer had changed, and with it, her actions. She could not keep doing the same thing over and over again. She could not keep walking the same path.

'I did love you, Ross.'

He smoothed his hand over hers.

She pulled away. 'And we can't be together.'

She didn't actually look at him when she said it.

'What?' he said.

'I—' she began, but he stopped her with a raised finger. Just like he always did when she spoke words he didn't want to hear.

'Don't shush me, Ross. I want to speak! I want to tell you how I'm feeling.' She pressed on. 'With you, I never have a fucking voice!'

His eyebrows raised. She had never sworn in front of him before.

'Somewhat ironic considering I work in advertising and my words are literally up there on television screens,' she continued. 'When it came to Mum, I never spoke about her, I was muted. I literally didn't speak for a month when she died.' A smile grew. 'Now I want to talk about her all the time. Now I want to celebrate her and it's all because of my ancestor, Temi.'

'Did you have a crash course in therapy or something?' he said, clearly not listening.

'Not yet, but as I said, I received a few messages from the past . . .'

'All that stuff you've been writing about online, is that it?'

'You have no idea.'

He squeezed her hand and this time she didn't pull away.

'Come home,' he said.

'I think we should just leave things here. Continue to walk in separate directions. Just as we have the last nine months.'

'I've been waiting, Landri. I never left.'

'More fool you, because I've been walking away and I still am. Even with that location tracker you installed on my phone.'

He flushed slightly.

'That's how you knew where I was.'

'Landri—'

'We will never be together again, Ross, because I have learnt to put me first.' She never thought she could say those words, reject him, because her greatest fear was always being abandoned by *him*.

'You should take this,' she said, reaching into her pocket and retrieving the little box he'd given her on that fateful night, perched on one knee.

'So that's it?' he said, pulling his hand away, a look of utter disbelief on his face.

The silence save for the sounds of the water felt so powerful, willing her to look at him. So she took in the handsome face, strong jawline, dark eyes, and all the features everyone else saw. The charm. A facade masking what lay beneath it all.

'You won't find anyone willing to put up with your bullshit like me, you know,' he said. The real Ross resurfacing.

'I hope not,' she said, turning to face the water. 'Because the woman you knew no longer exists.'

'It's not as if you're getting any younger, Landri.'

Hopefully wiser, she thought, not wanting to respond and prolong this conversation any further. Instead, taking a deep breath, she exhaled.

Then she walked away.

When she could no longer feel Ross's stunned eyes on her back, Landri thought about Temi, a woman who had experienced pain and trauma, just like her, but had also experienced love. A multitude of emotions jotted into that one notebook, reminding her of that certainty. Temi Masters had found love. True, unadulterated love.

The total opposite to what she had found with Ross.

Her great-great-great-grandparents Temi and Olu had found

each other at such a young age . . . and lost one another. A true tragedy. Yet at least they had loved.

She'd yet to feel such a privilege but, for the very first time, believed one day she would.

And, most importantly, felt she deserved to.

Chapter Seventy-Four

To satisfy what is expected of a woman can lead to a life full of falsehood and regret.

Mrs Adeline Copplefield,
'The Manual for Good Wives' (1893)

Dear learned women blessed with grace and resilience,

It can be burdensome to make wise choices when faced with the limitations of what is expected of you in our society. To be innocent in the eyes of a gentleman, whilst shrewd in your own; unknowing of most things, yet clever enough to decipher what is best; to submit all your worldly goods, whilst allocating elsewhere what he has permitted you, in case of marital abandonment.

Thus begins an assemblage of contradictions you may have or be about to consider, dependent on whether you are betrothed or already in marriage.

I can only dare hope you are able to make decisions which not only favour your husband, which is expected, but also you, the good wife.

It remains easy to reach an age where the mind fixates on what was or is a regrettable part of one's existence. However, such thoughts remain pointless and a waste of time that could be better spent reading a most satisfying novel!

Hence, there is no sense in thought upon thought, as there is certainly no way in which to change what has already occurred. The good, the bad and the dastardly. Perhaps the most pertinent question becomes: what can I do now for the betterment of what remains of my life?

Temi
1913

I waved over at the woman and the little girl, who quickly rushed over to me with widened eyes that reminded me of Amelia at such an age. I wasn't as fast as I once was and made no attempts to keep up with her.

'Muriel, are you coming for some lemonade today?' I said softly. She nodded and I held out my hand, which she took gently. Her mother smiled humbly and I waved her away as we slowly walked through the house and out to my beautiful garden. Eleanor had left long ago. Married Tommy, who now owned a thriving fishmongers on the high street, and had stopped employment soon after the birth of their third child. They visited me regularly. So as well as Muriel and the odd visit from Mr Crabtree and his dear wife Alice, I was never without guests. Of course, the loneliness would sometimes come. Creep up on me like the shivers, especially when alone with my thoughts of the past. With Amelia in Italy and Iyabo having made it clear that Africa was her home and she was not interested in inheriting this house as the firstborn child, my hope remained that my granddaughter Antonietta would be keen to inherit a house which meant so much to me and was instrumental in everything her mother Amelia was today. Of course, it wasn't helpful I had never made the trip to Italy and had only met her once when they travelled to England some years back. All I had was the hope that everything would culminate into something good.

All I had was hope. At my age, and with less years ahead of me than behind, I was at peace with that.

Once Muriel rushed off back to her home across the road, I

was grateful because an onset of sickness had gripped my stomach. Not enough to stop me from weeding, though, my favourite pastime. Lucky for me, these particular weeds had grown quite tall, as my limbs found it much more difficult to bend nowadays. I was grateful for their consideration.

My back did not thank me as I carried on with the weeding, regardless. However, the pain in my arm was not something I had felt until now.

I heard a sound. My ears prickling at the familiar term of endearment.

Tem-Tem.

I grabbed at the weeds. This wasn't the first time I'd heard his voice say my name in my head and in my heart over the years. I'd heard it last night and the night before too; this just sounded a bit more vivid than usual.

'Tem-Tem.'

The voice now sounded real.

Everything in me stopped as a feeling of light-headedness overcame me. I left the weeding and stood to my full height, a slight pull in my chest.

A figure walked slowly towards me. A child. Had Muriel come back? I instinctively held my hand out to her as she moved closer.

It was my sister.

Taye?

My sister lost to me when I was a child back in the old country.

Then, before I could even open my mouth to speak, another figure appeared and then another.

My mother.

Then Aunty Kike. My beautiful Aunty Kike.

Faces from the past. Was I dreaming? If so, this was the most wondrous of dreams – to be reunited with loved ones!

'Tem-Tem.' There it was again and feeling more powerful the

closer it got. Then I saw him, just as I pressed my hand to my chest to stem a shot of discomfort. Releasing the weeds in my hands, my body limp as I headed towards the ground. He caught me just in time, my eyes flickering, my mind confused. I began to float in between a dream state and reality.

Was this reality?

His breath danced across my skin. 'Tem-Tem.'

It couldn't be.

'Olu?' My eyes were closed but I could feel each of his fingers gently touching my face, gently stemming the single tear which ran down my cheek.

And then he kissed me gently. 'Thy lips are warm,' he said.

'Olu?'

'Olu,' he confirmed.

I opened my eyes to my husband, my only love. Still as handsome. Those long eyelashes I never thought I'd ever see again.

He lay beside me on the ground. 'I have come for you, my love.'

'This is an illusion,' I whispered.

He squeezed my hand gently and all the loneliness, the tears, the heaviness disappeared.

'Where . . . where have you been?' The words now formed in my head, unable to pass my lips.

'I have come back for you.'

For me?

I grazed my fingers across his cheek, his full lips curved into a smile.

'Tem-Tem, my love, my only love.'

He stood, pulling me gently to my feet. My back as erect as a young person's, the aches and pains no longer felt.

'Time to go now,' he said, just as a white bird with an orange ring around her eyes flew gently above us.

I was ready.

As we walked side by side, my thoughts moved to a balmy night, the sound of crickets and our heartbeats. Both of us, just children, ready to love each other with a vigour neither of us had ever known, believing it would be that way forever. Now, we had been given a second chance. My fairy tale had finally come true.

I closed my eyes, feeling the comforting warmth of the sun.

Now, I was home.

Epilogue

(The very last page of the notebook)

Despite everything, I believe fairy tale endings do exist.
They exist.
Princess Adekunbe Temitope Masters

Acknowledgements

2 pages

Lola Jaye